CURSE OF THE AKKERI

BOOK TWO OF THE MOONSTONE CHRONICLES

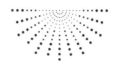

SARA C. ROETHLE

CHAPTER ONE

Elmerah

Elmerah was entirely sick of elves. She leaned against a thick post holding up one side of an antlioch pen, waiting with Alluin and Saida for the healer to emerge from a nearby hide tent. She didn't know what Alluin and Saida were hoping to hear. It would be the same news as yesterday. Merwyn's wound had healed, but his health was not improving. The healer suspected the Dreilore arrow had been poisoned, but with what, no one knew. The Akenyth Province in which the Dreilore dwelt was foreign to most. Few knew of their weapons and magics. Now the sun was beginning to set on another worthless day, and tomorrow promised to be no different.

She shifted her stance, stretching her long legs beneath thick black breeches and a long black coat, slit at the sides, leaving her cutlass in plain view. She was tired of inaction. Rissine had likely already rallied the Arthali to stand against the emperor. She'd venture back to the continent with an army in tow to find her inept younger sister had accomplished nothing.

"We'll have to leave him if his condition remains the same," Alluin muttered, his green eyes on the dirt at his feet. His rich brown hair was tied back from his face, the ends draping over his deep green tunic and brown breeches.

"No," Saida snapped, brushing a strand of long white hair aside. In her forest hued outfit she almost blended in with the Valeroot elves at the small settlement, and she was just as crabbish.

Elmerah had suffered through more than enough of bad elven attitudes. "Look, we have to make a choice. Either we sacrifice the fate of an entire continent to sit beside one ill Akkeri, or we move on. I didn't enlist with you lot only to live in an elven settlement for the rest of my life."

Saida glared at her, though her expression lacked a certain conviction. Deep down she had to know she couldn't wait on Merwyn indefinitely, but her deeply ingrained morals were holding her back. At least, that was how Elmerah saw it.

The healer, Vail, emerged from Merwyn's tent and approached, breaking the tension. She smoothed agile hands over her loose green dress as she reached them. In appearance, she could have been Alluin's younger sister, though the way she looked at him was definitely not . . . *sisterly*.

"Nothing has changed," Vail explained, speaking directly to Alluin, though Elmerah and Saida were right there. "He is conscious, but weak. His fever will not break. I fear this unknown poison will kill him in time."

Alluin and Elmerah both looked to Saida, whose face had turned a frustrated shade of pink. "*No*. That's just not good enough. We'll take him to Faerune where he can be treated by the best healers on the continent. Our scholars know more about the Dreilore than most. Perhaps they even know of an antidote."

Alluin shook his head. "He would slow us down and make us vulnerable. We don't need an extra life to protect."

Elmerah snorted. "At least we'd be *moving*. If he dies on the road, well, at this rate he's going to die anyhow."

Alluin turned his attention to her. "And when we're attacked, and Saida sacrifices her life to protect him? What then?"

She glared. "Well that would be her stupid choice, now wouldn't it?"

Vail watched them all with her jaw slightly agape. "I do not think he should be moved," she said finally. "He needs his rest."

Elmerah turned her glare to Vail, who wilted like a fragile flower. She held her hands up defensively. "That is simply my opinion as a healer."

Alluin gripped Elmerah's arm. "Leave her alone. She's done more to help him than any of us."

Elmerah begged to differ, considering they'd carted the sickly Akkeri all the way from the coastal inn to this remote southern settlement, but she chose to keep her mouth shut. Alluin was *kind of* on her side in the matter, and she wanted to keep it that way.

"Can I go in to see him?" Saida asked, her attention on Vail.

Vail nodded, but cast a wary glance at Alluin, then Elmerah, before gently touching Saida's arm. "I'll go with you."

Elmerah kept her gaze on Vail and Saida as they headed back toward the tent, not thrilled at the notion of another argument with Alluin in their absence. There had been *many* in the days prior.

She nearly jumped out of her skin as something bumped her back, then calmed as a fluffy antlioch head lowered over her shoulder. "I don't have any treats for you," she sighed, patting its head between the deadly, spiraling horns. She liked the antlioch. They were useful —not only could they be ridden, but they provided milk and wool—and they were fluffy and cute. Perfection in animal form, really, though she wouldn't admit her adoration of them out loud.

Alluin moved to stand shoulder to shoulder with her, ending her nice moment with the antlioch. Together they watched in silence as Saida and Vail entered Merwyn's tent.

"It's not that I don't *want* to save him," she sighed. "He's a decent enough little fellow . . . for an Akkeri."

Alluin nodded. "I know. We are not healers, and I doubt even if we made it to Faerune they'd see fit to aid him. They'll likely be too busy throwing stones at the two of us."

Elmerah smirked. "Hopefully stones are all they throw."

He smiled softly, though it didn't reach his vibrant green eyes. "We need to depart come morning. If anyone can convince Saida, it's you."

She shifted her stance, spotting Vail re-emerging from the hut. "Were you just in the same conversation as I? We're going to have to drag Saida out of here kicking and screaming. She won't leave that bloody Akkeri behind, though I'm not sure *why*."

"Saida is loyal, something you would know little about."

She gritted her teeth, trying to remember why she'd embarked on this unrewarding adventure to begin with.

Vail rejoined them. "If you think that is Saida's issue, you do not know her well."

Elmerah and Alluin both turned raised brows to her.

Vail glanced at the distant tent, then back to them. "Saida feels like a failure to her people," she explained, "and a failure to her fierce friends." She looked them both up and down. "She feels Merwyn is her last chance to prove herself of worth. Leaving him behind will take that away from her."

Elmerah sucked her teeth. "And she told you all of this?"

"She did not have to. Some of us choose to be at the center of things. Some choose to observe. I am of the latter ideology."

She wasn't quite sure, but she thought the elf might have just insulted her. "Alright, *oh wise one.* Since you seem to know so much, tell us how we can convince Saida to leave."

"That is Saida's choice," she replied. "If she is ever to take her place on the High Council of Faerune, she must learn what it means to lead. To sacrifice one for the good of many." With that, she turned and walked away.

Alluin stared after her approvingly.

"Bloody stupid elves," Elmerah muttered. She kicked a rock near her feet, then walked past Alluin, prepared to sulk alone in the woods beyond.

Alluin touched her arm before she was out of reach.

She turned toward him.

"I apologize. I should not have laid the issue with Saida on your shoulders. I've been—" he hesitated, "a bit on edge."

Yes, having half your kin slaughtered will do that to you, she thought. He had not mentioned his uncle, nor any of the other slain elves, since the night he'd found her during the storm, his hands still stained with the blood of his kin.

Her expression softened. "You would do well to focus

on the present. Just focus on what needs to be done today. It helps."

He nodded, seeming to understand what she meant. Focusing on the past, on those who were lost, was a sure way to become utterly ineffectual in the present.

He dropped his hand from her arm. "I'll try speaking with Saida."

She clenched her jaw. "No, I will. Finish conferring with your people. Rissine will be one angry viper if she finds no army of elves awaiting her return."

With a small smile, he turned away.

She watched him go, then glanced at the tent from which Saida was yet to emerge. She had no idea what she would say to convince her to leave. Maybe she could convince Vail to speak with her, since she *understood* what Saida was feeling.

Elmerah spat on the ground as she thought of Vail looking all twinkle-eyed at Alluin.

Bloody stupid elves.

Saida

S aida leaned forward in her wooden chair, looking down at Merwyn's sleeping face. His normally mottled skin was paler than usual, and glistened with a sheen of sweat. He looked like a Faerune elf that had died a week prior and had been left to rot in the sun. The strong fishy smell emanating from him helped the image along. The rough brown blanket pulled up to his chin prevented her from seeing if he'd grown thin with illness, though he was practically skin and bones even when healthy.

"I'm sorry," she said, though he likely couldn't hear her. If she hadn't been so intent on tracking down the emperor after spotting him in the woods, none of this would have happened. It was her own foolishness that had landed perhaps the only Akkeri with kindness in his heart in such a dire situation.

The final rays of sunlight cut across the dim space as the hide flap over the entrance shifted, making Saida's lone candle flicker. She turned to see Elmerah poking her head in, her thick black hair draped over her shoulder.

Saida steeled her expression, preparing for whatever insensitive thing the witch had to say next.

Instead of speaking, Elmerah moved into the shelter and stood beside Saida's chair. Her dark eyes peered down at Merwyn. "Any other creature would likely be dead by now."

Saida glared up at her. "He's not a *creature*."

"You know what I mean."

Her shoulders slumped. She *did* know what she meant. Until she'd met Merwyn, she'd viewed the Akkeri as vile monsters. Truly, she still did. Merwyn was an exception—and she'd nearly gotten him killed.

"You know," Elmerah began, seeming oddly hesitant,

"the elves will continue to care for him whether we're here or not."

"And when the war begins?" Saida questioned. "You promised Rissine that the Valeroot elves would fight alongside the Arthali. When the elves go to war, what of Merwyn then?"

Elmerah was silent, but Saida knew exactly what she was thinking. *Merwyn would probably be dead by then.*

"You know it's not your fault," Elmerah blurted suddenly. "Just as it's not Alluin's fault his kin were murdered," she added, "though I know he blames himself."

Saida braced her elbows on her knees, then leaned her chin in her palms. "It *is* my fault though. Merwyn begged me not to follow Egrin, and I ignored him."

"Merwyn knew he was risking his life from the start. It was his choice."

She shook her head slightly. She had no more arguments to offer, though deep down, her feelings would never change.

Elmerah's hand alighted on her shoulder. "I know it's unfair, but more lives depend on you than just Merwyn. In placing his life first, you are risking the lives of all in Faerune."

Saida straightened and blinked up at her, tossing her hand aside. "How dare you speak so callously!"

Elmerah rolled her eyes. "Look, princess, I tried being nice, now we'll try the truth. There comes a time when we all must accept that life is a big heaping pile of dung.

We cannot waltz through it without getting our boots a little dirty."

"And just what is that supposed to mean?"

"It means that you're going to have to do things you regret, but you just have to live with it." Elmerah turned her gaze back down to Merwyn. "You will recover from this regret, but if the Dreilore attack Faerune before we can warn them . . . " She shook her head and met Saida's waiting gaze. "You won't recover from that. You won't recover from hiding away in fear while your people fight for their lives. *Trust me.*"

With that, Elmerah turned and marched out of the tent, giving Saida a brief glimpse of the coming night. She stared at the doorway long after the witch left. She hated to admit it, but Elmerah's words were just what she'd needed to hear.

Thera

There shifted on her cushioned seat. She far preferred these meetings within the castle to those at the Crimson Jewel. A golden goblet of wine was at her fingertips, and a robust fire crackled nearby. It would have all been terribly comfortable if it weren't for her present company. The emperor, Egrin Dinoba, she did not mind. Nor did she mind his advisor, Daemon

Saredoth. It was the Dreilore Lord, Orius, who made her skin crawl beneath her emerald silk dress.

Egrin tapped his jeweled fingers on the table, breaking the uncomfortable silence. He turned his pale eyes to Thera. "You're *sure* she's no longer in the Capital?"

Thera nodded, pushing a lock of white-blonde hair behind her pointed ear. She wasn't quite sure why the emperor was so obsessed with Rissine. She wasn't *that* impressive. "The last I saw of her was the night I led Elmerah to the slums. I informed Rissine she was there, just like you requested."

"Yes," Daemon observed from his post behind the emperor's chair, "then she rescued her sister, and just . . . disappeared." He waggled his bejeweled fingers in the air, the gems almost as shiny as his straight blond hair.

Thera bit her lip. She hadn't told *anyone* what had happened with the Nokken. Those stupid creatures had tied her up and left her alone in a storehouse while they did who knew what to Rissine and Elmerah. She hadn't seen those particular Nokken, nor Rissine, again. She debated telling the emperor exactly what had happened—he obviously suspected her of deceit—but she needed to remain useful. If the emperor thought she secretly knew where Rissine had gone, he had reason to keep her around.

Egrin waved her off, then turned to Lord Orius. "Never mind the witches, I'm sure they'll turn up sooner or later."

"Yes," Orius agreed, a frown on his blueish gray lips. "Let us focus on *why* my people are still hiding in the woods. Why have we not begun our assault on Faerune?"

"All in good time," Egrin purred. "Soon Faerune will be perfectly primed for attack, and our victory will be ensured."

Orius smiled, his reddish eyes seeming to flicker with tiny flames, echoing the firelight dancing on his pure white hair flecked with tiny clear jewels.

Thera resisted the urge to clutch her twisting gut. She'd thought allying herself with the emperor the only way to ensure her continued survival in the Capital, but now she wished with all her heart she'd had the chance to flee with Rissine. She'd face a hundred Arthali if it took her away from the Dreilore.

Although, once her actions came to light, she'd rather face a hundred Dreilore than one Arthali in particular, once she realized her long-time associate had betrayed her . . . if she hadn't realized it already.

Merwyn

Merwyn's arms trembled as he pulled himself atop the antlioch. It had been difficult to remain awake as night fell. His fever plagued him so, and his joints were stiff and swollen. Even worse was his sadness to leave Saida behind, yet, he knew he must. She would not leave the Valeroot settlement until he was well, and he would never be well. The Dreilore poison would see to that. If he was anything other than Akkeri, he would have already been dead.

If he left, Saida would finally be forced to act. She would find Isara Saredoth, and with Alluin and Elmerah, she would save Faerune from the Empire. There was nothing more he could do for her now, and nothing she could do for him.

Settling himself onto the antlioch's fluffy wool, he guided it out of the pen. He hadn't the strength to dismount again and close the gate, but the other loyal creatures would not likely go far without riders.

He readjusted the supplies he'd pilfered, wishing he had the strength to end his burdensome life. Perhaps in doing so he might have ingratiated himself to the sky god Arcale. Instead, he'd stolen from those who'd helped him, and was escaping in the night. The Goddess of the Underworld would be quite pleased when she finally came to claim him.

CHAPTER TWO

Saida

S aida sat up in bed with a sigh. Though the first
trickle of sunlight had only just crept beneath the
hide flap covering the entrance to the small tent, she'd
been awake for hours. She glared at the mat across from
hers where Elmerah lay on her back, long legs sprawled
on top of her blankets, snoring loudly. She wouldn't
wake until she smelled the cooking eggs and smoked
trout the Valeroot elves enjoyed for their morning meal.

Saida stretched her tired arms over her head, then
stood, the hem of her thin night-shift fluttering to her
knees. First, she needed to get dressed, then she'd check
on Merwyn, just like she'd done every day since they
arrived at the settlement. It was her fault he'd been
pierced by the poisoned Dreilore arrow, so it was her

duty to see to him, even if Vail claimed her efforts did little good. Her shoulders slumped. She'd have to let that thinking go soon enough. Elmerah was right.

She walked across the hard-packed dirt floor to her small satchel of clothing. Though the elves had provided her with a few fresh tunics and leggings, she didn't have enough to keep the modest garments clean all the time. She could just imagine how her parents would react when she showed up dirty and bedraggled, dressed in clothes only servants would wear . . . at least in Faerune. The Valeroot elves did not seem to care about the finery of clothing. Rather than signaling status, clothes simply kept one from being nude, and the colors helped them blend in with the woods.

Once she was dressed she went outside, her spirits livening as cool morning mist coated her face. A few of the other elves were already up and about, starting the morning cookfires and feeding the antlioch.

She paused halfway across the cleared out expanse between structures as Alluin and Vail emerged from Merwyn's tent, worry creasing their tanned brows. Spotting her, Alluin approached, Vail trailing him with her head down.

Alluin tucked a stray strand of hair behind his ear as he reached her. "He's gone. Vail woke early to find the antlioch pen open, and one of them missing."

Saida swallowed the lump in her throat. "But he was in no condition to travel." She looked to Vail, hoping there had been some mistake. If Merwyn tried to travel in his state, he would die.

Vail bit her bottom lip, then replied, "The Akkeri are a strong race. While the poison is slowly killing him, he may survive for some time yet."

"Saida," Alluin began, placing a comforting hand on her shoulder. "You know why he left. Let us not refuse his gift."

She stepped back, pulling out of his reach. "*Gift*? He'll die out there because of us!" She gestured to the forest beyond the settlement, then realized she was standing in front of two Valeroot elves, the most skilled trackers on the continent. She lowered her arm. "We can find him. We must leave at once."

Alluin and Vail did not move.

"What are you waiting for?" she hissed.

Alluin's shoulders rose and fell with a sigh. "Saida, he does not want to be found. We need to move on to Faerune. We can avoid it no longer."

She opened her mouth to argue, but knew he was right, just like she knew Elmerah was right. She knew she had to face her mother. She had to explain to her parents why she'd run away from the duty placed upon her at birth. The fate of Faerune depended on her.

Alluin's hand landed back upon her shoulder. "Merwyn wants you to go to Faerune. He wants to do what's right."

She turned her gaze down to her boots—laced up tight to her knees—to steel herself for the bitter truth. It was her responsibility to convince Faerune that not only did they need to prepare for war, but to ally themselves with the Valeroot elves and the Arthali. They didn't listen to her at the best of times. Now, after running away, she'd be hard pressed to convince them she hadn't gone utterly mad.

"What's all this yelling and hissing about?" Elmerah's voice sounded behind her.

She turned to see the rumpled swamp witch emerging from their tent. Saida's knees felt weak. Her mother could perhaps be convinced that Alluin was a suitable ally, but Elmerah? *Suitable* was not a word Saida would use for her.

"Merwyn is gone," Alluin explained as Elmerah reached them. "He fled during the night."

"So we can finally leave?" She looked to Vail. "No offense, but I'm bloody tired of this place. I haven't had a proper bath in ages."

Vail pursed her lips in distaste, but did not reply.

Saida felt unsteady on her feet. She'd known all along she'd have to face everything she'd tried to escape. There was no other choice.

She'd only hoped to avoid it for a little while longer.

Alluin

lluin shifted his sore rump to a less flattened area of the antlioch's wool. They'd ridden all day without incident, other than the reluctant farewells at the settlement. Once they'd agreed to depart, it hadn't taken long to prepare three antlioch with supplies, and now they'd left the Valeroot settlement far behind. By Alluin's estimations, they were nearing the border of the Dracawyn Province and the Illuvian forests of the Nokken.

He thought back to Vail's warning upon his departure. The Illuvain forests were dangerous, but in a different way than the deep woods up North. Some claimed they were enchanted, but in reality, they were just filled with devious creatures like Fossegrim, ready to lure travelers to their deaths. He glanced at Elmerah riding at his side. She was practically beaming with excitement. She hadn't even thanked Vail for her hard work and kindness.

He looked past Elmerah to Saida. Her slender fingers toyed with the antlioch's thick wool, showing the nerves she refused to otherwise express. *She'd* at least been grateful. She'd promised Vail any favor she pleased at any time in the future, though in all likelihood they might never see her again.

He'd thanked Vail too, though he knew she had hoped for a bit more from him. Perhaps in another life, they could have spent more time together, but not in this one. Love had no place in his life, not if he wanted to honor his fallen kin. He would think of nothing else until he had carried out his uncle Ured's plan. He would love no one until Egrin Dinoba and Daemon Saredoth were dead.

The sun began its slow descent, casting flickering shadows through the surrounding oaks, illuminating their small rounded leaves in sudden spurts of brilliance. They would need to make camp soon. It would be best to wait and traverse the Illuvian forests in daylight.

"Do either of you hear singing?" Saida asked, startling him out of his thoughts.

Alluin halted his antlioch and listened, hearing nothing but the gentle hoot of an owl preparing for its nighttime hunt.

Saida dismounted her antlioch, her pointed ear tilted up to the sky.

"You must be going mad," Elmerah commented. "It was bound to happen sooner or later."

Saida scowled up at her.

Alluin sighed. "We may as well make camp. If we cross into the Dracawyn Province as soon as the sun rises, we should be able to reach the southern border before it sets."

Alluin dismounted, then began unstrapping the supplies from his antlioch's back. They didn't have much —they didn't want to weigh down the antlioch and slow their journey—just bedrolls, enough food and water to last a few days, and weapons. Many, many weapons.

Elmerah swung her leg over the antlioch's neck and

slid off, landing with a balanced thud on the forested earth.

While Elmerah piled twigs and branches for a fire, Saida unfurled her bedroll across the rocky ground scattered with oak leaves, then sat cross-legged on it. She glanced about warily, her fingers curled around a simple, Valeroot-crafted fighting staff at her side.

"Do you still hear—" Alluin began to ask, but the words froze on his lips. He heard it too. A sad, sweet melody in a language he did not recognize. "Everybody up," he ordered. "Be prepared." His arms felt weak, too weak to hold his heavy daggers. He was tired. He needed rest.

Elmerah sprung to her feet. "Oh bloody pig filth. It's a Fossegrim, isn't it?" She drew her fine cutlass, procured from a pirate captain, and glanced about. Unlike Alluin, she was seemingly unaffected by the eerie song sapping the strength from his limbs.

Saida remained seated on her bedroll, her eyes unfocused as she blinked up at them.

"I think so," he answered, his hands trembling around the leather-wrapped hilts of his daggers. He hadn't expected Fossegrim this far from the Illuvian forests, and only a day's ride from the Valeroot settlement. Even in the deep woods Fossegrims usually kept to the most remote territories, and only hunted at dusk.

He peered through the darkening trees past Saida as the Fossegrim came into view. It swayed as it approached. Long thin tendrils of moss and pale hair flowed over its head, covering its face. In the lessening light, the hair and moss appeared almost white, but he knew close up he would see tones of green and blue. It lifted long clawed hands, bobbing them in rhythm with the song that seemed to emanate from its very being, rather than from a mouth, for no mouth was visible on the swaying shape. Long mossy tendrils draped its spindly arms, seeming to float with its movements.

As Elmerah's blade lit with fire, Alluin snapped out of the Fossegrim's trance, still groggy, but somewhat freed from the sleep-like state the creature had cast upon him. That was how the Fossegrim hunted. They were highly vulnerable to direct attack, so they only killed once their victims were asleep. Saida slumped onto her side, not as lucky as he.

"Why aren't you affected?" he muttered to Elmerah, though his own voice sounded far away.

She snorted, and it seemed to echo in his mind. "Fossegrim are common in Shadowmarsh. Witches learn early to block out their song. You'd think with all the time you've spent in the deep woods, you'd have learned to do the same."

Listening to her speak helped him come to a little bit more. The Fossegrim continued its slow approach. He licked his dry lips, his gaze focused on the Fossegrim's long black claws. "How about you go ahead and kill it?"

"Witches also learn early on that sleep spells are not the Fossegrim's most deadly weapon. If I don't kill it quick enough, it will release its . . . spores. They can rot the flesh." She pursed her lips in thought. "If only I were better with a bow. We need a shot straight to the heart. That's the best way."

The Fossegrim stopped roughly twenty paces away. It seemed transfixed by Elmerah's fiery blade, despite its seeming lack of eyes.

Alluin tried to lift his arm toward the antlioch where his bow was strapped, but instead his hand went slack, dropping his dagger. He looked down at it, then past it to Saida, now curled up on her bedroll, fast asleep.

"You'll have to do your best to kill it quickly," he breathed, every word seeming to sap more of his strength. "I fear I will do no good here."

"Alright," she agreed. "I suppose lightning is our best bet, though I'll have to extinguish my flame, and I think that's the only thing keeping it at bay."

"Do it," he rasped.

He watched Elmerah's flame go out with a hiss as she lifted her blade to the sky. A rumble of thunder echoed, eliciting goosebumps across his arms. Despite their predicament, he couldn't help but marvel at her power. With a shrill cry echoing through the chorus of its song, the Fossegrim rushed forward. Elmerah's lightning would come too late, and he couldn't move to fight it—

An arrow sailed through the air and landed with a thunk in the Fossegrim's side. The creature's song cut off abruptly as it toppled over.

Elmerah lowered her cutlass, and the pressure of the oncoming storm began to dissipate. "What the—" she began as two men and a woman approached, each aiming a bow. All three had long, dark brown hair, and bronze skin close in tone to Elmerah's. Their clothes were mostly leather and fur, with a few roughly woven, undyed fabrics here and there.

"What are you doing here?" the female demanded as the older of the two men lowered his bow and knelt to retrieve his arrow from the dead Fossegrim.

Saida stumbled to her feet, then backed toward Elmerah, who was giving the newcomers a strange look.

"Answer me," the woman demanded, shifting her arrow so that it pointed directly at Elmerah's heart.

Elmerah didn't so much as flinch. Thunder crackled overhead. "Lower that arrow before you get yourself killed," she growled.

Raindrops began to patter across the leaves overhead.

The bow-wielding woman's jaw went slack as she seemed to finally really look at Elmerah. "You're Arthali," she gasped. "Pureblood?"

"Lower. Your. Bow," Elmerah demanded.

The woman instantly obeyed, as did the other man.

Elmerah glanced at Alluin. "They're Arthali halfbloods."

Saida rubbed her eyes, still seeming half under the dead Fossegrim's spell. "This cannot be. No Arthali live this far south. Neither the elves nor the Nokken would allow it."

The trio each glanced at each other, then the woman turned to Saida. "You would question our existence, when you travel with a pureblood Arthali? Are you an exile?"

Alluin shifted. This conversation was getting them nowhere. There was no possible way to explain to these people why a Faerune elf would travel with an Arthali, the two had been enemies for centuries. Any Arthali near Faerune's borders were hunted down and expelled.

"That's none of your concern," Elmerah interrupted. "From what clan do you hail?"

The woman bowed her head. "Different clans," she explained, slowly lifting her gaze. "I am Imra. My mother was from Northspire. Noa and Yahir," she gestured first at the younger man, then at the older, "hail from the Coldpeak clan. We dwell in the Illuvian forests, where witch hunters fear to venture."

"Are there any purebloods?" Elmerah questioned.

"Some," the woman answered.

Alluin's eyes widened. Pureblood Arthali living in the Illuvian forests? As far as most knew, the remaining Arthali clans kept to the far North across the Kalwey Sea.

"Take us to them," Elmerah demanded.

"Are you mad?" Alluin blurted.

Elmerah glared at him. "You know, you'll be seeing a lot more Arthali if Rissine is successful. You should wipe away your prejudices now."

He bit his tongue. He hadn't meant it as an insult, just that confronting bloodthirsty Arthali powerful enough to survive in the Illuvain forests was perhaps not the best plan for survival . . . which he supposed was slightly . . . prejudiced.

The three halfblood Arthali watched the exchange with interest.

Seeming to have fully regained her wits, Saida cleared her throat. "Perhaps we would be wise to visit these Arthali and secure safe passage through the forest." She glanced at the dead Fossegrim.

The older man, Yahir, stepped forward, his eyes on Elmerah. "We will gladly escort you, but the Faerune elf may not enter our borders." He aimed a glare at Saida. "Just as *we* may not enter *hers*."

The pressure of a storm returned to the air. For a moment, Alluin thought it was caused by Yahir, but the older Arthali flinched at the sound of thunder.

"I was not making a request," Elmerah stated cooly. "You will take us to the pureblood Arthali, *now*."

All three halfbloods bowed their heads, though Yahir did so reluctantly. Alluin was not sure of Elmerah's intent, but given the deadly gleam in her eye, they were not likely in for a warm welcome.

Elmerah

It was full dark by the time they reached the light of the fires. It was a larger encampment than Elmerah had expected. Since the exile, Arthali had fled *from* the main continent. She was interested to learn if these clans had been here all along, or if they'd arrived more recently.

The halfblood woman, Imra, walked at her side, casting wary glances from time to time. The antlioch stepped lightly behind them, their ears flicking in all directions trying to sense the dangers in the eerie woods. If only they knew the dangers were walking right in front of and beside them.

Alluin moved to Elmerah's side, opposite Imra. "Are we sure this is wise, walking right into their camp?"

It wasn't wise. She knew it wasn't, but the Northspire clan had been involved in her mother's murder. If the ones who killed her mother were here . . . they didn't need to know who she was. The halfbloods were obviously respectful. Saida and Alluin were likely safe . . .

She gritted her teeth then stopped walking. "If you and Saida want to remain here, away from the purebloods, I will understand."

Alluin stared at her for several heartbeats. Yahir and Noah had stopped to peer back at them.

"We don't need to remain behind," Saida answered, stepping forward and placing a hand on Alluin's arm. "If Elmerah can brave all of Faerune, surely we can remain by her side now."

Alluin nodded his agreement.

Elmerah rolled her eyes, ignoring the irritating fuzzy feeling growing in her heart. "Let's get this over with."

With hesitant nods, Imra and the other halfbloods

turned and led the way toward the fires and the quiet murmur of voices. Elmerah knew Imra was too young to have been involved in her mother's murder—especially as halfbloods were rarely tolerated among the clans—but she couldn't help her glare as she watched Imra's back.

They reached the first of the fires, surrounded by a handful of men and women, some were darker than others, but all were clearly Arthali. They looked up at Yahir, the elder of the group, though Imra was more dominant.

Yahir looked to the oldest female amongst them. "Where is Celen?"

Elmerah's jaw went slack at the mention of the name. It couldn't be . . .

The woman nodded out toward the darkness behind them. "He had last watch with Rissa. He should be back soon."

Elmerah fidgeted, glancing back at Saida and Alluin who waited silently behind her, avoiding the blatant stares of the seated Arthali.

Alluin was the first to turn at the sound of footsteps, but Elmerah barely noticed. A man around her age, one half of his face lost in scars, with close-cropped black hair and a rough-sewn fur coat, sauntered toward them. She was overcome by an odd feeling, one she hadn't felt since she was a too-skinny teenager. She felt compelled to rush toward the scarred man. To throw her arms around his neck and revel in the fact that he was still alive. Truly, when she'd left Rissine and the other

Arthali behind, never seeing Celen again was her sole regret.

Alluin

Alluin stepped aside as the newly arrived Arthali approached, though the man only had eyes for Elmerah. He walked right past Saida, and to Alluin's surprise, reached out and gripped Elmerah's arms. Alluin's hands hovered near his daggers, then the man let out a throaty laugh.

"Is it really you Ellie? At first I thought I was seeing a phantom."

Elmerah grinned a highly uncharacteristic, toothy grin. "When Yahir mentioned your name my heart nearly stopped. What in the name of Urus are you doing here?"

Alluin guessed the man was Celen, and clearly not an enemy, though he was previously under the impression Elmerah didn't have *friends.*

Letting out another deep laugh, Celen wrapped an arm around Elmerah's shoulders, an easy position since he was nearly a head taller than she or Alluin. "You should not invoke the God of War's name so lightly, Ellie. Let us find some food and whiskey and I will tell you my long, sordid tale. Although," he looked both Alluin and Saida up and down, "I'm daring to bet your tale will prove far more interesting."

Imra and Yahir waited behind Celen, who finally glanced at them. "What do you want?"

"We found them at the border," Imra explained, "she insisted we bring the elves."

His arm still around Elmerah's shoulders, he waved them off. "You were lucky this time. Bring elves here again and it will be both your heads." He glanced at Alluin and Saida and added, "No offense meant, you understand."

With that, he turned, guiding Elmerah deeper into the settlement while ignoring the stares of those who'd come out of their small wooden huts to assess the commotion.

Saida fell in to step beside Alluin as they followed closely behind Elmerah and Celen. She leaned in toward his shoulder and whispered, "*Ellie?*"

Though he was in an encampment full of both half-blood and pureblood Arthali, he couldn't help his snicker.

Elmerah glared at them over her shoulder, then whipped back around as they reached a wooden structure three times larger than any of the individual huts. Double doors were braced open, revealing a long row of cookfires beneath heavy iron pots. Two young Arthali tended the contents in the pots while an elderly woman chopped vegetables on a rough-hewn oak bench. Several more oaken benches stood outside the makeshift kitchen, though only one or two Arthali sat upon them with wooden bowls of cooked meat and root vegetables in their laps.

Celen signaled to a young man stirring one of the pots, then gestured for Elmerah to sit on a vacant bench.

Elmerah obliged, stretching her arms over her head. "I must admit, this is far from what I'd expected when Imra led us here."

Standing in front of Elmerah, Celen flicked his gaze to Alluin, then back down as he ran a palm across the scarred portion of his face. "You came to see if there were any Northspire witches, didn't you?"

Elmerah glanced back at Alluin and Saida, then back to Celen. "Yes, but there's no need to discuss that now that you are here. I know you would not ally yourself with *certain* Arthali."

Alluin wondered at their exchange as Celen smirked down at Elmerah. "You would still trust my loyalty after all this time?"

A girl in the makeshift kitchen emerged with four full bowls on a thin wooden platter. She silently offered a bowl to each of them, her gaze hidden behind her dark wavy locks. With a quick bow to Celen, she scurried away.

Alluin and Saida sat themselves on another bench. Judging by the way Celen boxed them out with his back, they were unwelcome in the conversation.

Elmerah set her bowl aside on her bench, watching Celen sit on the opposite bench, facing her.

"You'd not speak so easily with me now if any of those I seek were here," Elmerah replied to his earlier question.

Celen laughed. "No, I'd be hurrying the women and children away to avoid the destruction you would soon wreak. Now tell me," he shifted in his seat to encompass Saida and Alluin in his gaze, "what are you doing so near Dracawyn Province?" His eyes turned to Elmerah. "You know witch hunters roam the borders."

Elmerah snorted. "*You* don't seem too worried about that."

Celen shrugged. "The edge of the Illuvian forests is a good place to hide. We are far from the Capital, and just far enough from Faerune. The witch hunters stay on the other side of the forest, lest the Fossegrim and sun wyrms thin their numbers."

Elmerah picked up her bowl. "Speaking of the Capital, I should probably warn you—"

"Elmerah," Alluin hissed, unsure of just what she was about to give away.

She cast a glare at him, then turned back to Celen. "I was only going to say to be wary of Dreilore . . . and the Nokken for that matter."

Celen's strong jaw fell open. "The *Dreilore?*"

Saida darted a cautious look toward Alluin, her bowl of steaming meat seemingly forgotten in her hands.

He met her gaze with a frown. It was unlikely these Arthali were part of the emperor's schemes—they were hiding *from* the Empire after all—but Egrin had enlisted Rissine. There was no saying how far his reach went.

Elmerah lifted a hunk of meat with her fingers, tore off a bite with her teeth, chewed, and swallowed before plopping the meat back in her bowl. "Yes, they are hiding in the deep woods to the north, and also within the Capital. If it is possible to move further from the border of Faerune, I would."

Alluin shifted in his seat, now uncomfortable for another reason. While he instantly disliked Celen, Faerune still needed allies, and these Arthali were much closer than any Rissine might gather.

Saida cleared her throat, looking over at Celen. "Celen," she straightened her back and lifted her nose, "what are your thoughts on the Empire?"

Celen narrowed his eyes as Elmerah turned a glare at Saida. "Now is not the time to discuss that."

"No no," Celen soothed, leaning forward toward Saida. "Why would a Faerune elf, an ally of the Empire, want to know? Surely the opinion of a lowly exile does not interest you."

Elmerah sighed loudly. "Just answer her question, Celen. She won't relent until you do."

Celen addressed both Alluin and Saida. "I hope every day the Empire crumbles into ruin, taking any cowardly enough to accept Egrin Dinoba's protection with it."

Alluin sucked his teeth. "Easy for an Arthali to say. You had a choice other than death."

Celen straightened. "Far better to die, than to live like rodents in the Capital."

"Leave him be," Elmerah growled, her gaze on Celen. "You know nothing of his life." She nodded toward Saida. "Or hers."

Celen's anger seemed to melt away at her words. "I suppose I must trust your judgement, Ellie." He turned to Saida and Alluin. "Regardless, I believe you now know just what I think of the Empire, so perhaps you should answer a few questions of mine. What are you doing here, so far from your clans, and with an Arthali witch of all people? Though there is love in my heart for Ellie, I know she's not terribly agreeable."

Love in his heart? Alluin glanced again at Saida.

"Celen," Elmerah began, "can the other Arthali here be trusted? We have some . . . sensitive information, and I fear it is the only way to explain why the three of us are here together."

"I would never do anything to endanger you," he answered instantly. "You know that. Tell me your tale, and I'll decide if any of the others should know." As if on cue, the two nearby Arthali silently eating their meals stood and hurried away.

Alluin wondered if Celen was another Shadowmarsh witch, considering how the others seemed to fear him . . . though it was the females of the Shadowmarsh line who were the most powerful.

Elmerah leaned toward Celen. "I suppose I should begin my tale with meeting an elven priestess on a pirate ship, though there are certain parts later on that Alluin must choose to tell you." She turned back toward him.

Meeting her gaze, he swallowed the lump in his throat and nodded for her to go on. There would come a time in this tale where his kin would need to be discussed, along with his deceased uncle's plan. He'd simply have to trust Elmerah's judgement in trusting Celen with this information.

He found, to his surprise, that there was no one left alive he trusted more.

CHAPTER THREE

Elmerah

E lmerah tightened the rough blanket around her shoulders. She, Saida, and Alluin had been granted a hut for the night by Celen, but she'd requested the other two retreat before her. She needed to speak with Celen alone.

Now she sat at his side on the straw mat serving as his bed in the privacy of his small hut. They sipped from boiled leather cups of whiskey, though Elmerah's head had long since begun to spin.

"Are you sure you must depart come morning?" Celen asked yet again.

She emptied her cup in one long swill. "You heard our tale. You know I must."

"But to ally yourself once more with Rissine, after what she did to your mother?"

She couldn't quite meet his gaze. Celen was one of the few who knew the details of her sordid tale. When she'd found out what Rissine had done, he'd been the person she'd run to for help. He was the only reason she managed to escape Rissine's clutches with enough coin to survive on her own.

"The choices were limited," she explained. "After Alluin's kin were slaughtered, we needed a powerful ally. There are few in this land more powerful than Rissine, except perhaps the emperor."

"Yes," Celen breathed, resting his shoulder against hers. "For the emperor to have magic . . . " he trailed off. "You know he was spotted in Dracawyn Province last season? Several times."

Her back straightened as she twisted her shoulders toward him. "And you just thought to tell me this *now*?"

Angling his body toward her, the corner of his lip lifted in a half-smile. "Forgive me, I was a bit taken aback after learning the Dreilore would soon march on Faerune, but yes. As our nearest enemies, we keep a close eye on both the Nokken and Faerune. On several occasions my scouts claimed to have spotted a human man with jet black hair and pale eyes meeting with the Nokken. Some believed him to be the emperor, but I thought it mere speculation . . . especially once they started claiming that he disappeared into thin air at the end of his visits. No one ever saw where he came from, or where he went, and he most certainly did not pass through this forest."

Elmerah chewed her lip. *Just who—or* what—*exactly, was Egrin Dinoba?* "I'd say it likely was him. Though Alluin claimed he was seen traveling out of the Capital on many occasions, so I don't know about vanishing into thin air."

"Speaking of Alluin . . . "

Setting her empty cup on the hard-packed dirt near her boots, she waved him off. "Oh don't start."

"But to trust a Valeroot elf?"

Her shoulders slumped. She still was not entirely sure how she'd gotten herself into this mess to begin with, let alone how she'd come to trust Alluin and Saida almost as much as she trusted Celen . . . perhaps *more.*

"I'm tired of being treated like scum," she sighed. "As I imagine you're tired of hiding *here.*" She gestured around the small, lantern-lit space. "The elves are worthwhile allies, and if we can convince Faerune . . . "

"You may have convinced a single young priestess," he scoffed, "but I think your hopes are too high for the others. The Council leaders are old and closed-minded. They've been cloistered within their crystal walls for too long."

"Well one of them is also Saida's mother," she countered. "And I imagine the immediate threat to all their lives will help to convince the others."

"Perhaps."

"And what of you?" she pressed. "When Rissine returns to this land with the other Arthali, will you rally behind them?"

He turned and butted his shoulder back against hers. "You know, when my ship was first destroyed on that cursed hidden coral, I thought my life was at an end. Then when my crew found other Arthali in hiding, I realized perhaps there was another way. There was another life for me away from the sea, and away from Arthali politics."

She raised a brow at him. "But this?" She gestured at the hut's modest interior once more.

He chuckled. "I imagine your abode in your swamp was no finer."

"Perhaps not," she laughed, "but I do not think I can go back now, not even with Rissine's blessing. Egrin knows something about Shadowmarsh, and the reason his father ordered our clan to be killed, and I have a feeling it has something to do with why Faerune is next. I intend to see this through." She met his gaze. "And I'd hoped you'd want to help me."

"You know I would do most anything to help you . . . but Faerune? They're almost as bad as the Empire. They'd kill us on sight." He looked at her meaningfully. "They'll kill *you* on sight."

"Are you afraid?" she taunted.

He wrinkled his nose, tugging awkwardly at the scars littering one side of his face. "Hardly, but most who dwell here are halfbloods. They're weak. I'd rather not lead them to their deaths."

Her head was spinning from the whiskey. She wasn't

even sure why she was trying to lure Celen into this mad cause, but Celen had always made her feel safe, ever since she was a girl. "Then just you, and any other purebloods."

He placed a hand on her leg. "If you can convince Faerune to ally with the Arthali, maybe then we can come to terms."

"You already expressed your doubts over that notion. Your promise is empty."

He grinned, looking a bit eerie in the lantern light. "If anyone can manage such a feat, it's you."

She pursed her lips. "Fine. Once Saida and I convince the High Council, I will send a messenger to these woods, and you will come to meet me." She held out her hand.

He seemed to hesitate, then his shoulders slumped. "You know, I'm getting too old for these adventures." He lifted his palm from her leg and took her outstretched hand.

She grinned. "You're hardly older then me. You'll manage." Still feeling a little woozy, she dropped his hand and stood, casting aside the blanket from her shoulders.

He looked up at her. "You know, you could always stay here with me tonight."

She snorted. "I think not." She walked toward the rickety wooden door, then turned back. "But perhaps if you keep your promise, I might grow a little more partial to you."

The cool night air refreshed her wits as she let herself

out of the hut, leaving Celen to stew on his mat. Really, she was a bit surprised he'd made an advance toward her. She'd always viewed him more as a brother than anything else.

Shaking her head, she walked through the dark toward the hut where Alluin and Saida were hopefully asleep. They'd need to leave at first light, and she'd rather avoid questions about her private discussion with Celen. The scent of bitterroot drifted out from some of the surrounding huts, increasing her dizziness. She'd never been a fan of the pungent herb, and couldn't fathom why so many would choose to smoke it.

"It's late," a voice commented as she reached the hut.

She squinted in the near-darkness, making out Alluin's silhouette. "My how observant of you. I would have never realized."

Pushing away from the hut wall where he'd been leaning, he stepped forward. "Were you able to convince him? Will those here ally with Faerune?"

"We'll see," she said as she walked past him, more than ready to pass out for the rest of the evening.

He grabbed her arm, halting her. "Can we at least trust he'll keep all we've told him silent? The last thing we need is for the emperor to learn of our plans."

A flash of irritation warmed her cheeks. "If I'd thought that was a possibility I wouldn't have told him in the first place."

"We were surprised you did."

Oh, so now they were talking about her while she was away? She stepped back and faced him. "So let me see if I understand you. It was fine to blab all our plans to the other Valeroot elves, and to soon reveal all to Faerune, but we tell one Arthali and we're suddenly worried about sinking our ship?"

"That's not what I meant," he sighed.

Her jaw clenched. She really wished she hadn't had so much to drink. It tended to make her a bit . . . fiery.

She took a steadying breath. "Celen's scouts claimed to have seen the emperor meeting with the Nokken on multiple occasions. They claim he seemed to appear out of thin air, and vanished just as suddenly."

Alluin blinked at her, his face near enough for her to see his irritation leak away. "When was this? How many times?"

"Ask Celen," she said as she continued her advance toward the door.

She opened it, and he followed her inside. Saida's outline could be seen on the straw mat furthest from the door. There were two other mats, a pile of their belongings, and a dimly glowing lantern on the dirt floor.

Wishing she'd had a chance to wash up, but too tired to do it now, she flopped down onto the mat next to Saida's.

Alluin latched the door, for what little good it would do in holding the rickety wood closed against invaders, then took the third mat. "Many times my scouts followed

Egrin out of the kingdom," he whispered, "only to lose him quite suddenly on the road. Other times he wouldn't be seen within the Capital for weeks, but no one had noticed his departure. The only reason we knew he was meeting with the Dreilore was by word from our sentries near the border of the Akenyth Province. They heard whisperings from the local farmers of Egrin visiting the Salisfait mines."

Resting on her back, she stared up at the straw roof, the striated shadows shifting with the lantern's small flame. "So not only can Egrin crush the air from our lungs, form invisible barriers, and hold us immobile, he could also appear in this hut in the blink of an eye. *Lovely.*"

"Perhaps the Faerune scholars will have accounts of others with such magic."

"Perhaps," she muttered, slowly drifting off. She was quite sure once they reached Faerune, questioning the scholars would be the last thing on her mind. Staying alive amongst scheming elves who'd hated her kind for centuries would keep her plenty busy.

Saida

S aida was the first to wake, which wasn't a surprise considering the late night Elmerah and Alluin had.

She'd heard them whispering to each other, but had been too tired to note what was said.

She sat up and pawed at her tangled hair. Only one day back at their travels and she was an utter mess. Her parents wouldn't even recognize her when they reached Faerune the following day.

With a groan, Elmerah sat up and rubbed her furrowed brow. "Damned sunbrew whiskey. *Always* a mistake."

Saida laughed. Her parents would hardly even notice her when they had Elmerah to concern themselves with. "How was your time with Celen last night?"

Elmerah glanced at Alluin, still seemingly asleep, then back to Saida. "We can discuss that later." She threw aside the scrap of fabric serving as her blanket and stood, stretching her arms overhead where they brushed the underside of the low thatched roof. "Let's find a final meal then get out of this cursed forest before any more Fossegrim find us."

She walked across the hut and let herself out the rickety door as Alluin sat up on his mat and watched her go. He gave Saida an exasperated look, got up, then followed Elmerah. Saida stared at the empty doorway. She'd hoped eventually Alluin and Elmerah would stop conflicting, but it seemed they were only getting worse.

Elmerah popped her head back into the hut. "Are you coming, *princess*?"

Saida rose from her mat with a scowl. She liked it

better when Elmerah's attentions were focused on Alluin.

Once she'd gotten dressed and tended to her morning needs, Saida met Alluin, Elmerah, and Celen outside the cook-hut. Celen was accompanied by Imra and Yahir, both standing with arms crossed behind him while he lounged on one of the wooden benches.

"Toward Faerune?" she heard Elmerah ask as she reached her back. "Are you sure?"

Imra nodded. "Had I known you were at odds with the Nokken, I would have mentioned it earlier."

Elmerah glanced back from her perch across from Celen, landing her puffy-eyed gaze on Saida. "We should be on our way soon. A small party of Nokken were spotted heading toward Faerune well before we left the Capital. There's no saying what kind of trouble they've caused in that time."

A lump formed in Saida's throat. If the Nokken went to Faerune, it was surely upon orders from the emperor. An initial strike before the larger Dreilore assault?

A young female Arthali emerged from the cook-hut, its doors open just a crack against the chilly morning air. Her nose lifted to avoid eye-contact as she offered a bowl of porridge to Saida, causing her to finally notice the empty bowl next to Elmerah, and the mostly untouched bowl next to Alluin on a separate bench.

Elmerah was still watching her, awaiting her reaction.

Saida patted her wooden spoon on the surface of her porridge, having no desire to eat it. Her stomach was already filled with knots, leaving no room for food. "I should not have delayed us so long. Any damage the Nokken have caused is my fault."

Alluin retrieved his porridge bowl from his side. "No. If we hadn't ended up here, we might not have known the Nokken traveled that way. They can look like anyone. At least now, we'll be wary of any we meet."

Saida nodded and forced a bite of her salty porridge, though Alluin's words did little to soothe her.

Celen cleared his throat, breaking the heavy silence. "Imra and I will escort you to the edge of the forest. We know the safest paths, and can avoid any traveling Nokken. If your antlioch can carry two riders, we can likely make to the border by nightfall."

"We appreciate the escort," Elmerah laughed. "Elves seem to be highly susceptible to Fossegrim wiles."

Celen smirked. "Now now, not all of us are tossed to the dangers of the wilds as soon as we can walk."

Saida caught Alluin rolling his eyes, though he didn't comment. Thinking of the Fossegrim and how easily it had enchanted her, she was sure Alluin was just as grateful as she for the escort.

Alluin

The antlioch lightly swayed beneath Alluin, seemingly unaffected by the extra burden. Imra rode with him, barely touching his back, and Saida with Elmerah, distributing the weight of the riders as evenly as possible. Celen, giant that he was, rode Elmerah's antlioch on his own.

Alluin shifted, bumping Imra with his back. He tensed as she jerked away from the added touch, then let out a huff. He was hardly concerned with her at this point. He was more focused on the occasional tracks he'd spotted along their path, along with snapped twigs and trampled grass. A larger party had passed this way, hopefully more of Celen's clan, but it was impossible to say for sure.

Celen muttered something in a language Alluin didn't recognize, then to his surprise, Elmerah replied in the same language, perhaps one of the ancient dialects of the Northwestern Isles. As far as he knew, most Arthali only spoke the common tongue.

Elmerah leaned forward to peer at the ground ahead of her antlioch. "Alluin, did you notice the tracks?"

"Yes, but I assumed they were left behind by Celen's people."

Celen said something else in that strange language.

Elmerah snorted. "He says Arthali would never be foolish enough to leave such blatant signs of their passing."

Were *all* Arthali like this? "The Nokken then?" he questioned.

"The Nokken are deeply connected to the forest," Celen said in the common tongue. "This is something else. Are not Valeroot hunters among the finest trackers?" He said the latter with a bucket of sarcasm.

Refusing to acknowledge the implication that he was a lackluster hunter, he climbed down from the antlioch, leaving Imra to scoot forward in his place. The three antlioch halted as he leaned near the ground, running his nimble fingers across broken blades of grass, and measuring bootprints with his hand.

"Humans," he said as he walked along, keeping an eye out for any broken branches higher up that would imply the greater height of some Arthali. A few were broken. The travelers were tall, but that didn't really mean much. He peered back down at the prints. "Their boots are of similar design. All seem to be men, or women with particularly large feet. The depth of the indentations implies they are weighed down. Armor, extra supplies, or weaponry. They're tall. Definitely not Akkeri."

Celen said something else to Elmerah in that language, drawing Alluin's eye as her cheeks went pale.

"What is it?"

She glanced at Celen, then to Imra. "He says the only well-armed humans that would travel through these parts are witch hunters."

He walked back toward his antlioch. "But don't they keep to the borders of the province?"

"Most of the time," Celen explained, "unless they are hunting a particular witch."

"The prints are facing away from your settlement. Did anyone travel this way recently who the witch hunters might have tracked?"

Celen's eyes were dark with simmering rage. "Many travel to the smaller villages for supplies. It could be anyone."

Elmerah spat on the ground. "Or they could be looking for me . . . or Rissine. If Egrin has been visiting the Nokken in these parts, he could have easily paid a visit to the witch hunters."

She didn't explain further, but Alluin knew what she meant. Egrin had wanted to test her magic, to find its source. He had not likely been pleased about losing both her and Rissine.

Elmerah looked to Celen. "You should return to your clan. If we run into these witch hunters now, they may suspect there are more Arthali in the forest. If it's just me, and Egrin really did send them, they will know I came from elsewhere."

Celen shook his head and rubbed his brow. "Yes, they will have that knowledge right before they kill you. You don't want to face the witch hunters in these parts, Elmerah. They've grown far more clever than any we faced in the North. They have enchanted Dreilore weapons, and alchemic potions that can do as much damage as any natural magic. Some of the potions they drink to give them strength, and it eventually mutates both body and mind."

She shrugged. "I can handle them. Your duty is to those you've sworn to keep safe. I'm not the confused little girl you once knew."

Celen frowned. "You know that is not what I meant."

Imra watched the argument warily, clinging to the wool of Alluin's antlioch. By his estimation, they'd traveled half the distance to the border. She and Celen would barely make it back to the settlement by nightfall as it was.

"I will walk ahead on foot," Alluin offered. "If the tracks grow too fresh, we will take another route. I see no reason to confront the witch hunters. They are not our priority."

Celen watched him steadily for a long moment. His shoulders rose and fell with a heavy sigh. "You keep her safe. If the hunters take her, I will lay the blame upon your shoulders."

Alluin resisted the urge to laugh. "I'm quite sure Elmerah can take care of herself, but I'll watch her back none-the-less."

"How should I send word to you?" Elmerah interrupted. "I don't want to send a messenger only to lead witch hunters right to you."

Celen's scarred brow furrowed in thought. "Send someone to the border of the forest," he decided. "We will find them."

Alluin didn't question what the need for a messenger was about. His skin prickled with unease despite his assurances. He'd never encountered witch hunters before. The idea that small clans of humans could hunt down Arthali was absurd, and yet, the Arthali feared them.

Celen slid from his mount, as did Elmerah, Saida, and Imra. Celen and Elmerah embraced, and Celen whispered something in Elmerah's ear that Alluin's keen hearing couldn't quite pick up.

Elmerah nodded, then pulled away, her hands sliding down Celen's arms to linger at his elbows. "I look forward to seeing you again, we have much to catch up on."

"That we do, Ellie."

Alluin shifted uncomfortably. "We should go if we want to make it to the border by nightfall. Avoiding the witch hunters is sure to delay us."

With a final long look at Celen, Elmerah climbed atop her antlioch. "You won't have any issues reaching the settlement on foot?"

Celen laughed. "We've been in this forest a long time, girl. We'll be fine."

With a final nod, Elmerah gestured for Alluin to lead the way. He felt he could almost see her re-shielding herself behind her layers of sarcasm and disdain for others. Celen had brought something out in her, perhaps a hint of a younger Elmerah that hadn't existed for a long time.

He watched Celen and Imra depart, not surprised

that Imra had remained silent. Once Saida and Elmerah were both situated on their original antlioch, with Elmerah leading his mount behind hers, he began his tracking, his eyes glued to the ground. He focused his senses on the forest, ready to catch any slight shifts in sound or smell. If he could get a good idea of where the witch hunters were heading, they should be easy enough to avoid.

Aways behind him, he heard Saida whisper to Elmerah. "Are you sad to leave him?"

He could imagine Elmerah's glare as she replied, "He is a remnant of my past, nothing more."

He would have called her a liar, but knew her aim with her lightning was always true.

Elmerah

E lmerah huddled with her knees drawn to her chest, her bedroll wrapped around her shoulders. Saida sat next to her in the same position, close enough to steal a bit of warmth in the chilly night.

Stupid witch hunters, Elmerah thought, *robbing them of the opportunity for a fire*. They'd seen many tracks throughout the day, but had avoided any conflict thanks to Alluin. What unnerved her was that there were so many. What were all these witch hunters doing in the Illuvian forests, so close to Faerune? By Saida's estimations, they would reach the crystal walls by midday tomorrow. What were the chances they'd see the witch hunters at the walls when they arrived, or even inside them? With how the elves felt about Arthali, she wouldn't put it past them to work with the hunters.

Soil crunched almost inaudibly beneath a boot nearby. Elmerah and Saida both whipped their heads toward the sound, but it was only Alluin, returning from scouting the area, though Saida's night vision would have likely proven more fitting for the task.

"There is no one nearby," he explained. "You two should be safe to rest."

Saida glanced around doubtfully, then up to Alluin. "You need rest as well."

"I'll rest tomorrow."

Elmerah thought Alluin seemed rather crabbish since they first reached the Arthali settlement. Stupid elf probably hadn't liked being around so many of *her* kind, though she'd been forced to endure countless days at the Valeroot settlement.

She reluctantly removed her bedroll from her shoulders, releasing the bit of warmth she'd built up. She spread it on the ground right where she'd been sitting, then climbed in and rebundled herself, shifting uncomfortably as jagged rocks poked her shoulder and hip. She could feel Saida's eyes on her, but didn't look up. "Go to bed, princess. You have a big day tomorrow."

She imagined Saida was glaring at her, but her eyes were already closed, and she was quickly falling into a dark, still sleep. In her dreams she saw visions of witch hunters from tales her mother had told her when she was young.

Her body flinched often with faint utterances of concern because deep down, way deep down, she feared those tales were true.

CHAPTER FOUR

Elmerah

lmerah stood atop the grassy hill, peering up at the crystalline walls of Faerune. She couldn't help but let her jaw fall slightly agape. They really were . . . *crystal.* She'd heard numerous accounts over the years, but nothing could compare to the massive crystals jutting up out of the earth to form walls that would be impossible to scale. While the crystals were clear with faint hues of gray, blue, and purple, they were so thick one could only see hazy shadows where architecture spanned on the other side.

Alluin stepped up beside her. "They really are . . . *crystal.*"

She quickly closed her hanging jaw and rolled her eyes. "Of course they're crystal. They're not called the crystalline walls of Faerune because they're made of glass." She glanced over her shoulder at Saida, standing aways off with the three antlioch while they grazed, her back turned toward the looming crystal walls in the distance. "She's really not looking forward to this," she whispered.

Alluin turned to stand shoulder to shoulder with her. He shook his head, bringing to her nose the faint smell of dirt, sweat, and the mysterious scent of pine and vanilla that all Valeroot elves seemed to have. "Do we know why she ran away to begin with?"

Elmerah shrugged. "I never asked."

"You never asked? You're supposed to be her friend."

"Well she never asked why *I* ran away from home," she retorted without thinking.

"And why did you?"

She sucked her teeth. "Because Arthali are almost as annoying as elves." She walked away before he could ask any more questions, approaching Saida and the antlioch.

Alluin followed silently behind her.

Saida turned as they reached her.

Elmerah looked Saida up and down, noting her slumped shoulders and cowed expression. "Are you ready to go, princess?"

Saida seemed to force her gaze up from her feet, though it didn't quite meet Elmerah's eyes. "Yes. I should approach ahead of you. I do not want the guards to be startled." She turned away and pulled herself atop her antlioch, then started toward the city.

Elmerah gave Alluin a knowing look as Saida passed, then hurried up onto her antlioch to follow.

Soon Alluin's mount trotted to catch up to her side. "You should probably pull up your hood," he commented, "lest one of the guards atop the walls signal for arrows to rain down upon us."

She glared at him, but pulled up the hood of her black coat.

Saida was halfway to the gates ahead of them when the guards outside the walls started shouting, seeming to recognize her.

Alluin and Elmerah both watched as three guards rushed on foot toward Saida atop the antlioch, shouting things like, "Welcome home, priestess!" and, "Your mother will be thrilled to see you!"

Elmerah frowned, thinking what her homecoming would be like if she ever returned to Shadowmarsh. Probably something like, "Kill her!" or, "Curse the day she ever existed!"

Alluin cleared his throat to get her attention. She'd allowed her antlioch to halt while she watched the elven guards swarming Saida. "We should hurry," he pressed. "I don't want them to drag her in and leave us out here for the wolves."

She pulled her hood a little lower, then urged her antlioch forward. Saida had dismounted ahead and now conversed with three male elven guards wearing silver breastplates over charcoal gray tunics and breeches. All hair in varying shades of blond matched their alabaster skin.

She tucked a strand of dark hair into her hood. She was going to stick out like an eel in a nest of silverfish.

The guards parted as Elmerah and Alluin reached them. Alluin dismounted, but Elmerah thought it better she remain in a position to flee.

Speaking to the guards, Saida looked up to Elmerah, her eyes pleading for salvation. "These are the friends I mentioned." She flicked her gaze to the guards, then back to Elmerah. "We must go to see my mother at once."

"Lady Solana is not well," the youngest guard cautioned. "We should not overwhelm her."

Another guard, around Alluin's age with icy blond hair, stared up at Elmerah. His silvery gray eyes narrowed. "Kindly remove your hood, my lady."

She shifted uncomfortably.

Saida stepped toward him. "Malon, leave her alone. She is the only reason I am alive today."

The elf, Malon, shook his head. "Forgive me my lady, but we cannot just let *anyone* into the city, especially in times like these."

"Malon—" Saida began again, but Elmerah lifted a hand to stop her.

"I'm used to it," she sighed, then pulled back her hood.

All three guards stared at her sternly.

Malon cleared his throat. "If she has magic, she cannot come into the city."

Elmerah clenched her jaw. These elves were even worse than the humans in Galterra.

"I'll wait with her," Alluin offered, his eyes on Saida. "You should go to your mother. We don't have time to waste on petty arguments."

Saida shook her head, then turned to Malon. "Fetch my father. I'm sure *he* will see reason."

Malon's silver gaze remained on Elmerah. He raised a hand, signaling the youngest guard, who quickly turned and ran back toward the iron gates affixed between two massive crystals.

"My *thanks*," Saida grumbled to Malon, absentmindedly tugging at her dirty tan tunic.

Elmerah didn't comment. This wasn't the first time some blond muck-dweller looked down on her. It would have helped her ego a tad if it came from fear, but Malon's brow was free of sweat, his stance casual. The other remaining guard, flushed-faced with a reddish hue to his long blond hair, looked about ready to piss himself.

Muttering curses under her breath, Elmerah dismounted, then stretched her arms over her head, ignoring Malon.

It didn't take long for the young guard to return with a seemingly middle aged elf—it was difficult to accurately judge an elf's age, but he seemed older than the guards—whose eyes lit up behind thick round spectacles at the sight of Saida.

He hurried forward, outpacing the guard at his side,

then wrapped Saida in a tight embrace, lifting her from her feet. He spun her in a small circle, then set her down.

She laughed, then reached up and straightened his spectacles before patting down his short sandy hair . . . for what good it would do. It seemed to permanently stick out in all directions. "It's good to see you, father."

Her father nodded, seeming to have not yet noticed Elmerah and Alluin, though they stood just a few paces from Saida. "And you. While I'd love to hear all about your adventure," he finally glanced at Elmerah and Alluin, "*and* your new friends, we must go to your mother at once."

Saida wrung her hands. "It's that bad?"

Her father nodded. "The healers are flummoxed. Many others in the city have fallen ill." He looked again to Elmerah and Alluin. "Forgive me," he stepped toward them, "I am Ivran Fenmyar, Saida's father. You have my thanks for returning my daughter home safely."

Elmerah lifted a brow at Alluin, then turned back to Ivran. "Of course. She's been an unscrupulous terror. I'm not sure how you deal with her."

Malon and the other guards openly balked at her response, but Ivran merely laughed. "Very good. Let us all hurry to see Solana, then you can tell us of your journey."

Elmerah gave Malon a smug look, then sauntered past, fanning out the long hem of her coat behind her. "Be sure to properly tend the antlioch!" she called back.

She didn't look to see his reaction, but grinned as Saida and Ivran reached her side.

A moment later, Alluin joined them. He leaned in close to her shoulder. "Was it absolutely necessary to antagonize them?"

"Yes."

He sighed, but did not speak further, which was just as well because the crystal walls had once again caught her attention. The sun had shifted from behind the clouds, shining through the pointed crystal tips to bathe the grassy earth ahead in rainbows. It was stunning, and a bit dizzying.

Saida conversed with her father as they walked, and Malon and the other two guards grumbled behind them with the three antlioch, but Elmerah hardly heard any of it. She understood now why the Faerune elves were so protective of their homeland. It was pure magic, and not just visually. She could feel it thrumming up from the earth beneath her boots. She was sure if she closed her eyes, she'd still be able to distinguish each of the crystals butting together by their magical resonance.

Seeming to notice her state of awe, Ivran asked, "Can you sense them? I've always wondered if other magical races could sense them."

She nodded. "It's like nothing I've ever felt before."

She swallowed the lump in her throat, not speaking the second half of her thoughts. It was now quite clear to her why Egrin wanted Faerune to fall. There was unfathomable power here. If he could figure out how to harness it . . .

He would be unstoppable.

Saida

S aida found it somewhat hard to breathe as they waited for the iron-barred gates to open ahead of them. She was terrified of confronting her mother on *good* terms. Now to hear that she was gravely ill? She could not argue with her in such a state.

Once the gates had opened enough for them to walk through, her father led the way. The two guards whose names she did not know branched off toward the stables with the three antlioch, though Malon, as expected, followed them toward the High Temple. His heavy gaze made her back itch even more than the other elves staring at them as they walked past. Once her back was turned, she could hear them muttering her name.

"Are all the buildings here made of stone and crystal?" Elmerah asked, drawing Saida's attention.

She glanced at the surrounding buildings bordering the expansive cobblestone street bisecting this part of the city. She'd never really paid much attention to them, but she could imagine how someone who'd never seen them might react. Most were simple stone and brick, but with heavy carved granite, marble, and slate accents. The buildings nearest the gates were all single story, but there were some truly massive temples deeper in the city. The High Temple rose up above all, composed of more white marble than most.

"We don't have the dense forests of the North," she explained, "so there would never be enough wood to build a city like Galterra."

Ivran glanced back at them. "Our stoneworkers are rivaled by none," he added. "It is something in which the Faerune elves take great pride."

"It is pride well deserved," Elmerah replied, being uncharacteristically pleasant.

Saida slanted a look her way, but Elmerah's attention was on the architecture, seeming to hardly notice all the elves staring at her. Alluin, however, watched everyone they passed like a hawk, entirely aware of any and all dangers.

Saida lifted her brows as Elmerah picked up her pace to walk at her father's side ahead of them. She began asking more questions about the architecture, the mines, and the crystal gates.

Alluin finally tore his attention from their surroundings to stare in apparent disbelief at Elmerah's back. Slowly, he turned to Saida. "Are we sure we didn't pick up a Nokken in disguise along the way?"

"We must have. It's the only explanation."

"I can *hear* you," Elmerah snapped, interrupting Saida's father as he explained the process of supporting the heavy stone second floors in some of the buildings.

When Alluin and Saida silenced, she turned once more toward Ivran. "My apologies, please continue."

Saida glanced again at Alluin as they walked. He watched Elmerah's back with a small smile, clearly amused by her odd behavior.

Shaking her head, Saida looked up at the High Temple as they neared. Four guards stood on either side of the white-washed doors, one of the few common architectural components most often made of wood in the city.

They reached the steps leading up to the High Temple, where the six members of the High Council dwelt with their families. Saida had spent her entire life there, trapped in a role she did not choose.

Her father and Elmerah ascended the steps, reaching the white doors ahead of her and Alluin. The guards stationed there shifted uneasily, but would not prohibit her father from entering. One guard moved to open the doors, then stood aside while everyone entered.

Saida's shoulders relaxed as she stepped onto the white marble floors inside. While she was nervous to see her mother, this was still *home*. She was safe here . . . at least until the Dreilore attacked.

Her father led them through the expansive entry-room, lit by massive stained glass windows high up in the walls, then down a narrow hall leading to her family's quarters. He muttered to Elmerah about various aspects of the building, from the white stone pillars, to the carved moonstones embedded in the friezes depicting

Cindra and Arcale. There were some smaller depictions of Felan, goddess of the hunt, and Urus, god of war, but they were few and far between in comparison to Cindra and Arcale, the moon and the sun, fated lovers kept apart by their differences.

They reached the door to her family's quarters where two more guards were stationed. Nodding to her father, they opened the door and stepped aside. Saida instantly felt more comfortable as they stepped over the threshold and the door closed behind them, sealing them inside with her father's overflowing bookshelves and her mother's finely woven tapestries. Her mother had insisted she learn weaving from a young age, but she never took to it as much as the books.

Her father, always with an air of distracted energy about him, gathered up a few books that had spilled from the plush furniture to the exotic rug—imported all the way from the Helshone Desert—that was one of her mother's many prized possessions.

After surveying the room, Elmerah aimed a smirk at Saida. "And here you've been denying being a princess."

Saida glared, then turned toward her father as he tried to fit the fallen books back on a shelf. "Where is mother?"

Giving up and setting the books on the floor beside the shelf, he gestured to the bedchamber he and her mother shared. "She's in there with the healer." He glanced at Elmerah and Alluin. "Would you perhaps like some tea? I'm sure Solana would appreciate a moment alone with Saida."

Elmerah rubbed her stomach. "Perhaps something a bit stronger? And I wouldn't scoff at a meal."

Alluin nudged her with an elbow. "Don't be rude."

Saida's father grinned. "I'm sure we can rustle something up." He approached Saida and kissed her on the cheek. "Don't go running off again until we've had time to talk."

She nodded, her stomach clenched with guilt. Her father had always understood her better than anyone else, and she'd thrown that in his face by running off without saying a word. He'd probably been worried sick, but would never hold it over her.

With a warm smile, he ambled down the adjoining hall toward the well-stocked cellar.

Saida eyed Elmerah. "Don't steal anything, and be *nice* to my father."

Elmerah held a hand dramatically to her chest. "Why dear princess, you wound me."

Alluin rolled his eyes, then approached one of the bookshelves, running his finger across the aged leather spines.

Saida turned toward her mother's door. She could put this off no longer.

Ignoring Alluin and Elmerah quietly arguing at her back, she knocked on the door, but received no answer. Feeling ill, she gripped the handle and pushed down, letting herself inside.

The interior was mostly dark, with only a few candles flickering. The window, normally showing a stunning view of the well manicured gardens, was covered by a heavy cloth, blocking out the sunlight.

She shut the door quietly, then approached the large bed in the center of the room. She could see the outline of her mother's form beneath the white blankets. For her to be resting during the day meant her illness was far more serious than Saida realized. Her mother *never* slept during the day.

She glanced around the sparsely furnished room for the healer her father mentioned, but saw no one.

"Mother?"

No reply.

Fearing the worst, she approached the bed, then pulled down the blankets with a trembling hand.

Her mother groaned, then rolled over on her side, hiding her face beneath a curtain of shimmering, nearly white hair.

Exhaling in relief, Saida shook her mother's shoulder. "Mother, wake up. It's Saida."

Her mother startled, then sat up suddenly. Her hand shot to her brow, rubbing it as she winced in pain. "Saida? Is it truly you?"

Saida nodded, though her mother wasn't looking at her. "Mother, how long have you been ill?"

Her mother finally dropped her hand and looked up at her. She blinked, her eyes slowly seeming to come into focus. "It really is you. I thought perhaps I was having a dream. Where have you been?"

Saida shook her head. "We'll talk about that later. For now, you must tell me about your illness."

Solana sighed. "It started not long after you disappeared. Many in the city have fallen ill with the same malady. Some have perished." She fumbled to puff up her pillows.

Saida leaned in and helped her. "Where is the healer? I'd like to know what he or she is doing to help you."

Her mother waved her off as she rested her back against the pillows. "She went to fetch fresh bedding. She'll return soon. Now tell me, where have you been?"

Saida wrinkled her brow, though her mother's eyes were closed again so she didn't see it. "We'll talk about that later, once you're well."

Her mother cracked one eye open.

Saida met her partial gaze, then sighed. "Fine. I've been in Galterra, and we have much to discuss. Mother, I know it will be difficult to believe, but we can no longer trust the Empire. Faerune is in great danger."

Her mother's other eye opened. "Saida, we've had peace with the Empire since the Great War."

"Mother, you must believe me. There are Dreilore in the Capital slaughtering Valeroot elves. They will come for us next."

She turned at the sound of the door opening. The healer, dressed in loose white robes, entered the room with a pile of bedding in her arms, obscuring her face.

She used one foot to close the door behind her, then plopped the pile down in a chair beside the bed.

"Oh good," Saida's mother muttered. "Meara, my daughter would like to discuss my illness with you."

Her mother obviously wasn't taking the threat seriously, but that was the last thing on Saida's mind. "Mother! That is not your healer. That is one of the Nokken!" She shot to her feet, placing herself between her mother and the female Nokken.

The Nokken's eyes shifted nervously. Her fox ears twitched.

Her mother sat up. "Saida! What has gotten into you? That's Meara. You know very well the Nokken are not permitted within the crystal walls."

The Nokken slowly backed away, eyeing the door just as it burst open.

Alluin entered first, his hand on the dagger at his belt. "We heard yelling." He noted the Nokken without regard, then relaxed, stepping further into the room.

Elmerah stepped up behind him and resheathed her cutlass in a well-practiced, one-handed movement, then took a bite of the jelly-filled steamed bun in her other hand. "We thought you were being attacked," she lectured with her mouth half-full. Ivran stood in the doorway behind Elmerah, peeking into the room.

The Nokken had backed herself into the corner, her gaze on the open door.

Saida pointed to her. "Do you not all see the Nokken in the room!"

Elmerah and Alluin both looked at her like she was mad, then Alluin's expression turned grim. He narrowed his gaze at the cowering Nokken, then back to Saida. "The Nokken on the beach," he began, "the one impersonating Daemon Saredoth. I remember you telling me you never saw Daemon there, only the Nokken."

Saida's father turned to Elmerah. "Fetch the guards. They should be stationed outside the main door."

With a final curious glance at the Nokken, Elmerah nodded and hurried from the room.

Saida's mother glanced around the dimly lit room with semi-reflective eyes that seemed unable to fully focus. "Ivran, what is going on?"

Ivran moved toward the bed, his eyes on the Nokken. "Well my dear, I believe your healer is actually a Nokken, and our daughter is able to see through her illusion."

Finally the Nokken grunted in frustration, then lunged toward Alluin, who was blocking the door.

Alluin drew the dagger from his belt and pointed it at the Nokken's throat, halting her. "You are not going anywhere. You have much to explain."

The Nokken raised her hands in surrender and backed away, then aimed a glare at Saida. "How did you know?" she asked in a thick accent. "How could you tell?"

"I have no idea," she muttered, and truly, she did not.

Elmerah returned with the guards, who bound the Nokken's hands and escorted her from the room.

Elmerah stared at the empty doorway as they left. "I hope they'll properly question her."

"She'll be taken to the dungeons beneath the mines," Saida's father explained. "You may question her yourself if you like."

She nodded. "I may just do that."

Saida turned her attention back to her mother. "Mother, how long has that healer been tending you?"

Solana shook her head. "Since I fell ill. I had no idea what she was."

Saida approached the bed. "Was she around *before* you fell ill?"

She shrugged, her too-thin shoulders poking up like snowy mountain caps beneath her white dressing gown. "There are many healers in the city, several living in the High Temple. I cannot be expected to remember them all."

Saida's back stiffened. There could be so many more within the city. They might have looked like elves, but the guard, or *someone*, should have noticed the extra healers. "The Nokken are in league with the emperor," she explained. "I believe she was sent here to poison you and all the others who've fallen ill."

Her father gasped. "Saida, this is a grave accusation. Why would Egrin Dinoba want to poison your mother?"

She turned toward her father, hoping he'd hear her words more than her mother had. "The emperor has enlisted the Dreilore to launch an assault on Faerune. He has also allied himself with the Nokken, and I believe he sent them here to weaken us by poisoning our officials. He wants to ensure victory for the Dreilore."

Her father blinked at her, his eyes made large and bulbous by his thick spectacles. He turned to Elmerah. "Well then, I suppose you had good reason for wanting something a bit stronger than tea."

Elmerah smirked. "I like you, Ivran. You understand me."

"Saida," Solana interrupted, "What is an Arthali witch doing in my bedroom?"

"Let's find that drink you're after," Ivran said loudly, hurrying Elmerah out of the room before Solana could lose her composure.

Alluin looked to Saida and mouthed, *Good luck*, before following them out of the room.

Saida turned back to her mother. It was going to be a *very* long afternoon.

Alluin

Alluin, Elmerah, and Ivran retreated to the sitting room. Alluin was glad to have escaped Saida's mother's notice, at least for now. The situation was uncomfortable enough as it was, and Elmerah's oddly pleasant attitude toward Ivran was *not* helping.

The witch draped herself across an overstuffed chair as Ivran poured burrberry brandy from a bottle he'd retrieved before Saida started yelling about the Nokken. The plate of cold steamed buns sat forlornly on the edge of the low table stationed between the chairs.

"They'll be in there awhile," Ivran explained, nodding toward the closed door. "Saida left us without a word, not even a note, so we'd no idea if she was even alive or dead."

"She was kidnapped by pirates," Elmerah explained. "That is how she and I met."

Alluin watched her, surprised she didn't reveal that Saida was only in a position to be kidnapped because she'd been running away.

Ivran handed her a delicate glass of the purple-hued brandy. "How dreadful. Where are these pirates now?"

Elmerah took the drink and downed it in a single swill, then extended the glass to Ivran. "Likely in the Galterra stocks, I'd wager. We left them for the militia to find."

Ivran chuckled as he took her glass and refilled it. "That is good to hear." He looked to Alluin as he handed Elmerah the refilled glass. "Please, sit. Do not worry, Solana is too weak to charge out and question you."

Alluin managed a tired laugh, then slumped down into the nearest cushioned chair. He wasn't sure what he'd expected to find in Faerune, but it was not someone like Ivran. He understood now where Saida found her kind nature.

Ivran sat on the arm of one of two remaining chairs. "Now please, tell me more of why you're here."

Alluin glanced at Elmerah, who shrugged, then

downed her second glass of brandy. She set the empty glass on the table, then reached for the steamed buns.

It seemed he was on his own.

He turned back to Ivran. "Honestly, it is perhaps better for you to hear this from Saida. You may find what we have to say difficult to believe."

Ivran removed his thick spectacles, then wiped them with his tunic. "If you would have asked me yesterday, I would have found it difficult to believe the two of you would be in my sitting room, yet here you are. Just because I may doubt you, does not invalidate what is true."

Alluin pursed his lips, wondering if other Faerune scholars were just as odd.

"Oh get on with it," Elmerah sighed, leaning forward in her seat. "The emperor plans to attack Faerune, and he plans on using the Dreilore to do it. As Saida already deduced, that Nokken was likely sent here to poison your wife and the others, weakening Faerune before the main assault."

Ivran blinked at her. "That is not possible. The Empire and Faerune have been allies for decades. This alliance has brought peace to this land since the end of the Great War."

Elmerah shrugged, then settled back against her seat. "Believe what you like for now. You'll be forced to believe the truth when the Dreilore storm your crystal walls."

Ivran turned to Alluin. "Is this true?"

He nodded. "My people have been spying on Egrin

Dinoba for many years. He has been moving toward enacting his plan for some time now. Part of that plan was why your daughter was kidnapped. He hoped to trade her to the Akkeri in exchange for them attacking Galterra."

Now Ivran turned to Elmerah for verification, but she no longer seemed interested in the conversation. He turned back to Alluin. "Why would he attack his own city?"

"To scare them into accepting the new alliance with the Dreilore. I was there when the emperor made the announcement, as was the commander of the Dreilore, Orius."

Ivran pressed a hand to his brow and shook his head. "This cannot be."

Raised voices sounded within the bedroom. It seemed Solana was not taking the news as well as Ivran.

A moment later, Saida emerged, then slammed the door behind her. Her face was flushed, and tears rimmed her eyes. "She's *impossible*."

Alluin watched as Ivran moved to console his daughter. They hadn't even managed to broach the subject of alliances with Valeroot and the Arthali. Glancing at Elmerah, he knew the latter would likely be the thing that broke them all.

CHAPTER FIVE

Saida

S aida's fingers traced the words in the massive tome, propped open atop a wooden easel. The guards had been alerted there might be more Nokken in the city, and all healers and cooks of those who'd fallen ill were being questioned. Any who aroused the guard's suspicions would be detained until Saida could take a look at them. After her argument with her mother, she'd needed space, so she'd left Elmerah and Alluin in the care of her father.

She closed the volume with a heavy sigh, brushing the embossed title, *A Complete Compendium of Poisons and Antidotes*, with her palm. There were many similar volumes in the library attached to the High Temple, for what little good it did her. They might not even need an antidote—her mother could very well recover now that the Nokken could poison her no longer—but they also had found no evidence of what type of poison was used. If it was something more aggressive like the toxin the Dreilore used to tip their arrows, she might need an antidote to survive.

"You should rest," Alluin's voice said from behind her. "You need to be at your best for your meeting with the High Council tomorrow."

She turned to see him entering the quiet library. He seemed to fit well in the space, the earthy tones of his hair, eyes, and clothing blending in with the varying shades of leather binding the books, and the rich woods composing the shelves, podiums, and tabletops.

"Yes," she sighed, walking over to the nearest shelf to plunk the heavy tome she'd been reading back in its space. "Or, what remains of the High Council, we should say. Two have perished, and one is as ill as my mother. I'll only be meeting with Cornaith and Immril, and Immril is bound to oppose me."

Alluin scanned the nearest books. "She would oppose you, even with the evidence at hand?"

Saida bit her lip, then leaned against the heavy oak table. If her own mother didn't believe her, there was no way Immril would. "She had her eye on my father before I was born. She's held a grudge against my mother ever since. She's always opposed anything my mother has been in favor of, no matter her actual beliefs."

Alluin turned to her. "There must be something we can do to convince her, and quickly. We've no idea how long it will take us to locate Isara."

Saida's frown deepened. "Yes, Isara. If it were up to my mother, I'd have no part in finding her. She wants me to stay here to make sure the Nokken don't sneak back in." She could still clearly picture her mother's stunned expression when she'd told her she intended to leave Faerune again to search for Isara.

Alluin eyed her steadily for a long moment. "You know, that is not the worst idea."

Her fingers clamped down on the table edge on either side of her. "You would rather find her on your own?"

He shrugged. "With Elmerah. It will not be a pleasant journey, but she *has* come in handy."

Her chin drooped. "I cannot stay here. Now that the Nokken threat has been acknowledged, the guards will be more cautious. If I stay, I'll be little more than a nuisance, and I'll be doing nothing to help my people."

Alluin cleared his throat, but seemed hesitant to speak.

"What is it?" she sighed, pawing anxiously at a lock of her hair. "I'd think by now you could speak freely around me."

He nodded. "Yes, I suppose that is true. It is simply an uncomfortable topic."

Dropping her hands from her hair, she stared at him, waiting for him to go on. This entire day was a flurry of uncomfortable topics. What was one more?

He stepped forward and placed a hand on her shoulder. "While we can hope for the best, we do not know if your mother will recover. You may be required to take your spot on the High Council."

Her heart seemed to skip a beat. "She will recover. She's resilient."

Alluin shook his head. "You do not know that. You asked me to speak freely, so I will. Saida, your mother is quite ill, and she may not recover. You need to be prepared should such a thing come to pass."

Her mouth went dry. "You don't know what you're talking about."

He shook his head again. "You could not accept this with Merwyn, but you must accept it now. I once thought nothing harmful would befall my kin, but we are at war. Deaths are inevitable. We must all be prepared."

Tears welled at the back of her eyes. She wanted to argue with him, but she couldn't. He'd already suffered a nearly insurmountable loss.

She stilled her expression. "I am prepared to do what I must, but I will not remain behind to accept the role I was born to fulfill. I will not remain locked away in safety, making decisions I know little about. If I truly want to help my people, I need to find Isara and make her empress. Whether my mother lives or dies, that will be my course. And if she dies . . . " she shook her head. "I want to be the one to make Egrin pay."

Alluin watched her for a moment, carefully scanning her face, then nodded. "So be it. We will remain for one more day while the Nokken are caught and questioned, then we must move on, whether the High Council agrees or not."

Saida replied with a sharp nod. "Agreed. We should discuss this with Elmerah to ensure she's prepared."

Alluin laughed. "You'll find her in your bath. Once your father stopped badgering her with questions, she retreated there with a bottle of wine."

Saida imagined her mother's reaction to an Arthali swamp witch swilling wine in her bathtub and couldn't help but grin, though it soon faded with the realization that she might not live long enough to care.

Elmerah

E lmerah rested chin-deep in the steaming water, scented with herbs and rich oils. Having servants to fill one's bath was a new experience for her . . . as was having a bath at all. She'd bathed in cold streams far more often than in large iron tubs of heated water.

A sour expression pursing her lips, she took another swig straight from the bottle of wine. The elixir was more dark and smokey tasting than Valeroot wine, with hints of burberry instead of lavender.

She narrowed her eyes as the handle shifted on the nearby door. Her cutlass was on the marble floor with her pile of clothes, and she really didn't want to sit up out of the water to fetch it. Instead, she watched as the door cracked open, remaining covered by water made murky with powdered herbs.

Her shoulders relaxed when Saida's mother appeared in the doorway, helped along by a female elf in similar white garb to what the Nokken had worn.

"I hope you found yourself a proper healer this time," Elmerah commented.

Solana Fenmyar inclined her head, draping her white-blonde hair over her shoulder, then gestured for the healer to help her into the room. The healer clearly wasn't pleased. The blotchy red patches on her skin, matching the strawberry blonde hue of her short hair, showed her fluster.

Solana shuffled to a simple wooden chair by the washbasin and sat, her entire body seeming stiff with pain.

"I take it Ivran and Saida don't realize you're up and about?" Elmerah asked when Solana did not speak. "And by the way, I don't know how you do things in Faerune, but in the Empire, people tend to bathe alone."

Solana watched her steadily. She seemed a little more clear-headed than she had earlier, but still looked like death walking. "What do you want with my daughter? Why have you come here?"

Elmerah scowled, then took another swig of wine. She'd interrupted her bath for *this*? "You'd know those answers if you actually listened to what your daughter has to say."

"She's highly impressionable, and I know of your

kind. You would never help a Faerune elf unless you had something to gain."

Elmerah glared at her. She looked startlingly similar to Saida, only older, but the similarities stopped there. "Tell me, what do *you* think I want?"

Solana's pale gaze narrowed. The healer stood beside her like a statue, avoiding eye contact. "For all I know, you're in league with the Nokken. You've twisted my daughter's mind to believe the Empire would actually betray us, when it is the Arthali behind it all."

Elmerah snorted. "I see that poison has addled your mind as well. If the Arthali wanted to attack Faerune, they would not use the farce of friendship to do it."

"You speak as if you're not included in that."

Elmerah rolled her eyes. So much for a nice, relaxing bath. She tilted her head in Solana's direction. "Do you see any other Arthali here, or do you truly believe we're all connected?"

"I may be ill, but I am not blind. You are pure-blooded Arthali. You have blood ties."

"Blood ties," Elmerah muttered, sinking lower into the water. She kept her eyes on the ends of her hair floating around her. "Only a Faerune elf would speak of such things." She shifted her gaze to watch Solana from the corner of her eye.

Solana continued to watch her, though her body seemed to be slowly wilting. Stupid woman needed to be in bed.

"Look," Elmerah sighed, sitting up a little. "I'm going

to tell you a little story, but only because I don't want Saida to blame me when you drop dead from refusing to rest."

Solana pursed her lips, but did not interrupt.

"When I was a little girl," she began, ignoring the iciness that crept into her heart whenever recalling painful memories, "I had very close *blood ties*. I had a mother, and though she was harsh, she loved me, and I had a sister who was my entire world. One day, my sister brought me out on a fishing boat. I was very excited, as we rarely ventured out so far alone. We didn't return until nightfall, and things were very quiet. I still remember entering our modest little house, and finding it covered in my mother's blood. I still remember her lifeless body lying in her bed."

"What does this—" Solana began to interrupt.

Elmerah gestured to her with her half empty bottle. "No interruptions."

Solana scowled, but remained silent.

"After we found our dead mother," Elmerah continued, "Rissine—that's my sister—Rissine convinced me we needed to flee. We left on a ship the next morning with a nearby clan. I was devastated, but I still had my sister, and I knew she would always protect me, and of course she would never lie."

"Get to the point," Solana snapped. "I don't know what impression I've given, but I don't care about your childhood."

"And I don't expect you to," Elmerah sighed. "Rissine and I traveled together for many years after that. The pain of my mother's loss healed. That was, until one evening when I heard some of the others talking. *Whispering* behind our backs. They whispered that Rissine knew my mother was going to be killed. She took me out on that boat while it happened, then returned with me and acted like she was just as devastated as I." She sat up and met Solana's expectant gaze. "As far as I'm concerned, my sister killed our mother. We could have fled with her, but instead Rissine left her there to be murdered."

Solana's expression softened. The healer had even turned her eyes to watch Elmerah as she told her tale.

"So you see, Solana," she finished. "I don't give a badger's rear about blood ties."

Solana stared at her for several heartbeats. "Very well." She gestured for the healer to help her stand. "I'll leave you to your bath."

As Solana hobbled to the door, Elmerah cleared her throat.

Solana paused and turned back to her.

"I'd appreciate if you didn't tell anyone that little tale. I find pity irritating."

Solana nodded, then with the healer's help, opened the door and departed, shutting it gently behind her.

Elmerah slumped back down into the water, which was beginning to grow cold. She wasn't entirely sure why she'd finally shared her story with someone—especially with Solana—but it didn't matter. It was the past, and she was a stupid little girl no longer.

She would not be *anyone's* victim—*ever* again.

Not moments after Solana's departure, a crash sounded in the sitting area, followed by a scream.

Oh what is it now? Elmerah thought as she leapt from the tub, spilling her remaining wine as the bottle went rolling across the floor. Not taking time for breeches, she donned a loose silk bathing robe from a hook near the door, then flung the door open.

Two Faerune elves dressed in healer's garb stood over Solana, one male and one female, daggers poised. Solana's healer lay still near a toppled bookcase, unconscious or dead, Elmerah could not tell. The male nudged the female to look at Elmerah as Solana stared up at them in horror.

Elmerah considered her cutlass, which she'd left on the floor by the tub in her haste, then shook her head. "I was really enjoying that bath," she chided, then plucked an iron fire-poker from a nearby container. With a quick thought and a burst of magic, she encased its tip in flame.

To her surprise, the intruders ignored the implied threat and turned their attention back to Solana, who was scuttling back across the expensive rug. The female lunged just as Elmerah swung her arm, whipping a streak of flame at her. The male turned and intercepted the flame, protecting his comrade.

While he writhed on the floor, the female fell to her knees, plunging her dagger down toward Solana, who managed to lift a foot and kick the elf's hand where it held the blade. The main door echoed with a thud, rattling the chair braced under the handle. Whoever was trying to enter would not make it in time.

Elmerah hurtled across the room. Her bare foot connected with the attacking elf's cheek.

The elf fell aside, then something crispy and acrid smelling leapt upon Elmerah's back. The male elf. A dagger flashed near her face, then Solana was there, battering her attacker with a heavy vase.

Just as her attacker fell away, the door burst open, and three elven guards along with Ivran rushed in. The attacker who hadn't been lit on fire then battered with a vase tried to flee, but Elmerah chucked her fire-poker at her back, knocking her down before she could push past the confused guards. The male elf, singed and groaning in pain, curled up on the floor.

Solana swayed on her feet, but Elmerah caught her before she could fall. They both looked down to the singed elf at their toes. Russet hair flowed outward, replacing blonde, and his features slowly went . . . pointy. Where before was the serene, alabaster visage of a Faerune elf was now a sharp nose, thin lips, and pointed teeth.

Two guards hurried forward, tugging the injured Nokken to his feet, while the third aimed a gleaming spear at the Nokken Elmerah had knocked down with her poker. She recognized the third guard. It was Malon, the irritating elf they'd met at the gates.

Ignoring them all, Ivran approached his wife. "What happened? When I returned the door wouldn't budge. I heard the commotion, but the guards said none had entered."

"The window," Solana panted, pushing away from Elmerah to lean against her husband. "They came in through the window." She gestured across the room toward the strawberry-haired healer lying motionless on the floor. "Someone check on Nila."

More guards had come into the room to drag the two Nokken away. One of them branched off to check on Nila, though Elmerah was quite sure she was dead. Her chest did not rise nor fall with breath.

Solana cleared her throat, drawing Elmerah's attention. "You saved my life," she accused.

Elmerah furrowed her brow. "You say that like it's a bad thing."

Solana shook her head. "No, I am simply surprised. Perhaps I misjudged you."

"I get that a lot." She spotted Alluin and Saida as they appeared at the end of the exterior hall, jogging her way.

"Mother!" Saida gasped as she entered the room. She rushed past Elmerah and the guards, fretting over her mother like an old hen.

Malon watched the scene coolly as his comrades bound the hands of the uninjured Nokken, now no longer bothering with her disguise.

Alluin stopped beside Elmerah. "What happened?"

Elmerah turned to answer him, but his gaze was on

her thin robe, which had gaped open a bit during the tussle.

She tugged the fabric tightly around her, clutching the hem up near her neck. "More bloody Nokken of course. They came in through the window. Likely wanted to finish the job the poison was supposed to do."

Alluin's shoulders slumped, his gaze now on Saida and her parents. "This is our fault, we should have been more careful."

Elmerah rolled her eyes. "They were mad to come here again, now that we know their plan. They'll be executed."

He sighed. "Yes. It seems they wanted Solana dead enough to sacrifice their own lives to that end. They were in a hurry."

Neither had to speak what that might mean. If the Nokken needed Solana dead *now*, Egrin would soon act. He was trying to eliminate the High Council before the main attack, so there would be no one to guide the generals when battle ensued. With no one in charge, arguments would surely arise. It would be chaos. Elmerah watched the remaining guards as they ensured Solana was alright, then followed those carrying Nila's limp body out the door.

She sucked her teeth. No one seemed to care that Nila was dead, as long as the High Priestess was well. "We need to get out of this blasted city."

Alluin nodded, but did not speak, his gaze still on Saida.

Elmerah watched her too. She seemed . . . *young*, fretting over her mother. She had never really considered the fact that Saida was barely even an adult, and the weight of Faerune's High Council was already on her shoulders.

Thinking of the Valeroot elves depending on them, it was a weight she was beginning to understand all too well.

CHAPTER SIX

Saida

The High Council chambers echoed with every groan of wood and hiss of footsteps. Saida sat at the front of the main chamber, awaiting the arrival of Cornaith and Immril. They would be the only two members of the High Council to hear her plea, along with three scribes, and a handful of priests and priestesses. Alluin and Elmerah sat together off to one side, intentionally distanced from the Faerune elves in the room.

As Saida's gaze landed upon Elmerah, the witch tossed a lock of black hair aside and gave her an exaggerated wink.

Scowling, Saida turned to face forward as Cornaith and Immril entered and walked down the crimson rug spanning the center of the room. They walked past her, then climbed atop the raised platform and behind the lectern. They wore matching ice blue robes, as was customary for the High Council.

Cornaith straightened, fitting her silken blue robes regally across her strong shoulders. The tight braid cinching her white hair made her lightly lined features appear harsh, and there was no kindness in her watery gray eyes. "Saida Fenmyar, you have caused quite a stir as of late. First with your abrupt disappearance, and now with your . . . " she aimed her gaze past Saida, "*companions.*"

Saida gritted her teeth. She was here about neither of those things, and Cornaith knew it, but she'd likely try to focus the entire exchange on Saida's *shortcomings.*

A smug smile curled Immril's lips. She was a decade younger than Cornaith, though she looked no less severe with her golden hair plaited away from her face, leaving the back portion to cascade down the back of her robe. "Yes, and not only that, but you expect us to believe our closest ally has turned against us. Forgive me child, but we can hardly trust your judgment when you galavant around with Arthali witches."

Saida pursed her lips. Could anyone truly blame her for not wanting to join this antiquated council?

She stood. "I'm well aware of how my actions are viewed by some. Regardless, the threat to Faerune is real. It cannot hurt to prepare ourselves. Even if you think me a liar, we have nothing to lose in bolstering our defenses."

Cornaith scowled. "Nothing to lose in allying

ourselves with Valeroot and the Arthali? Child, you've gone utterly mad. The Valeroot elves are one thing, but the Arthali are our *enemies*."

Saida clenched her fists, silently praying Elmerah would keep her mouth shut. Her temper would surely not help matters. "Decades have passed since the Great War. The Arthali may be enemies of the Empire, but not of Faerune."

"Enemies of our allies are enemies of Faerune," Cornaith countered.

Saida shook her head. She was a fool to even try. They would never listen to her.

The double doors at the back of the room creaked open. All turned to observe the newcomers.

Saida inhaled sharply when she realized she'd stopped breathing. Her mother, accompanied by her father and three guards, entered the room. Solana leaned heavily on Ivran, her face pale and coated in a sheen of sweat.

Her heart thudding in her ears, Saida waited for her mother to reach the front of the room.

Once she did, she pushed away from Ivran to stand on her own. Saida could tell how much the effort to hold her shoulders straight and head high cost her. She cleared her throat. "High Council member Cornaith, and High Council member Immril, I implore you to hear my daughter's words. Just last night another attempt was made on my life. And this Arthali," she gestured back at Elmerah, "our *enemy*, as you would name her, risked her life to save me. If not for her, I would be dead, and Saida would assume her seat amongst you."

Both High Council members wore matching scowls. "Solana, your illness has made you brazen. Surely you cannot expect us to heed the wild ramblings of a child."

Solana smiled smugly. "You will heed them, as the fourth currently active member of the High Council has heeded them. Maedainn was slowly poisoned by the Nokken, just as I was. He believes the threat is real, and so do I."

Saida lifted a hand to hide her smile. With only four members of the High Council currently active, Solana and Maedainn accounted for half the vote. With half the vote on her side, the deliberations would at the very least proceed. There was hope. She couldn't quite believe her mother had been the one to give it to her.

Ivran helped Solana take another step forward, each placing a comforting hand upon one of Saida's shoulders. She lifted her gaze up toward Cornaith and Immril, awaiting their reactions.

The room fell utterly silent, save the distant sounds of the streets.

Finally, Cornaith cleared her throat. "The children of our two departed members, Seamonn and Illmadia, will be given a vote. If we are still divided at that point, we will review any evidence the Fenmyars are able to provide."

Elation zinged through her. Had she actually managed to achieve . . . *something*? Truly, she hadn't thought it possible. She'd run from this life because she believed it would be a life of never being *heard*.

"We will reconvene at midday," Immril announced, aiming a glare toward Solana. "If the votes cause this insanity to continue, we will hear from the Arthali witch and Valeroot hunter."

Saida's elation faltered. They wanted to hear from *Elmerah?*

She retracted her previous thoughts.

They were utterly doomed.

Elmerah

L ater that day, Elmerah fidgeted in the seat Saida previously inhabited. Another chair had been pulled up to her right for Alluin. She felt small and insignificant surrounded by elves, their expressions ranging from disdain to mild curiosity. They'd had a brief reprieve while the children of the deceased council members were sought out. The vote had come back one to one. Half of the High Council believed their tale, or were at least willing to learn more, while the others would sooner see her and Alluin crushed like insects beneath their silken slippers.

Ivran and Solana had both instructed Elmerah on just what to say, but she'd already forgotten half of it. Not that she was keen on taking their advice regardless. She'd swallow a venomous stingfish whole before she'd bow down meekly before elves.

With that thought in mind, she sat up a little straighter, squaring her shoulders toward the vacant lectern. She resisted the urge to look back in the crowd for Saida.

Alluin leaned in toward her shoulder, seemingly unaffected by the heavy gazes of those seated behind them, nor of those standing lined up against either wall. It seemed putting an Arthali witch on trial had gained the proceedings some attention.

"Are you nervous?" Alluin whispered.

"No."

"You can admit it if you are."

She tilted her head. "Now why in the name of Ilthune would I ever admit it?"

The mention of Ilthune brought on a chorus of whispers, and she realized she'd spoken too loud. Mentioning the tentacled goddess of the underworld would gain her no supporters here. Perhaps in a den of Akkeri, but not here.

The groan of an ancient door probably as old as Faerune itself signaled the arrival of Cornaith and Immril. Solana had returned to her chambers, too fatigued to aid them any further.

Cornaith and Immril walked toward the lectern with their noses held high, an air of sameness surrounded them despite the large gap in their ages . . . not that age mattered much to the long-lived elves.

It was Cornaith who acknowledged Elmerah. "As it seems the High Council of Faerune is equally divided on this matter, we will keep this short. Bring Isara Saredoth to us. If she supports your claims, we will consider an offer of allegiance with Valeroot."

Elmerah sucked her teeth. It was more than they'd expected, and it seemed she might get off without speaking, but the insult was just a bit too blatant. "And what of the Arthali? Surely you will not cast aside your most powerful potential ally against the might of the Dreilore?"

The chamber fell utterly silent at her words.

Cornaith glanced at Immril, who steeled her expression and leaned forward, spreading her palms across the smooth surface of the lectern. "We would have to be utterly mad to ally ourselves with the Arthali. Do not mistake me, we are *grateful* for your service to the Fenmyars, but that gratitude only buys you so much lenience."

Alluin had turned toward her, his eyes pleading that she not speak out of turn.

She stood and met Immril's judging expression with one of her own. "Truly? For it seems to me I could save a thousand elves and you'd still look at me like a crusting of sheep muck on your boots, though I doubt you've worked a field nor cared for livestock a single day of your pampered life. You would offer Valeroot a consideration if we bring you Isara?" She stepped out of Alluin's reach as he grabbed for her, walking as close to the lectern as the ornamental wooden divider would allow.

"I'd like to make an offer of my own instead. When the Arthali return to this continent, they can stand with you, or against you. I don't really care which you choose, all I know is that when this war begins, my people will not be the first to fall. Can you say the same?"

Immril and Cornaith both blinked at her, probably wishing they'd granted her a private audience instead of dragging her out for the elves to gawk at. Alluin had slumped down in his chair, defeated.

Cornaith tilted her head, observing Elmerah. "Very well. Bring us Isara, convince us the Dreilore are a threat, and we will *consider* the alliances of both the Arthali and Valeroot."

"*Cornaith*," Immril hissed. "That is not a decision you can make on your own."

Cornaith turned and lifted a brow at her. "Were you alive during the height of Arthali power? Can you say you've seen the destruction of their race firsthand?"

Elmerah's jaw dropped. Cornaith was much older than she would have guessed if she'd been alive when her people were at their most powerful. She knew elves were long-lived, but Cornaith had to be absolutely ancient.

Immril's jaw opened and closed, like a beached fish gasping for air. "You cannot mean it," she finally gasped. "You cannot mean to ally us with witches."

Cornaith smirked. "I only said we'd consider it." She turned toward Elmerah. "Does that work for you?"

She nodded. "Something tells me that's the best offer I'm going to get."

Cornaith turned next to Alluin. "And for you, Vale-root hunter? We've yet to hear you speak."

He stood, then bowed. "We will bring you Isara. My only request is that you make preparations to defend Faerune against the impending attack. I assure you, it will come, and *soon*."

Cornaith responded with a curt nod. Immril looked like she'd been kicked in the gut, or else she'd eaten some rotten fish. Elmerah couldn't help her grin. The Faerune elves were a lot of antiquated idiots, but she'd gladly save their hides if it meant redemption for the Arthali. She'd come to the conclusion long ago that it didn't matter how people saw her, how they judged her with a single glance, but now that the opportunity to prove them all wrong was within her grasp . . . well, she enjoyed proving idiots wrong almost as much as she enjoyed beating them senseless. The Faerune elves were wise to choose the former.

CHAPTER SEVEN

Saida

In her family's sitting room, Saida sat rigidly in a chair. It was finally time to leave Faerune, and she felt sick with worry. Though proper healers were tending her mother in the next room, and she seemed to be on the mend, there was no telling if the poison would have lasting effects, especially because it could not be identified. The captured Nokken claimed ignorance on the matter, and would not reveal who'd supplied it . . . yet. Saida had no doubt her kin would beat it out of them eventually, but by then it would be too late. Maybe it already was.

Saida looked to Elmerah and Alluin, muttering to each other as they packed their satchels full of supplies they'd gathered from her family's cellar. They would not be traveling far that day, just to a neighboring village where Isara was rumored to have gone on her way to the nearest Akkeri temples.

She glanced at the closed door to her parent's bedroom. She'd already said her goodbyes to her mother . . . though her mother had not said them to her. Despite her support of Alluin and Elmerah, she believed it Saida's duty to remain in Faerune. Should she need to take her mother's seat on the High Council, she'd be needed . . . but staying in Faerune was like admitting her mother would die. She would not let herself believe it.

And so, she would, yet again, leave behind someone she cared about. Another victim, poisoned by the actions of Egrin Dinoba. She startled when she realized Elmerah was staring at her.

"Are you sure about this? It is not too late to stay behind."

Saida sealed her lips into a tight line and nodded. They all knew the Dreilore might attack while she was away. Her mother's life was not the only one in danger. "I will not be of use here."

Elmerah pursed her lips. Her freshly laundered black coat, draped with her black hair, clung to her well-muscled curves. She didn't need the cutlass at her hip to look the part of an adventurer. "Your mother seems to think otherwise, and I know your father would like you to stay."

She clenched her fists. She might be small, and young, but she was skilled with a staff. She might not be as courageous as Elmerah, but she could hold her own.

"You know nothing of my parents. Do not presume to know what they want, and why." She regretted the words as soon as she said them, but she was tired of people telling her to stay. She was old enough to make her own decisions.

"Have it your way," Elmerah grumbled, lifting the leather strap of the stuffed satchel to her shoulder. She turned to Alluin as he did the same.

He straightened his freshly laundered tunic before lifting his forest green cloak from the nearby chair. "With that decided . . . *again*, we need to get moving. We should be able to reach Skaristead before nightfall." His gaze shifted to Saida's father, who entered through the main door behind them, several small glass bottles in hand.

Her father stopped beside her, then offered her the corked vials of liquid.

She took them, fearing he'd soon fumble and drop them. She'd definitely not inherited her fighting grace from her father's side. "What are these?"

Her father straightened his thick spectacles. "Medicines and a few antidotes." He pointed to her hands clutching the small vials. "The black one can be used if someone's heart has stopped. It may revive them, but can also do more harm than good. Only use it in the direst circumstances. The clear is the best our alchemists could come up with as an antidote to several well-studied Dreilore poisons, should the same fate befall one of you as it did your Akkeri friend. The green and brown ones you should already know."

She lifted her brows.

"Well, you should know them if you paid attention when I taught them to you."

Her eyebrows remained hopefully raised.

He laughed, glancing at Elmerah and Alluin. "If either of you ever have children, I hope they'll listen better than mine."

Elmerah snorted, while Alluin remained preoccupied double-checking his supplies.

Her father turned his attention back to her. "The green are strong herbs for illness caused by tainted water or food, the brown is silverleaf sap for treating wounds, though I should hope none will be incurred." He fished around in his pocket, then withdrew small vial with red liquid. "Store this one separately. A single sniff of this will knock someone unconscious for hours."

"Thank you, father," she said with a smile, moving to gently secure the bottles in her own satchel, sitting forlornly by the door since the previous night. With the bottles secure, she turned back to him. "Will the Dreilore antidote work for older poisoned wounds?"

Her father frowned. "You know that's not how it works, dear. You can counteract a freshly administered poison, but once they've been in your system for too long, they become like a disease, much more difficult to treat."

She sighed. She knew it was a stupid question when she asked it, but part of her hoped Merwyn could still be saved. "Then what of mother? The healers believe her likely to recover."

He nodded. "Solana is strong, and as neither her condition, nor Maedainn's has worsened since the Nokken were caught, we have hope they will survive, even if they do not fully recover."

She glanced again at the closed bedroom door, imagining that her strong, proud mother might not fully recover . . .

Her father's hand landed on her shoulder. "You saved her life, Saida. Without you, we may not have realized the Nokken were among us until it was far too late."

She hugged him to hide her tears from Elmerah and Alluin, hoping they didn't notice them. Neither would be caught crying no matter the situation, especially Elmerah.

Her father embraced her, then patted her back as she pulled away. "Do be careful, dear. I will try to soften the people of Faerune toward the idea of allying with the Arthali while you are away." He glanced back at Elmerah. "And if your sister comes, I'll see to it that she is not attacked on sight."

Her arms crossed, Elmerah replied with a curt nod.

Saida laced her fingers behind her back to hide their trembling. The first time she left home, she had no idea what awaited her. This time, she knew better than to be hopeful of an easy journey. At least with Elmerah around, she wasn't likely to be kidnapped by pirates.

Elmerah

E lmerah absentmindedly stroked her horse's russet mane. That morning, they'd left the antlioch behind in well-tended Faerune stables in favor of less conspicuous mounts. After a long day of riding, her rump missed the antlioch's fluffy wool. At least with the horses, and with hoods pulled up to hide their hair and features, the trio would not stand out . . . unless anyone looked too close. At least Saida would fit in well this near Faerune.

The smell of roasting meat was the first sign she had that the village of Skaristead was nearby. Soon enough the dying light revealed high wooden rooftops stained dark by the elements. She patted her horse again, hoping it would not be stolen. Though horses would draw little attention, such healthy animals would be coveted in any of the smaller villages.

The crunch of their horses' hooves on loose stones was the only sound as they reached the first buildings of Skaristead. A few curious glances darted their way, mostly elves with the pale coloring of Faerune, but a few humans too.

"That must be the inn," Alluin observed, pointing to a building larger than the rest, right at the end of the main path. The other homes fanned out around it, edged by what sounded like a blacksmith's workshop and a small stable with only one horse.

Elmerah hadn't seen any fields on the way in, so she imagined somewhere to the north or south would be the farms that supplied a measure of Faerune's crops.

Saida dismounted her sleek black horse, tugging up the chestnut brown hood of her loose traveling coat as it fell back from her head. "Let's hurry on and ask about Isara. Hopefully someone remembers her passing through."

Elmerah slid down from her horse, her eyes scanning the small stable for a hand.

Alluin approached and extended his reins toward her.

Her eyes widened. "Oh, I'm to wait with the horses now am I?"

His reins remained extended. "Arthali are rare this close to Faerune. They'll sooner chase you out of town than give you Isara's whereabouts."

She tugged her hood forward with an irritated grunt. It was always the same anywhere she went. Saida and Alluin could call her in if they needed to *scare* someone.

She took Alluin's offered reins, then held out her hand for Saida's.

At least Saida looked apologetic about it.

With a huff she led the horses toward the stables while Alluin and Saida headed toward the inn. She'd wait out of the way and would hopefully catch a stablehand at some point. Their supply of coin had been restocked by

Saida's parents at least, so they'd be able to afford a room at the inn that night.

She spat in the loose dirt turned up by horses coming in and out of the stables as she walked. Alluin would probably make her sneak in through a window.

Reaching the entrance to the stables, she let the horses have the full length of their reins to snuffle at sparse shoots of dead grass. Keeping the ends of the reins looped around one hand, she leaned her back against the tack room wall, crossed her arms, and waited. The sky overhead was a dreary gray, promising rain that hopefully wouldn't make the marshlands impassible the next morning. According to Ivran, that was where they'd find the first of the Akkeri temples Isara had gone to explore.

She scanned the few elves in the streets, going about their daily lives and never once glancing her way directly.

"Stupid elves," she muttered, sucking her teeth. She almost looked forward to the Akkeri temples, though she wished they still had Merwyn along. He'd know more than anyone else what sort of traps might lie in wait.

Her gaze stopped on a black-clad form standing between two homes across the wide dirt road. He was the only person in the village looking her way, and also the only one standing still. He seemed to be staring right at her, though his face was shrouded by a hood. He was big too, nearly Celen's height, and he probably weighed near as much as one of their slender Faerune horses. As she watched, his black-gloved hands clenched into fists.

She straightened, pushing away from the wall to place her free hand near her cutlass. The hairs at the back of her neck prickled in anticipation.

The distant inn doors creaked open, momentarily drawing her eye as Saida and Alluin emerged. She quickly darted her gaze back to the cloaked man, but he was gone.

"You look like you've seen a ghost," Saida observed as they reached her.

She searched the area where the man had been for a moment more, then turned to Saida. "Perhaps I have." An uneasy feeling washed over her. "What of Isara?"

Alluin shook his head. "They remember her passing through, but that was last winter. The last they saw of her, she was heading toward the temple not far south of here. We'll stay here for the night, then head that way in the morning."

Her stomach twisted at the thought of going to sleep with that black clad giant in the village, but with the storm coming in, they'd need the shelter. "Am I allowed to enter the inn now?" she asked caustically.

Alluin nodded. "We have the information we need, and there are just a few elves and humans inside, I don't imagine any will bother us. The innkeep instructed us to stable the horses ourselves. A guard stands watch at night."

She nodded, barely hearing his words. She scanned the village once more, but saw no sign of the black clad man. Perhaps he'd been a ghost after all, but the chill deep in her bones said otherwise.

Elmerah peered out the second-story window of the modest room she shared with Saida. Her icy fingers rested on the sill as she watched the darkness below. The window had no glass—not uncommon in smaller, poor villages—but it had shutters to ward away the cold. Said shutters were braced open, despite Saida's silhouette huddled in a ball beneath her blankets. For some reason, she expected the black clad man to appear below her window at any moment . . . she'd spot him right before he sent an arrow between her eyes.

She hadn't expressed her worries to Alluin or Saida—they'd think her mad—but she'd learned throughout her hard life to *always* trust her instincts. Now, they were telling her she was in danger.

A resounding *thud* sounded from downstairs, making her instinctively jump back from the window and reach for her cutlass. She waited perfectly still for several heartbeats, listening to the echo of heavy footsteps on the wooden floor of the common room. Her arms erupted in goosebumps beneath her coat.

Hearing the footsteps nearing the interior stairs, she tip-toed toward Saida's bed and gently shook her awake.

Saida pulled back her blanket and blinked up at her, her reflective eyes narrowed to mere slits.

Elmerah hovered over her, her focus on the footsteps. "Get dressed, then hide out of sight."

Saida didn't question her. She rolled out of bed, then crept across the room, her bare feet utterly silent on the floorboards.

Watching the door, Elmerah withdrew her cutlass with a dull hiss. If it was just an elf coming into the inn, she could feel like an idiot later. Better an idiot than dead.

The footsteps reached the top of the stairs, then echoed loudly down the hallway. Whoever was coming her way was big, just like the man she'd seen earlier. She wished Alluin was in their room so she could at least warn him, but he'd have to fend for himself.

She barely breathed as the footsteps stopped right outside the door. She didn't dare glance away to see if Saida was prepared. A gentle clicking sounded in the lock. One would think he would have made an effort to hide his footsteps if he planned on picking the lock, but she supposed footsteps wouldn't alert anyone else in the inn, a door crashing down would. She gripped her cutlass. Her flames were only a thought away, but for now, darkness would play to her advantage.

The lock clicked, then the door creaked open. A hulking dark form stood framed in the doorway for a brief second, then lunged into the room almost too fast for her to follow.

She hopped aside and lit her cutlass, hoping to stab the man in the back as he passed, but he was too fast.

She'd hoped he would assume she was fast asleep in her bed, but he'd somehow known she'd be waiting for him.

He whirled around like a dancer, deceptively graceful, meeting her cutlass with a dully glowing blue blade.

She caught a flash of a badly scarred face before her flames went out. His blade had to be enchanted. *Wonderful.*

She threw herself backward and rolled across the floor, out of the path of that glowing blue blade. He'd surprised her again with his speed. No one that size should move so quickly. She led with her cutlass as she came to her feet, aiming to shove it upward through his belly, but he pivoted back.

The tip of her blade sliced through his shirt, missing the skin below.

"Down!" Alluin's voice shouted from behind her.

Ignoring the possibility of an oncoming attack, she dropped to the floorboards, distantly registering an arrow whizzing through the air. A grunt drew her eyes upward. Her attacker's shadowed form, dully illuminated by his glowing blue blade, rocked back with the force of the arrow striking him in one shoulder, just as a flash of white leapt over her, preceding a staff blow right to his face.

Saida threw herself toward Elmerah as their attacker reeled backward, but no attack came. The intruder turned and ran past Saida toward the open window. Enchanted blade in hand, he dove through the opening.

Elmerah scrambled to her feet as Alluin rushed past her, bow still at the ready.

Together they braced themselves against the windowsill and looked downward, but Elmerah saw only darkness.

Saida shoved her way between them, looked down, then shook her head. "Gone. We might be able to follow the blood trail."

Elmerah leaned back. A fine trembling had overcome her entire body. "No. We'll let him go for now. If we leave this place quickly, we might be able to avoid any more of them."

"Any more of who?" Saida asked.

"Witch hunters," Elmerah breathed. "That man is surely one of many, and they're not just hunting witches. They're hunting me."

Saida's reflective eyes flickered as she met Elmerah's gaze. "Do you think—"

She nodded. "Yes. I think Egrin sent them. That man had a set of shackles at his belt, and I'd bet my life they were enchanted. Witch hunters are trained to kill Arthali on sight. This one wanted to take me alive."

Alluin continued to peer out the window at her side. "That would mean Egrin knows we're here, and perhaps even knows whom we seek."

Elmerah gripped the windowsill tight enough to turn her knuckles white, and took a final look outside. The stars glimmered occasionally from behind clouds heavy with moisture. She imagined the dark streets below filled with witch hunters.

She hadn't felt much fear in her life, not *real* fear. She was powerful enough to protect herself . . . but witch hunters? They were the stuff of Arthali nightmares for a reason. Many thought they'd disbanded since the Arthali exile, but now she was beginning to sense the truth.

They hadn't disbanded. They'd simply been biding their time, growing more powerful in preparation for the day the Arthali would return to this continent. What was more, she'd seen a similar glowing blade before, green instead of blue . . . in the hands of a Dreilore warrior.

Alluin

Alluin glanced over his shoulder, scanning the thin walls of the night-dark stable. The horse before him stomped its front hoof, sensing his unease. There was an elven guard—hired by the innkeep—outside too, but just the fact that he hadn't seen anything odd when the inn was well within sight made Alluin sincerely doubt his skills.

His nimble fingers quickly fastened the girth beneath his horse's belly, securing the saddle. With the other two already saddled, he led all three horses outside. They would get drenched traveling through the coming storm, but he'd seen the look of fear in Elmerah's eyes. He'd never thought to see her so frightened of *anything*.

Finding Elmerah and Saida waiting outside where he'd left them, he offered them their reins. If they were wise, they would eliminate the stablehand, leaving no one to say which direction they'd gone, but he had no desire to harm an innocent, let alone someone who may become a potential ally once Faerune went to war. The young stable guard in question was leaning his back against the tack room, shoulders hunched beneath his wool coat, seemingly asleep standing up.

Even if they did kill him, there was still the innkeep left to reveal that they'd been asking about Isara and the Akkeri temple.

Not a word was spoken between them as they mounted their horses and rode off into the night. There was no choice but to take their chances and come what may. The scent of rain filled Alluin's nostrils. The rain would wash away old tracks behind them, but would make new ones far too visible in the mud.

As previously discussed, they would travel east, back toward Faerune, before verging off to the south. Hopefully any witch hunters who tried to follow would assume they'd scared them enough to run to Faerune for protection, not to an old Akkeri temple where they'd be more vulnerable than ever.

They rode in silence well into the night. The first drops of rain hit as they reached a rocky ravine that, according to a map procured from Ivran, should lead them in the general direction of the temple. It was a small blessing the rain chose now to come. The rocks ahead would bear no hoof prints.

As Elmerah's horse slowly passed his by, he cleared his throat.

She turned toward him, her features darkened by her hood.

"Are you well?"

She tugged on her reins, allowing Saida to ride past. "The Dreilore and the militia of the Empire are one thing. They will always have self-preservation in the forefront of their minds. The witch hunters are like the Akkeri. It doesn't matter how many we kill, they will keep coming until I'm dead . . . or locked in Egrin's dungeon, if that's his intent."

"We won't let that happen to you."

"Then you will die with me," she breathed. Her boots tapped her horse's sides, ending the conversation.

He took up the rear, glancing over his shoulder periodically to ensure none followed. The witch hunters with their enchanted weapons and manacles might have Elmerah scared, but he saw no reason to fear them more than the Dreilore.

As far as he knew, they were only human . . .

Weren't they?

CHAPTER EIGHT

Saida

I t was well past dawn when they reached the Akkeri
temple. The rains had come and gone, leaving them
cold and damp. Saida leaned forward in her saddle while
her eyes scanned for the entrance to the temple. The
salmon pink walls were made of rough coral, pockmarked and oddly formed, with large appendages jutting
out here and there. Where the walls, if one could call
them walls, met the boggy ground, moss and slime
seeped up over the coral. Overhead the walls met with
the gleaming sun where the temple had formed into the
steep hillside, guarding the caves within. There was no
way such a temple could be built, it had to be magic,
though as far as she knew, the Akkeri had little magic,
save their dark rituals in dedication to Ilthune.

"Alright," Elmerah said. "Who will be keeping a

lookout for the witch hunters, and who will be going inside?"

Alluin's green eyes scanned the coral. "We'll have to find a door first, but I will go inside."

Saida shivered at the thought of entering the temple, but she wanted to do her part. She looked to Elmerah. "It makes sense for me to go in as well. I'll be able to see better than you if we get lost in the dark."

"And I can conjure a flame," Elmerah added, shifting in her saddle to look toward Alluin, "which means *you* must be the lookout."

Alluin shook his head. "I'll not send both of you into danger. We have no idea what might lurk inside."

Elmerah and Saida both stared at him.

He stared back, commencing the battle of wills.

It wasn't long before Alluin lifted his hands in surrender. "Alright, alright. I'll find a place to keep watch out of sight, and try to slip inside unnoticed if anyone approaches. But first, we need to find the entrance."

Elmerah turned to Saida. "This is where you come in, princess. If you can see through illusions, you should be able to see through whatever is guarding the entrance."

Saida leaned back in her saddle, wincing at the soreness of her rump. "We don't know that I can see through illusions, just the Nokken's disguises. And why do we believe there's an illusion here to begin with?" She scanned the rough coral, spanning way up into the hillside.

Elmerah followed her gaze. "There's magic here. I can

sense it. I assume it's what's hiding the entrance from view, unless we are at the wrong place entirely."

Alluin dismounted, then walked forward through the mushy yellow grass, his boots making a slight suction sound on the soggy earth. "Look," he pointed, "there's a difference in the soil here leading up to the wall. I think it once was a path."

Saida followed the demarkation with her eyes. Sure enough, it led right into the solid coral. She climbed down from her horse and led it behind her, doubting she'd be able to suddenly *see* the entrance. Reaching the coral, she smoothed her hand across the surface then recoiled, wiping a slimy substance on her pants.

She scanned the surface with her eyes instead. "I don't see anything. If only Merwyn were here."

Alluin approached her back. "He might not have known how to enter either. This temple was likely abandoned well before the Great War."

Elmerah reached Saida's other side. Trailing her reins in one hand, she reached up with the other and gripped one of the odd appendages. She pulled down on it and it moved, dropping flakes of coral from the seam.

Saida jumped back as the solid wall in front of her let out a deep rumble, then shifted, breaking apart mineral sediment that had sealed it together. The section shifted back just enough to let out a wash of musty cave air from within.

Elmerah wiped her hand on her black breeches. "Not

an illusion after all, though I *do* feel magic here. Perhaps it's something inside. It feels . . . dark."

Saida and Alluin both stared at her.

"Well?" She gestured to the slight opening. "*Push*."

Muttering under his breath, Alluin braced his shoulder against the slimy, crumbling door and pushed. Flakes of minerals and small chunks of coral rained down upon him as he forced the door further inward through the collected mud. Once there was a wide enough opening to walk through, he stepped back.

He dusted off his clothing as he turned to Elmerah. "Don't go too far in if it seems risky. Judging by the state of the entrance, I imagine it was a long while ago that Isara visited this place, if she even made it inside at all. We promised Saida's parents we'd keep her safe."

Saida bit her tongue, waited for her sudden irritation to ebb, then replied, "We'll be fine. We won't take any unnecessary risks. Now let's go before we change our minds."

With a small smile that Alluin likely found infuriating, Elmerah handed him her reins.

Saida did the same. She didn't know where he'd put the horses while he was hiding on lookout, but trusted he knew what he was doing. Turning away from him, she leaned forward and peered into the dark opening, nearly gagging at the potent musty odor. While she could see well in the darkness, it was so pitch black inside, she couldn't even gauge the size of the space.

Taking a final deep breath of clean air, she stepped inside, her eyes slowly adjusting to the darkness. The first thing that caught her attention were the carvings. She could barely make them out, but could see the outline of curved tentacles, and a large, strong female body. Ilthune, the tentacled goddess of the underworld.

A flame came to life behind her, then Elmerah walked past, holding her blazing cutlass aloft to light up the stone carvings. "It seems we're in the right place. Only Akkeri would put such a thing in their temples, though I never took them for artisans." She continued onward toward a tunnel leading deeper into the cave.

Saida took one last look at Ilthune, then followed. The tunnel ahead was perfectly still—not even rats scurried about—so hopefully they would encounter nothing *living* deeper in.

"I don't think we'll find much here," Elmerah said without looking back. "I'd say that door has been sealed for a very long time. I don't think Isara made it inside, if she came here at all."

"She left Faerune last winter. We cannot rule out the possibility she visited this place, as deserted as it may seem."

"Maybe we'll find treasure." Elmerah and her flame disappeared around the bend ahead, prompting Saida to hurry and catch up with her.

"That's not what we're here for," she whispered, wishing Elmerah would keep her voice down. If there *was* something down here, some dark magic or nocturnal monster more horrifying than Saida's worst nightmares, her blabbering would draw it right to them.

Suddenly Elmerah's flame went out, and Saida's eyes had to readjust to the darkness. "Elmerah?"

"*Shh.*"

Saida opened her mouth to speak again, then she heard it. A faint hissing like something dragging across the stone beneath their feet. First one long hiss, then another like . . . feet? No. *Many* feet. Many huge, dragging feet.

She nearly screamed when something touched her, then realized it was Elmerah. Elmerah's fingers dug into one shoulder, turning her back in the direction they'd come.

A strange sound like an arrow leaving a bow echoed through the cave and Elmerah's hand was ripped away.

"Bloody bootlicking cur!" she cried out, her voice suddenly further into the cavern.

Wishing she hadn't left her staff with her horse, Saida drew a dagger and rushed toward Elmerah's voice. She found her hacking at a sticky white substance with her flaming cutlass. A big white glob covered her chest. Tugging at the other end of the glob was the largest spider Saida had ever seen. Elmerah hacked away at the last clump of spider silk just before the creature could tug her toward its giant mandible.

The spider lifted an abdomen larger than a horse over its head. White silk spewed toward them.

Elmerah's flaming cutlass whipped down, clouding

Saida's vision and sense of smell with an acrid black smoke as the webbing burned.

"Run!" Elmerah shouted to Saida. She spread her legs and bent her knees, holding her flaming cutlass out in front of her. She watched the spider with a calm eye.

Saida was about to obey, figuring she'd be more of a hindrance than anything else, then her blood turned to ice. Deep within the cave shadows, more giant forms shifted, lifting up legs longer than Elmerah was tall as they cautiously sidled forward. Elmerah could handle one spider, but many? She'd never make it out alive.

They needed a distraction so they could run.

Unfortunately, not a single thing came to mind.

Alluin

Alluin leaned forward from his perch in one of the few trees, debating his options as the three black-clad men approached, leading stocky warhorses behind them. If there was any doubt in his mind the witch hunters were after Elmerah specifically, they were gone now. All three were nearly as big as the man who'd attacked Elmerah at the inn, though he surely could not be among them, having taken an arrow to the shoulder before vaulting out a second floor window.

Alluin didn't think they'd spotted his party's horses,

tethered deeper in the marsh amidst thick vegetation, but they'd surely see him if he tried to run into the temple ahead of them now. No, it was better to watch and wait. Maybe they would send just one or two inside, and he could quietly take care of whoever remained to keep watch.

The three men barely glanced at their surroundings as they reached the temple entrance. Were they idiots, or just that confident? Thinking of Elmerah's fear, he assumed the latter, then watched as two of the men handed off their reins to the third, who stationed himself with his back against the coral near the entrance while the other two ventured inside the temple.

So there would be no sneaking up, apparently.

He glanced back at his bow, knowing it was his best choice, but what if he was mistaken? What if these men weren't more witch hunters, but simple treasure seekers? He knew the chances were exceedingly slim, that the coincidence was too high . . . but his uncle had taught him never to shoot a man unawares. One should face his opponent with dignity.

Of course, doing so might risk Saida and Elmerah's lives.

No time for indecision now. He grabbed his bow, hopped down from the tree, and knocked an arrow as he approached.

The remaining man turned a bored, cool gaze toward him. His features were all mashed up like clay, whether from childhood disease, or injuries, was difficult to say. Either way, he didn't seem to mind the arrow pointed at his heart.

Alluin stopped walking, his muscles tense from keeping his bow drawn. From this distance, the witch hunter would know his shot would not miss. "What do you want?"

Still leaning casually against the coral with the horses at the end of their tethers, the man spat on the ground. "We've no quarrel with you, elf. We want the witch. Do not get in our way."

"Who sent you?"

The man grinned, a sickening gleam in his eye.

This was useless. He needed to get inside to Elmerah before the others reached her.

Alluin sensed something behind him, then dove aside as something whizzed past his ear. He rolled across the soggy ground, soaking his shoulder in muck, then came to his feet and redrew his bow. The witch hunter lay slumped against the coral, an arrow sticking out of his chest. His eyes, which had gleamed with malice just a moment before, stared lifelessly at the cloudy sky.

Alluin whipped his bow around, coming to settle on a elf about his height, with long silvery hair braided back from his face.

Malon, the elven guard from Faerune, approached, another arrow knocked and ready to fly. He wore simple clothes in earthy shades, including a chestnut travel coat similar to Saida's, all perfect for traveling undetected through the wilds. "Where is Priestess Saida?"

Alluin's brows raised as he lowered his bow. "You tracked us?"

"To trust Saida's life in the hands of an Arthali witch is folly."

Alluin turned to look down at the witch hunter. If Malon was going to loose an arrow on him next, he would have done it already . . . and he would likely be dead. The arrow had pierced the witch hunter's heart. A perfect killing shot.

He shook his head. "We're wasting time. There are two more witch hunters inside."

Malon reached his side and looked down at the dead man in disgust. "Let's go." He strode confidently past Alluin and into the temple ahead of him.

Alluin followed, reluctantly reminding himself that Malon could see in near darkness. He would be needed to locate the others.

They entered a large cavern adorned with ornate carvings, echoing dully with sounds of commotion further in. Malon hardly seemed to notice the carvings. Alluin wasn't even sure he noticed the sounds. Malon's long legs strode onward toward a tunnel leading deeper inward, barely perceptible to Alluin in the minimal light.

He hurried after him before he could get left behind. Once they were in the tunnel, the distant echoes grew louder. He heard Elmerah shout, "Get down!"

Malon took off like a silverfish in the presence of a

whale, his footfalls silent, or at least, covered by the noise ahead.

His bow gripped in one hand, Alluin threw himself forward, trusting his instincts to protect him from any cracks in the ground or low hanging stalactites, which he could not see at all. He sensed something solid ahead of him a split-second before he would have run into Malon's back. A small measure of light from the cavern ahead outlined the two witch hunters, silently watching as Saida and Elmerah were cornered by giant spiders. The dull light he'd noticed was from Elmerah's flaming cutlass.

"Let the spiders kill her," one of the witch hunters said, his words barely perceptible over the sound of hissing and giant legs. They were not yet aware of Alluin and Malon behind them.

"He wants her alive," the other said. "No matter how many of us die in obtaining her."

"Then you go," said the first. "I'm tired of playing lapdog."

I don't have time for this, Alluin thought. He could shoot them with an arrow, but they'd be more valuable in distracting the spiders. He launched himself toward the nearest witch hunter, shouldering him out into the larger cavern. Two spiders turned with loud hisses toward the noise, raising their front legs defensively. He heard Malon curse as the other witch hunter turned back behind him, then there was a clang of steel, but Alluin was already running toward Saida and Elmerah.

He dove to the ground, sensing a gust of air overhead as long spider legs grabbed for him. Holding his breath a moment, he rolled back up to his feet and kept running, maintaining a death grip on his bow, though he'd lost a few arrows from his quiver to the dark cavern floor. He reached Elmerah and the protective glow of her fire. The spiders remained cautiously distant, watching the blaze.

"Come to die with us?" Elmerah asked, her hands clenched around the hilt of her flaming cutlass. Before he could answer, she added, "At least you brought some witch hunters to die too."

The commotion had faded where he'd left Malon. One witch hunter was nowhere to be seen. The other was backed into a corner by one of the larger spiders, and Malon was against a different wall. The witch hunter glared at Malon as if their predicament was entirely his fault.

"Can we edge back toward the entrance?" he asked.

Elmerah shook her head. "Every time we try to move they attack."

The spiders' hisses were growing louder, more impatient. This stalemate would not last for long. "Well we can't all just stay like this."

"They are Ayperos." Malon's voice was calm and even despite the spiders edging toward him. "Demons summoned to protect treasures."

Elmerah brandished her cutlass at a spider reaching a leg out to test her. The movement caused a collective hiss, followed by the rasp of shifting legs. "I'm so glad to know the name of the things that are going to eat me," she said caustically as she backed closer to Saida.

The remaining cornered witch hunter snorted. "Of course the witch is involved with demons."

"I didn't summon them," Elmerah snapped. "Now be quiet until I can make it over there to kill you."

The witch hunter snorted again. This was getting them nowhere. The spiders watched them with rows of little round eyes glistening in the firelight from Elmerah's cutlass.

"The Ayperos," Malon began, the strain in his voice making it clear his patience was wearing thin, "will only attack when there is a treasure to guard. Capture their treasure, and you will become their new master."

Alluin gritted his teeth. "A lot of good that does us. Do you see a treasure in here?"

"It will be within the largest monster," Malon added.

"Of course it will," Elmerah muttered.

"There," Saida pointed to one particularly large spider in the center of the group. "That has to be it."

As if understanding her words, the spiders began to hiss louder.

Alluin darted his gaze toward Malon, then back to the spiders. He was good with a bow, but he could admit, Malon was better. "Do you think you can hit it with your bow?"

"Perhaps, but someone will still have to wade in and cut the treasure out of it."

Alluin sighed. The witch hunter was silently watching

them all. Looking for an opportunity to get them killed? No, he was the one that said someone wanted Elmerah alive.

"Just shoot the bloody spider," Elmerah snarled. "I can't hold this flame forever, and I have a feeling once it goes out, we're all dead."

Malon glared at her, but lifted his bow. He knocked an arrow, drew back his arm, and aimed.

"Wait," the witch hunter pleaded. "If you fire upon them they may all attack. Grisham is already dead."

Grisham had to be the other witch hunter. Good riddance.

"Only one way to find out," Malon said curtly, then loosed his arrow.

The largest spider crumpled to the ground with a surprisingly soft thud. The rest reacted instantly. The cavern became a flurry of hairy legs and bobbing abdomens. A stream of spidersilk shot toward Alluin, narrowly missing his chest as he hopped aside.

"Watch my back!" he shouted to Elmerah. "I'll get to the carcass!"

He tossed aside his bow and drew a dagger from his belt, sticking it deep into a spider's front leg as it lunged for him. He narrowly avoided an attack to his back as Elmerah appeared behind him. The spider fell in a hissing, flaming heap at her feet.

"Go!" she urged. "I cannot hold them back for long."

He could no longer see Saida, Malon, or the witch hunter in the chaos, but if he could reach that one dead spider he could stop it all . . . hopefully. He ran forward, ignoring his instincts to react to oncoming attacks as Elmerah intercepted them instead. If she fell and he didn't notice, he was as good as dead. Dozens of sets of long legs clacked and hissed across the ground. He could barely see the one dead spider in the flickering light. Sometimes things would disappear from sight entirely as Elmerah rammed her flaming cutlass into a spider's underbelly.

One arrow after another landed with solid thunks around him, but Malon would run out of arrows soon.

He reached the spider. The witch hunter was already there, blade in hand.

He leered at Alluin. "Whoever gets the treasure becomes their master?" he taunted.

Another spider lunged at Alluin. He jumped aside, but no attack from Elmerah came. He glanced back. He could see flashes of dancing flame, surrounded by other spiders.

The nearest spider hissed and shot webbing at him, trapping his boots against the stone. The witch hunter began hacking away at the dead spider's abdomen, searching for the treasure. Alluin slashed at the attacking spider.

"Hah!" the witch hunter howled triumphantly. He held a circlet above his head, dripping spider blood and other fluids down his arm.

All movement in the room ceased. The spiders turned

toward him. He grinned. It was all over for them. An arrow thunked into his chest.

Alluin had to suppress a giggle brought on by the mixture of anticipation and sudden elation.

The witch hunter hunched over, his free hand grasping at the arrow shaft. He aimed a final hateful look at Alluin—though his eyes weren't quite focused—then crumpled over, dead. The circlet clattered to the ground.

Her cutlass still aflame, Elmerah walked around the dead spider blocking her way, then picked up the circlet. Spider blood dripped from her hair, and blotted her hands and face. She held her cutlass near the goo-covered circlet as she observed it.

Saida edged cautiously around the waiting spiders until she reached Elmerah's side. Malon remained back near the wall, bow gripped in one hand. Alluin's eyes widened as he noticed a small shining wisplight hovering over Malon's other hand. He knew the Faerune elves had more magic than Valeroot, but he'd never seen it up close.

Saida peered at the circlet through a veil of hair streaming with spider silk. She swatted at the sticky silk, unable to tug it free. "This must be something special if it was worth summoning demons to protect it."

Alluin watched the spiders warily. They did not attack, but he couldn't quite bring himself to trust them. "Speaking of said demons. Perhaps we should depart."

Elmerah held her cutlass out toward the waiting

spiders. "If they're through attacking us, we still need to search for signs of Isara."

Alluin looked around until he spotted the other dead witch hunter, killed by the spiders. "I think if Isara made it this far in, all we would find is a corpse."

Malon slung his bow over his shoulder and approached, bringing his whisp-light with him. His eyes were on the circlet in Elmerah's hand. "Is that . . . moonstone?"

Elmerah held it up. The band was gold, tarnished with age, curved into a perfect delicate circlet, much thinner and lighter than a crown. It was simple, if finely made, with tiny clusters of moonstones along the front, leading up to one large stone in the center. Spider liquids had seeped into the seams.

Saida cast a knowing look at Malon.

"What is it?" Alluin asked, shifting impatiently. Everyone else might be fine with all the beady, glistening eyes watching them, but he most certainly was not.

"This circlet is of Faerune design," Saida explained, "and our rare moonstones are only used for the most special pieces."

"So what is it doing here?" Elmerah asked. "And guarded by demons?"

Saida looked to Malon, who shrugged. "Probably stolen by Akkeri. This is one of their temples, after all."

Elmerah pursed her lips, looking down at the circlet. "We'll take it with us. Maybe the Faerune scholars will have more to say. Now let's finish our search and move on. I want to reach the next village by nightfall." Her gaze turned down to the dead witch hunter, then up to Alluin. "Were these the only two? It would have been useful to capture one alive. Find out why they're hunting me."

"They said someone wanted you alive," he explained, then added, "a man, it was a *he* they mentioned."

She nudged the witch hunter corpse with the toe of her boot. "Hmph. They're going to end up with a lot of dead witch hunters if they keep this up."

All the spiders watched in silence as she turned toward the back end of the cavern and walked past them, the circlet swinging in one hand with all the care one would give a cheap trinket. If it bothered her to come so close to death all the time, she most certainly didn't show it.

Saida

After a fruitless search, the group rode far away from the Akkeri temple. Saida would have preferred to stop and clean the spider blood from her hair, but there was no saying what lurked beneath the fetid marsh water, nor how many other witch hunters might be nearby. They'd hidden the third body within the temple, and had taken the three witch hunter horses. Two they would set loose well away from the temple, and the third now carried Malon, who'd followed them to the temple on foot.

Saida eyed him askance. Had he really come just to ensure her safety? He'd never seemed to care about her previously—in fact, she'd only learned his name when he'd been promoted to Guard Captain last year—and it wasn't like she was terribly special. He was one of only five Guard Captains. His duty was in Faerune, not here with her.

Malon's gray eyes flicked her way and she whipped her gaze forward.

He cleared his throat. "Fallshire is not far off, but are you sure you want to rest there? We are quite a conspicuous party, and there may be more witch hunters lying in wait."

"Don't you dare deprive me of a bath, Malon!" Elmerah called from further ahead on the rutted path.

Alluin rode silently at her side. He hadn't spoken since they'd left the temple. Saida suspected he was a bit shy of spiders.

Malon visibly clenched his smooth jaw. "I was right not trusting her to protect you," he muttered, low enough that only Saida could hear.

She squirmed in her saddle. "I daresay I trust her more than I trust you."

He startled, then turned wide eyes to her. "Truly?"

She lifted her nose, feeling oddly guilty, as if she were betraying Faerune in some way. "She has saved my life many times. You have done so only once."

A smile tugged at the corner of his lips. "Oh? How many more times must I save you?"

She blushed, realizing how ridiculous she sounded. "I only meant you have not earned my trust, Malon."

"Nor you mine, priestess. Nor you mine."

She turned away. They rode in silence as the night shadows slowly closed in around them. Thinking of witch hunters and giant spiders, she shivered.

Malon stared off into the growing darkness, his reflective eyes occasionally flickering when she caught him at just the right angle.

Elmerah and Alluin quietly conversed ahead.

Saida longed to pull the circlet from the small satchel she wore as a waist pouch, but did not dare observe it out in the open. If anyone saw . . . she shook her head. Moonstones amplified elven power tenfold. Any Sun Priest or Priestess—those with magical power to begin with—would jump at the opportunity to don the circlet. Unfortunately, for her it was useless. She had none of the magics she was supposed to, save seeing through Nokken disguises.

"Did you recognize the circlet?" she asked suddenly.

Malon turned toward her, his shoulders gently swaying in rhythm with his mount.

"I mean other than it being of Faerune origin," she clarified. "You knew about the Ayperos. If you've studied myths so extensively, perhaps you know more about this circlet too."

He frowned. "The Ayperos aren't mere myth, as you've clearly seen."

Goosebumps tickled up her arms. Demons were supposed to be myth. She'd thought the spiders normal beasts like wyverns or trolls, but Malon had been right about the treasure buried within the largest monster. "That doesn't answer my question," she said out loud. "Did you recognize the circlet?"

"Just because I knew of the Ayperos, does not mean I've extensively studied myths, demonic or otherwise. You know full well I am no scholar."

And you're not much for pleasant conversation either, she thought. "You still haven't answered my question."

His back stiffened, ever so slightly. "No, I did not recognize it specifically, but you and I both know it is extremely valuable. It is dangerous to travel with such an item, especially when we don't know who summoned the Ayperos to protect it."

"You think whoever did it is still alive? I assumed it had been in that temple for ages."

"Ayperos will only remain in this realm as long as their summoner is alive."

She bit her lip. For someone who claimed to not have studied the myths extensively, he knew quite a bit about demons.

"There," he said, pointing past Elmerah and Alluin further down the narrow path.

She looked up, catching sight of smoke plumes from

the distant town of Fallshire billowing up past the last light of sunset.

"Keep that circlet well hidden," Malon advised. "We'll rest for a few hours and leave before first light."

Saida couldn't help but smile. If Malon thought he was suddenly going to be in charge with someone like Elmerah around, he was in for a rude—or violent—awakening.

CHAPTER NINE

Elmerah

Elmerah leaned back in her chair, a smug smile on her lips. Fallshire was a modest town, not interesting at all, but the ale at their sole inn was decent. She also didn't mind the warm fire, and comforting murmur of conversation.

Malon sat across from her at the round wooden table, next to Saida, glowering. Stupid elf had thought to tell her she'd have to go to bed with no supper, and no ale.

Elmerah swirled the amber liquid around in her boiled leather mug, then scraped the last remnants of steamed eel from her plate and stuck them in her mouth, intentionally smacking her lips louder than necessary.

Malon turned to Saida, whose hair was still wet from washing away the spider blood. "Is there a secret to putting up with this insufferable woman," he gestured to Elmerah, "or have you simply forced yourself to become deaf when that grating voice comes out of her lips?"

Alluin chuckled and sipped his ale. He was stationed between Elmerah and Malon, clearly not choosing sides.

Elmerah took a long swig from her mug, then offered Malon a sweet smile. Her voice was appealingly toned, sultry even. Stupid elf just couldn't hear her right with his pointy ears.

Malon glared at her. "We shouldn't be sitting out in the open like this," he said, keeping his voice low in a final—at least she hoped it was final—appeal. "It's not safe. You're being hunted."

She drummed her fingers on the table for a moment before answering. "You do realize what we're doing out here, don't you? It can be a bit difficult finding someone who's been missing for several seasons when you hide in your room and don't talk to anyone."

He gestured toward the bar. "So go talk to someone then."

"Fine." She stood. Truth be told, she wasn't looking forward to hearing another person say they had no idea where Isara was, but if it would take her away from Malon, she'd manage.

Alluin pushed his empty mug away. "I'll come along and make sure you don't kill anyone."

She rolled her eyes and turned away. The small tavern was bustling for such a remote village, not that she could blame anyone for imbibing. She'd want to be drunk out of her mind too if she had to live and work in a place like this. A few elves and humans glanced at her and Alluin as they passed. Most of the elves had the fairer complexion of Faerune, while many humans were darker complected. Likely some of the bloodlines of the Helshone Desert and other regions of the Far South creeping in. For once, Alluin stood out more than her.

She reached the bar and smoothed her hands across the pockmarked surface. The wood was soft and old, lined with countless dents and creases where plates and cutlery had been knocked around. Alluin stationed himself at her left, as the place on her right was occupied by an older female elf hunched over a dram of whiskey. She stank of sweat and manure.

The barkeep, an aged human man with thinning dark hair and a round belly from too much ale, caught her eye and approached. He didn't speak as he reached them, and the glassy look in his eyes told her he really didn't care what they had to say.

"We're looking for a human woman named Isara," Elmerah explained. "Have you heard of her?"

Recognition flickered across his face before smoothing away. He leaned his elbows on the bar. "How bad do you want to know?"

Elmerah eyed him dangerously. "I asked my question first."

This seemed to confuse him. His lips twisted into a gross pout.

The drunk elf on Elmerah's right turned toward

them. "Buy me a drink and I'll tell you. It'll cost you much less than worming any information out of Tully here." She gestured with a crooked thumb toward the barkeep.

Tully, scowled at her. "Don't make me throw you out on your bony arse, Nissa."

Nissa laughed. The pungent smell of whiskey worked its way toward Elmerah's nostrils. "I'm your most loyal patron, Tully, and I swaddled you when you were but a mewling babe. You'll do no such thing."

His face turned rubyfish red, but he straightened and backed away. "Have it your way, you old hag." He headed further down the bar, no doubt intending to swindle other patrons.

Elmerah fished a silver gull from the pouch at her belt, then held it up. "Isara?"

Nissa grinned, crinkling the slight lines on her face. "You'll find her out at Ravenstooth Farm. She works there for room and board."

Elmerah could have kissed Nissa if she didn't smell so awful. Perhaps their search could finally come to an end. She held the coin up, but slightly out of reach. "Anything else you can tell us about her?"

Nissa eyed the coin greedily. "Well, she's mad as a whipfish, for starters. Goes around talking about demons and curses."

Elmerah glanced at Alluin to see his brow wrinkled in concern. While she was turned away, Nissa snatched the gull from her fingertips, faster than she seemed.

She turned back to Nissa with a smirk. "Enjoy your drink, Nissa. My thanks for the information."

She turned back to Alluin. "Shall we?"

He raised a brow. "You want to go to the farm tonight?"

"Don't you?"

"I suppose so," he laughed.

She leaned her back against the bar. "What's so damned funny?"

He grinned. "Ravenstooth farm. Ravens don't have teeth."

Her eyes widened. "Are you drunk?"

He laughed again, then pushed away from the bar. "It's been a long day."

She followed after him back toward Saida and Malon. "An especially long day for someone who's afraid of spiders."

"I told you that in confidence," he chided. "Now shut up."

She shut up, but couldn't help her grin as they reached the table and looked down at the pair of Faerune elves. "It seems we're in luck. Let's go."

Alluin

The night was clear and quiet as they reached the top of the steep incline leading to Ravenstooth farm. Alluin *hoped* it was Ravenstooth farm. The barkeep hadn't been terribly pleased with them. He could have easily given them false directions. They'd left the horses stabled at the local inn in favor of traveling the rocky path to the modest farmstead on foot.

A few chickens clucked in their coop as the four of them passed, Elmerah and Saida leading the way, with Alluin and Malon bringing up the rear. Malon had of course argued against visiting the farmstead at night, but where Saida went, he went, so he had little choice. Alluin, however, preferred the more secretive meeting to escape the notice of any spies Egrin might have in the area. If Egrin knew they were after Isara, he'd likely eliminate her.

"Why would the cousin of the emperor stay here?" Malon asked, his reflective eyes scanning the main house, not far ahead. "Surely she can afford more suitable lodgings."

Alluin's eyes followed the lines of moonlight glinting at the roof's edge. It needed to be rethatched, and he doubted the rickety plank walls held back the cold. The exterior hearthfire casting a gentle glow on the haystacks would need to remain lit day and night just to ward away winter's breath. It was all rather . . . modest, for the emperor's cousin.

"I take it you never met her then?" Alluin asked Malon.

Malon shook his head. "No. I saw her scurrying about the Faerune libraries a time or two, but she mostly kept to herself. Odd girl."

Remembering Nissa's words, Alluin squirmed. Neither he nor Elmerah had mentioned the drunken elf's comments to Saida and Malon. If Isara was as mad as Nissa seemed to think, everything they'd sacrificed might be for naught.

Elmerah and Saida, having reached the house, turned back to them. Elmerah cleared her throat expectantly.

He felt even more squirmy under her scrutinizing gaze. He was the one who'd led them all on this wild hunt. If Isara could not be used . . .

Elmerah crossed her arms as he approached. "The moment is finally here. Do you care to do the knocking?"

He looked to Saida, then nodded. Saying a silent prayer to the hunt goddess Felan, he approached the sun-faded door and knocked.

Footsteps sounded within. A moment later the door cracked open, and a woman that had to be at least one hundred years old peered out at them through thick, hazy spectacles. She was tiny, far shorter than Saida, almost the size of a child, with charcoal gray hair tied in a knot atop her head.

"Forgive me for disturbing you—" he began.

"Girl!" the old woman shrieked, then turned away and walked back toward a cozy, ancient stuffed chair.

Footsteps clattered across the floorboards, then a willowy girl of medium height came to a skidding stop in front of the doorway. She wore wire-rimmed spectacles almost as thick as the old woman's, if a bit less hazy. Her curly blonde hair shone in the candlelight illuminating the home. The hair seemed far too rich and lustrous for her tattered maroon dress.

"That's her," he heard Malon mutter behind him, but he didn't need the information. The girl was nearly the mirror image of her brother, Daemon Saredoth, except with curly hair rather than straight, and only slightly more feminine, which said more about Daemon than it did about her.

She blinked at them, her eyes made large by her lenses. "Can I help you? It's rather late for a visit." She peered past Alluin then gasped. "Is that an Arthali witch?"

"What of it?" Elmerah growled.

Isara jumped back as if stung, but quickly seemed to regain her composure. "An Arthali witch and a Valeroot hunter, you both must come in. I have so many questions to ask you."

She turned away and headed toward the small kitchen area, fully visible from the door by lantern light.

Elmerah stepped up to Alluin's side. "Well, Nissa was obviously right."

He clenched his jaw. It seemed so. No sane person

would invite four strangers so readily into their home without first learning why they'd come to call. Especially not when one of those visitors was an Arthali witch.

Elmerah walked past him into the home, followed by Saida and Malon, the latter of whom gave him an infuriating wink.

With a heavy sigh, he followed them in, then shut the door. The old woman had settled into her chair, and seemed to be fast asleep.

"Don't mind her," Isara said, gesturing toward the old woman. "She'll be out for the rest of the night." She walked into the kitchen area and placed a copper kettle onto the dusty wooden table dominating the center of the floor, then filled it with water from a lidded clay jug. "Who would like some tea?"

Elmerah moved toward the stone hearth, much smaller than the one outside, near the old woman's chair. She hooked an unused footstool with her boot, scooted it against the wall, then sat. There was no other seating in the small space, save two wooden chairs pushed in against the wooden table. Dried herbs decorated the kitchen, and a few farming tools lined the back wall, and that was it. Alluin spotted one door further in that must have led to the bedroom.

Malon crossed his arms and leaned against the wall near the door, leaving Saida and Alluin to wait around the table with Isara as she opened a delicate wooden box filled with dried herbs. Alluin hoped the herbs were actually meant for tea, and they weren't all about to be poisoned.

Alluin cleared his throat. "Just to confirm, you are Isara Saredoth, are you not?"

She looked up from the herbs, her pointed jaw slightly agape. "Oh don't tell me my brother sent you."

Elmerah snorted from her seat across the room. "Hardly."

Isara's eyes remained glued to Alluin.

"No," he said, wondering just what he should tell her. He'd waited for this moment for so long, but now his mind was coming up utterly blank.

"We come to you on behalf of Faerune," Saida interjected, "as your long-time allies."

Isara's gaze shifted to Saida, then back to Alluin. "Why would anyone from Faerune come to find me? I daresay the scholars were glad to see me go."

Saida bit her lip, now seemingly at a loss.

Alluin felt the same. How did you tell someone you wanted to murder her cousin and brother so that you could make her empress of the Ulrian Empire? Perhaps it was best to weigh her further before sharing any sensitive information.

He smiled encouragingly. "We mean you no ill will, I assure you. How much do you know of what's going on in the Empire?"

The kettle of water lay forgotten near Isara's fingertips. "Are you here to call me crazy like all the rest then?

What do you want to hear? That I think my cousin is a demon?"

Elmerah was suddenly at Alluin's side. He hadn't even heard her move. "Demon, you say? Do go on."

Isara seemed unsure, but continued, "I believe Egrin is a demon, or another type of immortal being. Everyone says it was his father who defeated the Arthali during the Great War, but it wasn't. It was Egrin himself."

That's it, Alluin thought. *She is utterly mad.*

Elmerah stepped nearer, her gaze intent on Isara. "Have you any proof of this?"

Isara paled a bit. "You mean, you believe me?"

Elmerah gripped the edge of the table and leaned forward. "Your cousin has a type of magic I've never seen, and there have been accounts of him visiting different places, but no one sees him come or go, he simply appears. I don't know that I believe he is a demon, but I'm willing to hear your theories."

Isara's eyes lit up. "Arcale preserve us, I can't believe I finally found someone willing to listen, and an Arthali witch no less. After my father died, I thought I'd be alone with my knowledge forever."

Alluin stepped back, willing to let the situation play out. Saida and Malon were both watching Isara, but he had no way of knowing if they believed anything she was saying. He thought Elmerah was being a bit gullible, but then again, she'd experienced the emperor's magic more closely than anyone else, except perhaps Saida.

Isara smoothed her hands across the dusty tabletop,

then pulled them away, wiping her palms on her dress. She stared at Elmerah. "How do I know I can trust you? What if you were sent by Egrin?"

Elmerah lifted a brow. "If Egrin had his hands on an Arthali witch, do you think he'd send her this far south where she could easily disappear into the wilds?"

Isara licked her lips. Her entire skinny body seemed to tremble. "Alright. I'll tell you what I know, but Arcale help you if you're lying to me. I might not have the same power as Egrin, but we do share a measure of the same blood."

Elmerah held up her palm. "I'll swear to whatever god you'd like me to swear to, that I mean you no harm."

Isara glanced past them to the old woman in her chair, then nodded. "Let's go to the bedroom. I can show you my father's research. He was the one who first suspected what Egrin truly is. When he was killed by the Dreilore, I picked up where he left off." She stepped away from the table and walked toward the only other door in the home, grabbing a lit candle in an iron holder on her way.

Elmerah was the first to follow.

Alluin met Saida's gaze across the table.

She shrugged, then mouthed, "What do we have to lose?" before following.

Malon went after her, leaving Alluin alone for a moment in the main room with the old woman. Could Egrin Dinoba really be a demon? He wouldn't have thought it possible, but after seeing the Ayperos in the

Akkeri temple . . . maybe greater demons really existed too. Egrin's atrocious actions surely suggested an evil nature.

He could hear shuffling papers and Isara's soft voice from the bedroom. He supposed he could at least hear her out . . . it wasn't like he had any better options.

He followed the others into the faintly candlelit room. It was cleaner than the rest of the house, but more cluttered. Stacks of books and papers dominated every surface, from the small desk, to the only chair, to the trunk at the foot of the modest bed. Isara sat on the floor before the trunk, flipping pages in a heavy tome by candlelight. Malon and Saida stood at her back, lighting more candles decorating the shelves on the walls, while Elmerah perched on the bed.

Isara stopped flipping pages with a triumphant, "Hah!" She looked up to Elmerah. "Here it is, come have a look for yourself."

Elmerah crawled forward on the bed to look at the book upside down.

Unable to fight his curiosity, Alluin stepped forward. Within the book, taking up the full righthand page, was a detailed sketch of Egrin Dinoba. His haunting icy eyes seemed to stare at each of them from within the prison of the page.

Isara pointed to the small caption below the picture. "Look at the date."

Elmerah snatched one corner of the tome and turned it upside down so she could read it. "Soren Dinoba, ruler of the Ulrian Empire." She turned her eyes up to Isara. "So Egrin looks a great deal like his father. This proves nothing."

Isara stared up at her. The candlelight reflecting off her spectacles made her seem almost blind. "Have you personally encountered Egrin?"

Elmerah frowned. "Yes, I've had the misfortune."

"Let me guess, he questioned your magic, where it comes from?"

Elmerah hesitated, then nodded. "How did you know I had magic?"

Isara tilted her head, her hand resting absentmindedly on the ancient book. "Don't all Arthali?"

"Yes," she replied, "but only to an extent. Some gifts are as small as predicting the weather and the tides. Most would not consider that magic."

Isara seemed to have forgotten everyone else in the room. "It *is* magic though. Egrin knows that, and he wants it. It's why he attacked Shadowmarsh. He hoped to attain some of the most powerful magics known to the Empire."

Elmerah's expression soured, but Alluin was finally beginning to feel hopeful. Isara's story was lining up with Elmerah's experience with the emperor, only he'd claimed it was his father who destroyed the Shadowmarsh Clan.

Isara seemed to scrutinize Elmerah, as if she could peer right through her skull and steal her innermost thoughts. Her head tilted further, reminding Alluin of a sea crane. "You wouldn't happen to be a Shadowmarsh witch, would you?"

Elmerah pursed her lips. "So what if I am?"

Isara scrambled to her feet. The ancient tome went toppling to the dirty rug atop the dirt floor. "Not only an Arthali, but of the Shadowmarsh Clan? I have so many questions for you! And a warning," she added hurriedly, "you must stay *far* away from my cousin. He'd probably cut you up into little pieces if he thought it would give him the key to your magic."

Elmerah lifted a brow. "You know, most who learn of my heritage are more apt to run the other way than to ask questions."

Isara waved her off. "If you wanted to kill me, there isn't much I could do to stop it. It would be a waste of my time to worry about such outcomes."

Elmerah looked to Alluin. "So do we think she's crazy, or no? I keep changing my mind."

Isara looked to him. "C-crazy?"

Malon *hmphed* from his post against the far wall. Saida glared at him as he explained, "The village folk seem to think you quite mad."

Alluin expected Isara to wilt at the accusation, but she only stood straighter. Her gaze was on Alluin as she said, "But you don't think me mad, else you wouldn't be here." She turned to Elmerah. "You know of Egrin's magic. You know what he can do."

"Isara," Alluin began patiently. "Why did you flee the

Capital? Why not live in wealth and esteem with your brother and cousin?"

Her jaw fell open. "You're asking me why I wouldn't want to remain a servant to a demon and his closest ally? It was my father's life's work to uncover the truth about Egrin, and I shall carry on with it as long as I am breathing."

Alluin flicked his gaze to Elmerah, then back to Isara. Saida had stepped forward, leaving Malon to sulk in a corner.

He took a deep breath. "What if we told you we share the same purpose? That not only do we wish to uncover the truth about Egrin Dinoba, but to depose him, and to make you the next Empress of the Ulrian Empire?"

Isara's eyes widened so much he thought they might pop out of her head, then they rolled back into her skull. She swayed on her feet, then thudded to the floor, landing in a limp heap.

"Why Alluin," Elmerah said tersely, "I believe you've killed her."

CHAPTER TEN

Saida

S aida peered down at Isara, now tucked beneath the
threadbare blankets on her bed, still unconscious.
Malon hovered over Saida's shoulder, far too close for
her liking. Alluin and Elmerah had gone outside to make
sure no one had followed them from Fallshire.

"You can't possibly believe this frightful creature is
our only hope," Malon commented. "Just look at her.
Even if she weren't half-mad, she's certainly no empress."

She turned toward him, only then realizing just how
close he'd been standing. The open hem of his travel coat
brushed her back. She stepped away, butting the backs of
her legs against Isara's bed. "I'm well aware of what you
think of our plan, but we're going through with it."

"I implore you to reconsider."

Isara let out a low groan, drawing Saida's eye, but she

did not wake. She turned back to Malon. "Why do you care? Why are you even here, Malon? If our plan is so foolish, surely I'm not important enough to protect. You have little to lose if I die."

His expression softened, and for a moment she almost thought she'd hurt his feelings, then his sharp jaw stiffened once more. "You have a duty to Faerune, priestess. If your mother dies, you will be needed. To continue with this plan is utterly selfish."

Heat crept up her neck. "My mother is not going to die!"

"The words of a scared child," he chided.

Though her heart pounded furiously, she forced her shoulders to straighten. "You would do well to remember your place, Malon. I may be a magic-less Moon Priestess, but I still outrank you. To speak to me in such a way is a violation of the oath you swore to the High Council of Faerune."

He bowed his head, conceding her point, albeit grudgingly.

She tried to slow her breathing, but she feared her emotions were written all over her face. Was she being selfish? Her presence hadn't helped Alluin and Elmerah to get to this point . . .

"Do you really think my mother is going to die?" she asked, instantly wishing she could take it back. It was another child's question, and she'd shown Malon more than enough weakness already.

"No," he assured, "I do not think she is going to die."

She observed him, wondering if he was just humoring her.

"What happened?" Isara groaned behind her.

Saida quickly looked away from Malon, a blush burning her cheeks. Isara blinked up at her, trying to see without her spectacles, she realized.

With Malon standing silently at her back, she fumbled the spectacles from a nearby pile of books. "You fainted," she explained, handing them to Isara.

Isara sat up and adjusted her spectacles. "My apologies, I have a tendency to be a bit excitable."

"Hmph," Malon muttered behind Saida.

She ignored him, keeping her attention on Isara. "Do you remember what was said before you fainted?"

"You mean that wasn't just a dream? You actually intend to murder my cousin?"

"*And* your brother," Malon added.

Isara gasped. "No! Egrin I understand, but I will not let you harm Daemon."

Saida chewed her lip. This was exactly what they'd feared. They could not expect Isara's cooperation when they intended to kill her only immediate family.

"If we eliminate only Egrin," she explained. "Daemon will become emperor. There's much you do not know. They're both working with the Dreilore to destroy Faerune."

Isara went utterly still. Saida wasn't even sure she was breathing.

"Is she about to faint again?" Malon asked caustically.

Isara turned her gaze up to Saida. "My brother would never ally himself with the Dreilore. They murdered our father. Daemon may be a pompous mule, but he loved our father."

"It is the truth," Saida forced herself to say, realizing that in a way, she was breaking Isara's heart. She might have run from her cousin and brother, but that didn't mean they weren't still her kin.

Isara's head slumped over her hands grasped in her lap. "Then he has fallen farther then I would have thought possible." She shook her head, seeming to come out of her fugue as she turned back to Saida. "But why would Egrin break his treaty with Faerune?"

She shrugged. "All we've come up with is his obsession with foreign magics. Elmerah's sister worked closely with him for a time, and this is what she believes."

Isara wrung her hands. "It makes sense, I suppose. The moonstone mines are the source of Faerune's power."

"How do you know that?" Malon snapped.

Isara didn't react to his tone. Her gaze had gone distant. After a long pause, she spoke, "Elven moonstones, Dreilore metals, and the Arthali. It seems whatever he's been planning all this time may soon come to pass."

Malon moved forward to Saida's side. "And just what might that be?"

Isara's gaze shifted to him. "That I do not know, but a

demon is gathering immeasurable magics. Is that not enough?"

A lump formed in Saida's throat. If Isara was right . . . Faerune would never give up their mines willingly. If Egrin wanted their moonstones, he would have to kill every last elf to get them.

She had no doubt he'd do just that.

"I will help you," Isara breathed. "I will not harm my brother, but Egrin must be stopped. Perhaps if we can defeat him, Daemon will come to see reason."

Saida leaned forward and placed a hand over Isara's. "We accept your terms."

She knew she'd be hard pressed to convince Elmerah and Alluin to spare Daemon, but Faerune was running out of time. They had to stop Egrin Dinoba. If the Empire fell to another ruler, one with the same prejudices prevalent in the Capital, then so be it. At least Faerune would be safe.

Elmerah

Elmerah stood with hands on hips, freezing her wits off in the dark night while Alluin circled the final barn. He'd circled every cursed structure on the entire farm. *Twice.*

"You know," she called out, "if there were any witch hunters out here, I imagine they would have attacked by now."

Alluin finished his inspection and returned to her. "We cannot be too cautious, especially now that we've found Isara."

"If we were being cautious, we wouldn't have left Malon in there with her and Saida."

"You think he's up to something?"

She shrugged. She didn't like haughty elves at the best of times, and Malon was the haughtiest of them all. Perhaps it was her prejudices speaking, but . . . "Why is he here? Why is a Guard Captain shirking his duty to watch over a single priestess?"

Alluin turned his gaze toward the main house, its windows dully glowing from the warm light within. "You may have a point, but I do not see what his aim could be. Thus far, he has done exactly what he said he came here to do."

Elmerah followed his gaze. "Perhaps he's in love with her. Love can turn even Guard Captains into idiots."

Alluin laughed. "That it can. Let's go back inside and see if Isara has awoken."

They walked side by side back toward the front door. Elmerah was just about to push it open when Alluin grabbed her arm.

She turned to him, sensing his tension.

He held a finger to his lips, then gestured for them to retreat the way they'd come. He stopped near a decrepit tack room. "I heard voices inside," he whispered.

"Yes," she whispered back, her gaze on the seemingly

peaceful house, "I'm not sure why you find that out of the ordinary."

He shook his head, following her gaze. "Not voices I recognize. Let's go around back, see if we can peer through Isara's bedroom window."

He hurried back toward the house, his footfalls making only the slightest rasp through the dry grass. She followed after him, stepping lightly.

She noticed the voices he'd mentioned as they crept toward the glowing window, high up in the wall near the low thatched roof. She, however, recognized one of the voices. She snatched Alluin's wrist before he could rise up on tip toe to look in the window, then dragged him backward.

Once out of hearing range of the house, she forced him to crouch. "Egrin is in there," she hissed.

Alluin's eyes widened, glinting in the dim moonlight. "Are you sure?"

Goosebumps erupted down her arms beneath her coat as she recalled her confrontation with the emperor in the slums of Galterra. "I'm sure." She almost asked what they should do, but bit her tongue. Alluin would know no better than she. The last time they'd faced the emperor, they'd barely escaped with their lives, and it was only because they had antlioch to ride away on. They'd left their horses back in Fallshire.

"We have to get Saida and Isara out of there," Alluin said finally.

She didn't bother mentioning that they should probably save Malon too. "I'll distract Egrin, you get them out."

"Absolutely not."

She eyed him steadily through the fog of her breath, her legs tiring from crouching too long. "He won't kill me, at least not right away. If I'm unable to escape, you must meet with Rissine and tell her what happened. I hate to admit it, but she'd be my best hope of rescue."

"No," he said again.

She shook her head. She wasn't a lover of altruism, but— "There is more at stake here than our lives. You must get Saida and Isara back to Faerune. I'll distract him while you escape, and if I can come after you, I will. If not," she shook her head, "just find Rissine."

He clung to her arms. "Elmerah—"

She nodded. He didn't need to say the words. "I know."

They stood. "I'll go in through the front," she explained. "I'll try to get Saida and Isara out of the room. Once they're out, convince them to run. Saida won't want to leave me behind." She couldn't quite manage a smirk. "We both know how sentimental she can be."

She pulled away from him, then trotted toward the front door, her hand on the cutlass at her belt. She knew as soon as Egrin was able to focus his attention on her, her magic would be useless, so she'd need to act quickly.

She reached the front door with Alluin just behind her, took a deep breath, then slowly opened it and peeked inside. The fire still crackled in the hearth, and the old woman still slept in her chair. The voices deeper within had gone silent. Did they know she was here? Would they attack her as soon as she stepped inside?

She supposed the answers didn't matter. She crept inside, wincing as her weight made a floorboard creak. She barely breathed for several heartbeats, but nothing moved. She drew her cutlass, encased it in flame, and charged Isara's door, throwing it open and launching herself inside.

A female Dreilore near the door threw herself aside, out of the path of Elmerah's flaming cutlass. Isara, Saida, and Malon were all herded against the far wall beneath the window with two male Dreilore aiming green-glowing blades at them. To their left stood Egrin, dressed in all black, a smug smile on his thin lips.

Elmerah took it all in a moment before she whipped fire Egrin's way. "Get out!" she shouted, hoping Saida realized her words were meant for her. Egrin waved an arm and her flames evaporated without even a hiss of smoke. She charged him, ignoring the Dreilore as Saida and Malon took the opportunity to rush them.

Her cutlass was only a hair away from Egrin's neck when her entire body froze, and the air was sucked from her lungs.

Egrin's grin widened. If he was fazed by how close he'd just come to death, he didn't show it. Or maybe he just let her get that close to mock her. Either way, she couldn't move or breathe.

"Stop it!" Isara screeched.

Elmerah was released so suddenly she toppled to her knees. Her cutlass clattered across the floorboards. She looked up to see Egrin turn a stunned expression toward Isara.

Malon had been backed once more into a corner, his body shielding Saida as the three Dreilore edged in. The two elves hadn't even stood a chance against the ancient warriors with their enchanted blades. Enchanted to do what, was anyone's guess.

Egrin's body gave a slight shake, like a bird settling its feathers. He looked at Isara. "It seems I've underestimated you, cousin. Perhaps you are more talented than Daemon after all."

Elmerah would have liked to hear more, but instead drove her fist up into Egrin's groin.

He doubled over with an *oof*, just as an arrow whizzed through the open doorway and thunked into the back of one of the male Dreilore. It seemed Alluin had found his bow.

She dove across the room for her cutlass as Egrin staggered toward her, his arms outstretched. Suddenly the air was torn from her lungs again, only to be restored a moment later with a satisfied grunt from Isara.

"Grab the witch!" Egrin ordered. "Ignore the others."

The two remaining Dreilore lunged for her. She rolled onto her back, kicking out. Her boot knocked the female Dreilore in the cheek, but the male deftly evaded her kick then grabbed her leg. "Saida!" she shouted. "Go!"

Elmerah watched upside down as Malon threw Saida

over his shoulder and ran toward the door, his movements slowed by her struggles. Isara remained with her back pressed against the wall, wide-eyed.

Elmerah kicked her free leg at the male Dreilore, but his grip did not relent. Her only advantage was that Egrin wanted her alive, while she wanted both him and the Dreilore dead. Her grin was the only warning the male Dreilore had before she filled her body with magic to the point of bursting. A weapon helped to direct her flames and lightning, but she could still wield them without her cutlass.

Her magic erupted in a wave, scalding the male Dreilore's skin. It would have set his clothes aflame too if they weren't leather, which unfortunately, they were. The female had scrambled to her feet just in time to catch the edge of the flame. She screamed, then the air was knocked from Elmerah's lungs again.

She heard Egrin's voice beyond the two cursing, hissing Dreilore. "Undo my magic again, Isara, and I will have her killed. I may want you both alive, but my patience is not endless."

Lovely, she thought. *Perhaps she'd overestimated her value.* Her lungs began to feel like hot pokers were scalding her from the inside. It wouldn't be long before she lost consciousness, and she couldn't even shout at stupid Isara to do something. At least Alluin, Saida, and Malon had escaped, unless they were lurking somewhere beyond her slowly graying vision.

The last thing she saw was Egrin dragging Isara by

the collar of her maroon dress as he came to stand over her. "You should have run while you had the chance."

If she could have spoken, she would have agreed with him.

Saida

"We can't just leave her!" Saida shrieked as Malon dragged her along by the wrist.

Not only had they left behind Elmerah, but they'd lost Isara. Egrin would kill her before he'd let her fall into their hands again. Her boots scraped against rocky earth as Malon dragged her onward, following after Alluin, who ran with his bow gripped in one hand. They were headed not back west toward Fallshire, but further east toward the barren wilderness.

"Stop!" she begged, but Malon's iron grip was unrelenting. If she could manage to gather her wits, she might be able to escape him, but her body just kept urging her to pull against his grip. "Alluin!" she called out to the form jogging through the darkness ahead of them. "We cannot leave her!"

"Quiet, priestess," Malon urged. "You know if we go back, we will not survive the encounter, and we will not be able to help your friend if we're dead. At least this way, someone will know where she is. We will get her back."

His words finally sank in. He was right. It would do Elmerah more harm than good if they went back now.

She stopped fighting against his grip and started running at his side. Soon they caught up with Alluin. "If he kills her," she panted, "I will never forgive either of you."

Alluin didn't reply, and all she got from Malon was an exasperated glance.

They ran on through the darkness until Saida thought her legs might soon turn to jelly. She was coated in sweat despite the chill night. They'd left most of their supplies behind, save Alluin's bow, and the few other weapons both he and Malon kept strapped to their persons. She had her small satchel looped around her waist like a belt-pouch, but all it contained was the moonstone circlet. Malon had her larger satchel containing a fire-striker, a bit of food, and the few vials of medicine from her father.

Saida staggered against a spindly tree, bracing herself as she panted, then lifted a trembling hand to wipe the sweat from her brow. The tree was sticky with moisture and sap, but she couldn't bring herself to push away. Bile threatened at the back of her throat.

"Are you well, priestess?" Malon asked. He stood straight, his reflective gaze on their surroundings.

"No," she rasped. "I'm really not."

Alluin stood a few paces away, watching them.

She wasn't quite sure her feet would carry her, but she took the risk and marched toward him. "Why did you let her charge back in like that? You both should have stayed away."

Alluin avoided her accusing gaze. "You truly think I had any choice in the matter? She knew Egrin wanted her alive, and she chose to use that leverage to help you escape."

"He wants me alive too," she snapped.

Finally he looked her in the eye. A fine sheen of sweat coated his brow, but she had a feeling the tension wrinkling his skin had nothing to do with physical weariness. "Does he? Perhaps he once did, but he missed his opportunity to deliver you to the Akkeri. You are useless to him now."

The word *useless* stung. She gritted her jaw. "Fine. What do we do now?"

He gestured to their dark surroundings. "We walk."

She clenched her fists. Somewhere far behind them, Elmerah was probably tied up being tossed into a carriage. Or maybe Egrin would use his dark magics to transport her back to the Capital in an instant. Either way, Saida knew she stood no chance of saving her. The only person who could stand up to Egrin's magic was Isara, and she was lost to them now too. Would he kill his own cousin to protect his legacy?

She shook her head and followed after Malon and Alluin as they led the way further away from Ravenstooth Farm. Isara was as good as dead.

CHAPTER ELEVEN

Elmerah

A harsh rattling awoke her. Elmerah's eyes slid open just a crack. She was in a carriage, her head resting in someone's lap. Across from her were Egrin and the two surviving Dreilore. With a hiss of breath she tried to sit up, but hard metal bound her wrists behind her back. *Son of a Dreilore wench, they were magic-nullifying shackles.* Her cutlass was missing too.

She flexed her abdomen and rocked to lift herself upright. Isara winced apologetically at her side. Her spectacles were askew on her face, fully revealing one wide eye. "I would have helped you up, but my hands are bound." Sure enough, her wrists were pinned behind her, just like Elmerah's.

She turned toward Egrin and the Dreilore. "Where are we going?"

Egrin smiled, the harsh shadows of the carriage making him look menacing, though really, he didn't need the help. "Does it matter?"

The two Dreilore watched her with blank expressions, their fiery eyes seeming dull in the dark carriage. She would have spit on them if her mouth weren't bone dry.

"What do you have to lose in telling me?"

Egrin shrugged. "Nothing. You will not escape me this time, but if I don't tell you, I get to watch you *squirm.*"

"I don't *squirm,*" she snapped, then turned toward Isara. "Do the shackles nullify your magic too?"

Isara shifted in her seat, her gaze on her lap. "No, mine are just normal shackles. My . . . skills are useless when Egrin isn't doing anything. The shackles don't work on me anyway."

Elmerah bit her lip. *Lovely.* If the shackles didn't work on Isara, such things would likely not work on Egrin . . . not that she'd be given an opportunity to test her theories.

Egrin cleared his throat, drawing her eye. The carriage gave a jump over a particularly rocky area, then continued ambling along. "Did you really hope to murder me and place my dear cousin on the throne?" Egrin asked.

Elmerah's eyes flew wide as she turned toward Isara.

"He was going to harm you!" she blurted. "I had to tell him!"

"He wasn't going to harm me," she sighed.

Egrin laughed. "Losing a hand or a foot won't hurt your magic, Elmerah. Magic is your only value."

She fought to hide her discomfort, but found herself *squirming* in her seat. Curse it all. "What do you want, Egrin? Where are we going?"

"We're going to Faerune to watch it burn, then we will return to the Capital where I will have all the time with you I desire. I will lay your soul bare, then I will kill you."

She stared at him. Cursing him now would only provide amusement.

"Or," he began, "there is another option."

She scowled. "Go on."

"I know you desire asylum for your people. This is something I can easily offer you."

She laughed, rocking back in her seat. The uncushioned wood bit into her shoulders. "Do you think me a total fool? You would never lift the Arthali exile."

He tilted his head. "Why not? The people of Galterra have come to accept the Dreilore as allies," he gestured to the Dreilore on either side of him. "They will accept the Arthali just as easily. You are far less exotic, at least to the untrained eye."

She clenched her jaw. "And what, you'd make us your loyal lapdogs, just like the Dreilore?"

The female Dreilore lunged forward, rage contorting her narrow features, then halted mid-motion. Her red-orange eyes seemed to bug out of her head, then she dropped to the rattling carriage floor. She recovered quickly, then resumed her seat, hanging her head to drape her long white hair over her features.

"As I was saying," Egrin continued, raising his voice as they hit another rocky patch, "I will gladly lift the exile. All you must do is aid in destroying Faerune, and grant me the secrets of your magic willingly."

"No."

"You would rather die?"

She curled her lip. "You'll kill me regardless. I'm not an idiot. At least this way I can be a complete thorn in your paw until you do."

Egrin settled back against his seat and steepled his fingers before his face. "You certainly are odd for an Arthali."

She shifted her shackled hands, trying to find a more comfortable position. She knew she wasn't getting out of this one, not unless Alluin could find Rissine in time. She hated to admit it, but Egrin's offer tempted her more than she'd let on. She even almost believed he'd follow through on it. He'd allied himself with the Dreilore after all.

She caught Isara's eye as the carriage ambled onward. There was a look of resolve there behind the lifted side of her smudged, foggy lenses. Maybe, just maybe she might be useful. If they could disable the Dreilore, and if Isara could hold off Egrin's magic long enough for her to run.

"Do you really think my cousin will help you kill me,

let alone kill her own brother?" Egrin's tone was mocking.

Elmerah didn't reply. Perhaps it was wishful thinking, but at the moment, it was all she had.

Saida

The first rays of sunlight seemed to sap the strength from Saida's limbs. They'd bypassed Fallshire, wanting to avoid any more of the emperor's men, which meant leaving their horses behind, but she'd not let Elmerah's sacrifice be in vain. They had to find Rissine.

They were finally back on the path leading back to the Akkeri temple. It was the shortest route to Faerune that would keep them off the main roads. If they were apprehended before they could find help, Elmerah and Isara were as good as lost. They might be lost already.

Alluin's hand alighted on her shoulder. She stopped walking. At first she thought he'd noticed her dejected expression, then his fingers clamped down, warning her.

Malon, his pale skin marred with purple beneath his silver eyes, looked questioningly at both of them.

Alluin removed his hand from Saida's shoulder, then unlooped his bow from his arm. "Get off the path."

Saida moved to obey, but froze as a low eerie howl cut across the surrounding marshlands. All the hissing and chirping insects went silent.

Another howl.

Fear tickled her throat, echoing her heart's nervous patter. "Wolves?"

Malon grabbed Saida's arm and pulled her close to him, his free hand on the shortsword at his belt. "Not wolves," he explained. "Bonehounds. I recognize their call. They are the trackers for the Akkeri."

A dart of movement drew Saida's attention to the left. The creature was small, about the size of a sheep, with wiry gray hair, a long canine snout, and beady black eyes. Another creature darted across the path ahead of them.

Malon wrapped his left arm around Saida, then drew the sword from his belt with his right. "Stay close, priestess. If we do not move, they will not be distracted from whatever the Akkeri have sent them to hunt."

Alluin moved close to her other side, his bow at the ready. "But what would the Akkeri be hunting this far inland? This close to Faerune?"

Saida glanced at him. She knew the Akkeri wanted her for their ritual. They believed marrying her to their High King would break the curse that made them the grotesque, bloodthirsty creatures they were. Was their desire to break the curse enough to lure them into places they would be killed on sight?

More bonehounds darted through the scraggly trees surrounding them, their small paws nearly silent on the sodden ground. They seemed to be . . . circling.

Malon watched them calmly. "They should move on soon."

"Um—" Saida began.

"They may be after Saida," Alluin finished her thought.

Malon's arm around her tightened. "That would have been nice to know . . . *prior* to this moment."

The bonehounds tightened their circle, close enough now that Saida could see tears in their flappy ears, and scars on their muzzles and chests, parting their wiry fur.

Her heart thundered in her ears. "What do we do?"

Alluin shook his head. He had an arrow knocked, but not aimed. "There are too many of them."

Something moved beyond the hounds at the edge of the down-sloping path. Several humanoid forms of medium build, slightly hunched, approached. The sun behind them made them stand in stark silhouette, though Saida knew what features would be revealed as they neared. Pale, mottled skin, sparse hair, and too-thin frames, like Faerune corpses left to rot in a bog.

The Akkeri whooped and hollered as they realized what their hounds had found, and more grotesque forms trotted into view. There had to be at least twenty of them. Saida held her stomach, feeling the urge to vomit.

Malon whispered in her ear, "You need to run, priestess. I will provide a distraction."

She barely heard him, for amidst the nearing creatures was the largest Akkeri she'd ever seen. He was at least a head taller than Malon or Alluin, likely even taller than Celen if she recalled his height correctly. Not only that, but he was muscular, built like a mountain. The thin, sickly-looking Akkeri seemed like children scurrying out of the path of his thick leather boots. He wore dark breeches and a gray woolen tunic crisscrossed with studded leather straps. His shaved head revealed pointed ears curving upward from a deeply scarred face.

She wasn't sure at what point she'd started to tremble, but it seemed almost uncontrollable now. This had to be their High King, their *Konnungar*. The Akkeri leader Egrin had promised her to wed.

"Saida," Malon said more firmly. "When I say run, you must go."

She tried to take a steadying breath, but fear crushed her chest. "No."

"Sai—"

"No," she said again, then pulled away from him.

Elmerah had known Egrin wouldn't kill her, and she'd used that knowledge to save them. Now she had the same opportunity with the Akkeri. She would not be a coward. Not now.

The giant Akkeri said something to those surrounding him in their guttural tongue. Crude weapons were raised as a few Akkeri stuck spindly fingers into their mouths and whistled. The bonehounds' tattered ears perked up, then as one, they leapt away toward where two Akkeri herded them off the desolate path.

"Little elves," the High King said in a lisping voice. He sounded just like Merwyn, like his lips were too dry and thin for speaking, only his voice was deep. It was a voice she imagined an elder bear would have if it could speak. "Which one of you has my circlet?"

Her jaw dropped. The circlet? Did he not realize who she was?

"Circlet?" she questioned, careful to not look down at the satchel hanging from her waist.

He took a step forward. The other Akkeri waited silently, all watching their king. "The circlet stolen from a spider's belly. I can sense it. You killed the Ayperos."

"What do you want with it?" Malon demanded.

The Akkeri king sneered, revealing rotted teeth. He said something else in Akkeri, then added in the common tongue, "Keep the girl alive, kill the others."

"Wait!" She started to step forward, then felt a tug on her shoulder as Malon pulled her back. She struggled against him. "I'll give you the circlet, just don't hurt them."

The Akkeri stroked his ruddy chin with long, meaty fingers. "What status do you hold in Faerune, girl?"

She hesitated. He obviously didn't know she was the specific elf he needed, but that knowledge might be the only way she could keep everyone alive.

"I am a high priestess," she answered.

The Akkeri tilted his head, then said something in his language to the others. The lesser Akkeri closed in around them, bringing with them the odor of rotten fish.

Malon lifted his sword, and Alluin his bow, for what little good they would do.

"Wait!" Saida said again, and the Akkeri stopped. She

looked to the High King. "I am the Moon Priestess you seek. Spare my friends and I will go with you willingly."

The king grinned. The Akkeri surrounding him chattered and whooped in excitement. "You may as well keep the circlet!" The High King called over the chatter of his kin. "You will wear it as we take our marriage vows."

Saida gulped and shrunk back. The thought of marrying the vile creature gave her chills.

"Bind and gag the others," the large Akkeri ordered in the common tongue for Saida to hear. "We will bring them along. If the priestess shows any inclination of breaking her vow, we will pluck out their eyeballs and string them up by their pointy little ears."

Alluin edged close to Saida's shoulder. Through gritted teeth, he asked, "What exactly do you think you're doing?"

"Saving your lives," she hissed.

Malon backed away as the Akkeri edged near.

"Don't fight it," Alluin said. "All you'll get is bruised and bloody, and they'll take you regardless. Save your strength."

Malon shook his head. The sweat glistening on his brow caught the murky sunlight. "I will not let them touch me."

The High King had turned away, confident his subordinates would do as they were told.

Bony fingers gripped Saida's arms. She flinched, then closed her eyes, forcing her breathing to slow. She could get through this. She'd play along for now, and would find a way to escape when the time came . . . she hoped.

She opened her eyes to see two Akkeri approaching Alluin with leather binding straps in hand. He remained calm, at least outwardly, though tension seemed to radiate through his jaw.

Malon slashed his sword at the nearest Akkeri. The creature dove out of the way, as two more Akkeri jumped on Malon's back. In an instant three more leapt atop him, one catching his blade against its thigh. The single creature shrieked and fell back, but there were too many of them.

Saida tugged against her captors. "Don't hurt him!"

"Take prisoner," one of the Akkeri holding her hissed, obviously less fluent in the common tongue than the High King had been.

She relaxed hearing that, even as Malon was piled upon by more Akkeri. Alluin calmly allowed himself to be bound. She wondered if he felt just as ill as she did watching Malon get beaten into submission. He'd probably never forgive her for the humiliation, but she'd had no other choice.

Her knees went weak as another realization dawned on her. With the three of them held hostage by the Akkeri, there would be no one to tell Rissine what happened to Elmerah. She and Isara would be on their own to free themselves from the emperor, just as she, Alluin, and Malon would be to free themselves from the Akkeri.

She couldn't quite decide whose situation was worse.

Rissine

Rissine lifted the monocular to her eye, her legs braced wide against the sway of the ship. She shifted slowly from left to right, taking in the crystal walls, then the grand architecture, then finally the distant, whitestone docks. She knew the elves had already spotted them. The only thing left to be determined was if Elmerah had reached them first. Were they sailing straight toward enemies, or allies? The swirling tattoos on her arms were bare to the murky sunlight. There was a chill in the air, but the sun felt good after weeks spent sailing the Kalwey Sea.

She lowered the monocular, then turned toward Zirin, the first to join her ranks. His long black hair was braided back from his strong-boned face, as was customary for the Winter Isles clans. He wore a rough-spun tunic, adorned with snow leopard fur at the collar and cuffs. His breeches were thick wool, made for blocking out the cold winds and moisture of his homeland.

He sucked his teeth, then spit on the deck. "What do we do now?"

She fought the urge to roll her eyes. He wasn't the most . . . refined, amongst them, but the Winter Isles clans could control the winds. They came in handy when one needed to sail great distances.

"They'll send an envoy," she explained. "We will wait here."

"And if they do not welcome us?"

She cast a wary glance across the ship. She'd gathered two dozen pureblood Arthali together. Not as many as she'd hoped, but for now, they would have to be enough . . . she just had to ensure they didn't turn against her.

She lowered her voice. "Then we shall dock elsewhere and search for my sister. If Faerune will not join us, we will join with the Valeroot elves to tear down the Capital stone by stone."

Zirin bared his yellow teeth. "And what if they *do* welcome us?"

"Then old hatreds will be forgotten. We know who our true enemy is."

She lifted the monocular again, spotting the envoy. Four sets of oars propelled the modest vessel across the choppy waters near the docks. She could see only four elves on the vessel besides the oarsmen: an older elf wearing round spectacles and scholar's robes, along with three armed guardsmen.

She lowered the monocular and turned back to Zirin. "Lower the ladder. I'll go down and talk to them myself."

Zirin's dark eyes bulged. "The elves cannot be trusted. You should force them to board where you will be protected."

Rissine glared. "I do not *need* protection Zirin, and I am in charge here. Remember your place."

Zirin bared his teeth again, but at her continued glare, finally backed down. "Do not expect a rescue when the elves throw you to the sharks."

She stormed past him, the trinkets and tiny gems at her waist tinkling with every step. Elmerah better have done her job, because she was more than ready to get off this cursed ship and away from these foul-mannered Arthali.

Others on the ship watched her silently as she strode across the deck, then threw her leg over the railing. The elven entourage was just reaching the ship's side. She descended the ladder confidently, but halfway down couldn't resist a look at the elves below.

The spectacled elf blinked up at her with an odd smile, while three of the oarsmen moored the boat to the ship.

She continued her descent, then hopped aboard the secured boat, keeping hold of the rope ladder should she need to make a quick escape. She could sense the eyes of half a dozen Arthali staring down at her from the ship's railing.

"My," the spectacled elf said, straightening his silken robes, "you do look quite a bit like Elmerah. I am Ivran Fenmyar."

Rissine's shoulders relaxed. "I'm glad to see my sister reached you first. This could have been a rather *uncomfortable* encounter."

He removed his spectacles and wiped them on his robes. The robes probably cost more than every cheap jewel on her fingers and at her hips. "I'm afraid it still is a bit . . . uncomfortable."

She looked to the other elves, but all the oarsmen had their eyes on their laps, and the three guardsmen stared straight ahead.

Her fingers itched for her cutlass. "Do go on," she said through gritted teeth.

"Oh no no!" Ivran babbled as he fumbled replacing his spectacles. "I did not mean that you are unwelcome, only . . . well, you're a bit unwelcome. You see, your sister, my daughter, and their friend Alluin were sent on a mission to retrieve someone. No decisions are to be made about alliances until they return."

She tilted her head. "Your daughter is Saida?"

He smiled warmly. "Ah, so you've met. Saida has convinced me of her claims, but the High Council, they can be a tad stubborn. I'm afraid I cannot invite you into port until your sister returns."

She crossed her arms and cocked her hip. "And what are we supposed to do until then? We haven't docked in a week."

Ivran stepped back as much as the small, crowded boat would allow. "I do apologize for the inconvenience. If you would be kind enough to cast anchor here, I can have some provisions rowed out to you."

She scowled. Leave it to Elmerah to take off before

she could arrive. "Very well," she sighed. "When is my sister expected to return?"

"Soon, I would hope. Dreilore have been spotted in the Illuvian forests. It's only a matter of time before they reach our crystal walls."

Her jaw dropped. "The Dreilore are nearly upon you, and you would still turn us away?"

He smiled sadly. "Not away. I would like to welcome you right here to our little part of the sea."

She blinked at him. "Was that supposed to be a joke?"

"I find levity the best medicine for tense situations."

She shook her head. "Alright, Ivran. We'll wait here, but don't expect us to rush to the docks when the Dreilore come to kill you all."

His face went a bit green. "Let us hope Saida returns before it comes to that."

Saida

Saida licked her cracked lips. Before her, on a spread of ragged furs, lay an unappealing plate of cured silverfish, pickled squid, and steamed rainbow clams. Across from her sat Hotrath, the High King of the Akkeri. A small hide tent had been erected for their meal, though no furniture or other comforts were provided. Hotrath almost managed to seem harmless, hunched over his wooden plate with his legs crossed, sucking steamed clams from their iridescent shells before tossing them aside.

"Eat," he commanded, gesturing to her plate with a meaty hand dripping with saliva and clam juice.

Her stomach turned. She'd been taken away from Alluin and Malon before she could see what *they'd* be fed, or if they'd be fed at all. "I'm not hungry," she lied.

Hotrath scowled. At least, she thought it was a scowl. It was hard to tell with his drooping skin, thin lips, and eyes so pale and milky he looked blind. "You'll need to acquire a taste for Akkeri foods. You'll be eating them the rest of your life."

She reached out and plucked a single clam from her plate. "So I'm not to be murdered after the . . . ceremony?"

Hotrath sucked up another clam and flung the shell, dripping juices all over the already stained and matted furs beneath them. The smell of old fish was almost overwhelming. "Perhaps once our curse is broken, you will no longer look at us like writhing insects."

He seemed to be content with her picking up a clam instead of actually eating it, so she kept it in her hand. Merwyn had thought that once the Akkeri curse was broken, they'd be more or less like Faerune elves. "Do you really believe that you are cursed?"

Hotrath gestured to his ugly visage. "Do you have a better explanation?"

She was hesitant to anger him, but answered with her honest thoughts. "Trolls have skin similar to yours, and other creatures bear unsettling odors. It does not mean they are cursed."

He slammed a fist on the ground, catching the edge of his plate and flinging silverfish and roast tentacles through the air. "You would compare us to monsters!" he hissed.

"You kill indiscriminately," she replied without thinking. "You pillage helpless villages and merchant vessels, and you plan to force me into marriage. How else should I view you?"

That seemed to calm him. "The bloodlust is part of our curse, and elves kill too. The shores were piled high with Akkeri corpses during the Great War."

"You were trying to destroy Faerune," she said tersely. "Protecting one's homeland is not the same as killing for riches."

"Spoken like someone who has never been poor, nor hungry."

She pursed her lips. She'd always been taught that Akkeri were stupid creatures, and most seemed to prove that generalization true, but not the High King, nor Merwyn. "What if forcing me to marry you does not break your curse?"

He watched her for a moment, for the first time seeming entirely interested in what she had to say. "How has a Faerune elf come to know so much about our beliefs?"

She finally dropped the clam back to her plate, since

he no longer seemed focused on making her eat. "I met an Akkeri once. He told me."

"A tall tale at best."

She glared. "It's true, though he didn't believe a forced marriage would break your curse. He thought, if the Akkeri were to gain the favor of the Skygod, that they would have to cast aside their bloody ways. They would have to live as Arcale would want, and only then, might the curse be lifted."

"Who was this Akkeri? He should be put to death for such talk."

"He was poisoned by a Dreilore arrow. I do not know where he is now . . . but I imagine it is too late to punish him." Her voice trembled as she said the last.

Hotrath didn't seemed to notice. "Dreilore poison will not kill us. Nothing seems to kill us save beheading, fire, or electrocution. We are not trolls. We are *cursed*."

She sat up a little straighter. "Truly? You can survive even the most toxic of substances."

His milky eyes narrowed in suspicion. "If I did not know any better, I'd say you cared for this Akkeri."

She lifted her nose. "He was a friend."

She fell back in surprise at his sudden laughter, so loud it made her ears ring. She braced herself on her elbows, then sat back up.

He finished laughing, then pushed aside his mostly empty plate. "Finish your food, priestess. We have a long journey ahead of us, and I only need one of your friends alive to force you into compliance."

She gulped. She'd been wondering if he'd realized that. "If you hurt either of them, I will not comply. I will do everything in my power to destroy you."

He stood, towering over her. His feet were so large and his legs so thick, she had a sudden vision of him squishing her beneath his threadbare boots. "Such loyalty, priestess. I wonder if they would do the same for you."

He turned and walked through the hide flap leading out of the tent, leaving her alone.

She shivered, knowing her threat was in vain. He was the High King of the Akkeri, the king of monsters. He could summon demons to guard his treasures and left a sea of corpses in his wake. She shook her head. It didn't matter who he was, she had to figure out a way out of this.

She looked down at her plate. If she tried to escape now, Malon or Alluin would be killed. She picked up a stiff salted silverfish, plugged her nose, and ate it. She'd play along for now, and at least she had one reason to be glad. Merwyn might still be alive, and letting him escape her company might have very well saved his life since it kept him away from Hotrath.

It was a cold comfort at best, but it was better than nothing.

CHAPTER TWELVE

Elmerah

Elmerah struggled against her shackles. Morning had waned into evening, and she *desperately* needed to relieve herself. She didn't know where Isara had gone, only that she'd been taken from the carriage by Egrin, leaving her alone with the two Dreilore. She would sooner die than piss herself in front of any of them.

Her stomach growled loudly.

The female Dreilore smirked.

"Remove these shackles and I'll slice that smirk off your lips."

Her bluish lips smoothed into an indignant frown. "You won't be cutting anyone, *witch*."

"We'll see," she muttered, though the Dreilore was probably right.

The carriage door to her right swung outward, revealing four more Dreilore. They must have reached their camp, though that didn't explain why she'd been left in the carriage all this time.

"Bring the witch," one of the male Dreilore outside said. "Her lodgings have been prepared."

She leaned forward to look out at him. "I've been in this carriage all day, and most of last night. I'll be needing to make a stop along the way to these . . . lodgings."

The Dreilore just stared at her with his strange burning eyes. Three other male Dreilore stood behind him. All wore dyed-black leather, their version of armor. Would these be the soldiers who would soon attack Faerune? Did this mean they were somewhere near the elven city? Thoughts of Celen and the Arthali camp flooded her mind.

The female Dreilore in the carriage with her stood, then kicked Elmerah's boot. "Get moving. No stops."

She winced as she stood. It was probably fortunate she hadn't been given any food or water, else she'd never make the walk.

Two of the Dreilore outside took hold of her arms as she stepped down from the carriage. She took a quick look around, noting the dense surrounding oaks, and narrow, rutted dirt path, barely passable by carriage. If she had to guess by how long they'd traveled, they were at the southern edge of the Illuvian forests. Mostly east, and just a bit north of Faerune, south of Celen's encampment.

One of the Dreilore jerked her arm hard enough she thought it might pop free of her shoulder. She gave him an evil glare, but had no choice but to be prodded along. Trying to escape now would be futile.

They walked her around the carriage and deeper into the woods. She could smell cookfires, but only faintly. They had a far walk ahead of them.

"Did I mention I was in that carriage for a full day and most of the previous night? I don't know much about Dreilore, but I imagine our body processes are the same, if you catch my meaning."

One of the Dreilore said something under his breath. It sounded like a curse, but she'd never really know as she didn't speak their language. He gestured to the female Dreilore from the carriage. "Help her. If she tries to escape, cut off her feet. Dinoba was clear that he only needs her living, nothing more."

Elmerah flexed her wrists against her shackles. It was a risk she was willing to take.

The female Dreilore replaced the male at her side, then led her off the freshly worn path into the trees. She barely went a few paces, affording Elmerah little privacy.

"Can we go no further? I wouldn't put it past your colleagues to peep."

The female Dreilore shoved her shoulder, knocking her into a tree. "They have no desire to see you, witch. Now hurry up."

She pushed off the tree trunk, regaining her balance. "I can't pull down my breeches with my hands shackled."

The Dreilore lifted her thin white brows. "Would you like me to do it for you? I do not have a key to your shackles, nor would I ever dream of unlocking them."

"It was worth a try," Elmerah sighed, then started wiggling her pants down on her own.

To her surprise, the Dreilore turned her back. Well, not terribly surprising, she supposed, with several male Dreilore just a few paces away, she had little chance of catching any of them off guard. She debated shoving the woman and making a run for it regardless, but had to think better of it. Not enough to risk her feet over after all.

After finishing her business and awkwardly pulling up her pants, the female shoved her back toward the path, and it was onward toward the encampment. Her captors spoke little as they walked, leaving Elmerah to ponder their surroundings, and her dire fate. Would Egrin begin his torture that night, or did he want her to watch Faerune crumble first?

It was full dark by the time they reached the encampment. They were so deep within the forest she expected a Fossegrim to slither out at any moment. She almost hoped for one, as the Dreilore, not native to this region, might not be immune to the creature's song.

Countless Dreilore watched her as she was marched through the canvas tents and cookfires composing the camp. She was marched all the way to the end of the line before being shoved into a tent, no different from any of the others. She braced herself as she went inside, then straightened. The tent was empty except for a large iron cage. *Lovely.*

One of the Dreilore stepped forward and opened the cage. It was tall enough for her to stand, but not wide enough for her to lie flat.

She turned toward the female Dreilore. "You're going to have to make good on your threat of chopping off my feet if you expect me to go in there."

Sudden pain shot through her legs as something hit the back of her knees, crumpling her to the ground. Unforgiving hands grasped her biceps, and she was unceremoniously dragged through the dirt and tossed into the cage. The door slammed shut, and one of the Dreilore looped a padlock around the corner bars, then locked it in place.

The female Dreilore smirked. "I'll take your feet later, witch, if there's anything left of you after Dinoba has had his fill."

She watched them all depart. If she ever got these cursed shackles off, that female Dreilore would be the first to taste her lightning.

With a heavy sigh, she slid her arms back down the bars of her little prison until her rump hit the solid iron bottom, then tucked her knees up against her chest. Her shoulders and wrists ached from being bound for so long, and she'd hoped she'd at least be imprisoned with Isara.

She should really learn to stop *hoping* all the time.

The hours waned on. The Dreilore in the camp all spoke in their foreign tongue, yielding no hints to what they planned. She had almost nodded off when the white tent flap finally opened, revealing Egrin and another familiar face. *Thera*.

Remaining seated, she looked the exiled Faerune elf up and down. "I'm surprised you're still alive, traitor."

Thera bared her teeth. Dark bruises marked the skin beneath her blue eyes, and her pale hair hung unwashed and limp over her modest dark woolen dress. "At least I'm not the one in the cage."

Elmerah laughed. "You'll wish you were safe in a cage if Rissine ever finds you."

Thera's skin, still perfect despite her bedraggled appearance, flushed. She opened her mouth to reply, but Egrin motioned her to silence.

"You are here to observe, Thera. Tell me if you see anything I cannot."

Elmerah lifted her brows at Egrin. "You mean you aren't all-knowing and all-noticing?"

He laced his fingers, flipped his hands, and cracked his knuckles. "Thera is a Moon Priestess, or she would have been had her mother not been exiled. She can see through certain magics."

Her brows lifted further. A Moon Priestess just like Saida? And with the same gifts?

"So why didn't you give her to the Akkeri instead of Saida?"

Thera's face turned beet red.

Egrin laughed. "She was under the protection of Rissine at the time, and Rissine promised me a different Moon Priestess, one of high standing within Faerune, not a besmirched exile."

Elmerah leaned her head back against the bars, observing Thera. "Yes, I imagine the Akkeri wouldn't have wanted such a dishonorable lout."

Egrin laughed again. "I imagine not, but it is of little consequence now. I got what I wanted from the Akkeri. If they attack Galterra again, the Dreilore will put them down." He gestured to Elmerah without so much as glancing at Thera. "Remove her shackles."

Thera reached into her belt pouch and removed a heavy iron key, then stepped toward Elmerah's cage. "Reach your hands out."

"Make me."

Egrin sighed. "Remember, the Dreilore's enchantments only neutralize *your* magic. I can crush the air from your lungs with or without the shackles."

She stuck her tongue out at Egrin, but obeyed and stood with her back against the bars, sliding her shackled wrists through one of the openings.

She couldn't help her sigh of relief as her hands were freed. She stretched her arms above her head, then side to side.

"Now attack me with all you have," Egrin instructed, "and I'll see to it you're fed come morning."

She reached out for her magic and felt it coursing through her. There was little chance any of her attacks would land, but she'd sure as salt and air try.

Elmerah

Elmerah groaned. She tried to turn over before she got a boot to the back of the head, but she couldn't bring herself to move. She was too tired. Everything she'd thrown at Egrin had been easily deflected.

She sensed him as he crouched beside her. "I don't understand it. It's as if the air itself fills you with magic, yet I can't feel it being pulled from our surroundings."

She turned her head, resting her cheek in the dirt. The white tent, anchored to the ground by heavy stakes, fluttered and tugged at its bindings with the wild gusts of wind outside. She hoped the wind had been enough to drown out the sounds of her struggle. The Dreilore had seen her humiliated enough. Beyond Egrin stood Thera, holding a lantern aloft, her face utterly dispassionate.

Elmerah winced as Egrin's hand landed on her shoulder. She prepared herself for more torture, but it didn't come.

He shook his head and withdrew his hand. "I simply do not understand it."

Elmerah coughed, sending up a faint puff of dirt from

the hard-packed earth. "Well if you're done figuring it out, maybe you should just let me go."

He leaned closer. "Or maybe you should just tell me how you do it."

His closeness sent shivers of panic through her. "That's like asking a fish how it manages to breathe. Can you explain where your magic comes from?"

He stood. "No, I cannot, which is why your magic interests me so. We are not like other beings, who draw their magic through the earth, and filter it through objects. We simply . . . are."

Tired of straining her eyes upward to see him, she took a deep breath, held it, then rolled onto her shoulder, curling up around her bruised belly and cracked ribs. She did prefer to filter her magics through weapons, but it wasn't absolutely necessary for her. "So you're telling me you don't even understand your own magic? You'd think in all the time you've been alive you would have figured it out."

He smirked down at her. "I see Isara has been waggling her loose lips."

Elmerah stared up at him.

"Very well," he sighed. "To answer your question, no, even with the centuries I've lived, I have not figured it out. I have learned a great many other things though, things you could hardly comprehend. And I can use the magic of others. Not always a great feat, considering enchanted Dreilore steel can be wielded by any who possess it."

She debated sitting up, but was pretty sure she couldn't manage it. "Are there others of your kind?"

His expression darkened. She must have hit a nerve. "There used to be." His voice was short and clipped.

He turned and walked toward the tent entrance, pausing a moment beside Thera. "She's not strong enough to attack you now. Replace her shackles and put her back in her cage."

Thera's eyes widened and her upper lip trembled, the small movement clear in the lantern light. She reached for the shackles at her belt with her free hand as Egrin exited the tent.

Elmerah licked her cracked lips. Once the shackles were returned to her wrists, she'd be all but defenseless. She tried to summon her magic, but there was nothing left. It was a wonder she was even conscious. She was getting stronger, but not strong enough to withstand Egrin's torture and still be well enough to fight.

Setting her lantern aside, Thera knelt behind her.

She closed her eyes as cold steel sealed around her wrists. "Why do you do his bidding? The Dreilore I understand, but you? He treats you like a slave."

Thera retrieved her lantern and moved so Elmerah could see her clearly. "I do his bidding because I am smarter than you. Soon you'll be dead, and I'll still be alive. Perhaps someday I'll escape him, but for now, at least I have protection."

"What will you feel when Faerune is destroyed, I

wonder? Will it hurt you to hear the screams of your kin?"

"My mother was an exile," Thera snapped. "And so am I."

Elmerah snorted. "And so am *I*, but I still wouldn't stand and let Egrin destroy the Arthali. Did the little children elves exile your mother? Did their poor mothers and fathers? I don't think so. It was the High Council. You will allow innocent elves to be slain for the crimes of six priests and priestesses. Egrin may be a monster, but as I see it, you're the true demon here."

Thera's lips sealed into a tight line. She'd struck another nerve. Lovely. "I'll enjoy watching Egrin kill you."

Elmerah lifted the shoulder she wasn't laying on in the barest of shrugs. "Maybe, but my death won't be the one you'll remember in your nightmares until the day you die."

Thera stormed toward the exit. "Put her back in the cage," she said to someone outside as she walked past.

Two male Dreilore came into the tent. It was clear by their smug smiles they'd been listening in. Apparently they didn't like Thera any better than she did. It was probably the only thing they'd *ever* have in common.

Alluin

Alluin glared at his Akkeri guards. The four vile creatures chattered on in their language above the buzz of a thousand swamp insects, making lewd gestures toward him here and there. They occasionally threw one Malon's way. However, since he was unconscious, they were far less entertained.

They were in the center of the crude camp, deep in the swampland. More Akkeri had awaited them there, bringing their number to nearly forty. Only one tent stood casting a shadow across the soggy ground. Alluin knew Saida was inside. He'd seen the Akkeri leader exit, but not her.

He shifted his shoulders against the leather straps binding his arms against his sides. Moisture snuck up the rear of his breeches from the soggy ground. He could almost feel sorry for himself if it weren't for the fact that Elmerah was in an even more dire, and likely uncomfortable, situation. Just what did Egrin Dinoba have planned for her? He could at least hope that she was still alive. Egrin had wanted her alive for a reason.

Malon groaned. He squirmed on the ground, trying to sit up, but the Akkeri had bound him from shoulder to ankles with leather straps. His face was bruised and bloody, matting his silver-blond hair against his scalp.

Noticing Malon's struggle, one Akkeri swaggered up. The thin scraps of cloth hanging limply from his scrawny body left little to the imagination. Another guard said something in their language, then all three laughed.

The Akkeri before Malon kicked him in the gut.

Malon grunted, reflexively curling his body to protect his belly.

The Akkeri spat on him. "Filthy elf, not so fine now?"

Malon glared up at him. "If you're hoping to insult me, you should perhaps gain a better grasp of the common tongue. You sound like an imbecile."

The Akkeri spat again, this time missing Malon's shirt. A glistening glob of mucous-filled spittle coated the dead grass near his shoulder. "Female Akkeri wait on ship. Give you to them, then we see who em-bee-seel."

A few of the Akkeri milling around the camp had stopped to watch the spectacle. They edged closer, like wolves sensing weakness. The penned bonehounds at the edge of camp whimpered in anticipation.

"Enough of this!" a deep voice boomed.

Alluin looked over his shoulder to see their leader approach, though he didn't so much as glance at Alluin or Malon.

"Night will come soon. We will continue on until we reach the ship, then you can do as you please with the elves."

The Akkeri surrounding him cheered, eliciting more yips and whimpers from the bonehounds.

Alluin squirmed. Their leader had spoken in the common tongue on purpose. He knew they couldn't escape. He'd let Saida think they were safe until he had her on his ship, then there would be no escape for any of them.

His eyes darted around the camp, searching for a way out. His gaze fell upon one Akkeri, smaller than the others, cheering not half as fervently. He almost thought he recognized him, though it was difficult to say. They all looked nearly the same.

He had just written the sense of recognition off as hunger and fatigue addling his brain, then the Akkeri's eyes landed on him. Almost imperceptibly, he nodded.

Elmerah

Elmerah lay in an awkward ball, her shoulders and knees braced against the bars of her too-small cage. She thought that if she let herself fall asleep, she might stop breathing, though the dark shadows of the tent continued to lull her toward oblivion.

Egrin had forced her to drain every last ounce of her magic, yet still believed she'd been hiding something from him. She *wished* she'd been hiding something. It would have made it slightly less humiliating when she'd collapsed, and Thera had replaced the magic-nullifying shackles.

She forced air deeply through her lungs, then let it out again. Her entire body ached. Egrin had not been lax in punishing her for failing him. Her ribs were cracked, and she'd probably be pissing blood if she managed to live long enough.

Moonlight cut across her face. She winced, distantly noting the sound of the tent flap falling back into place, bathing her once more in near darkness. Someone approached, then knelt before her cage.

"It's alright," Isara's voice soothed. "I'm not here to harm you."

"You're not here to help me either," Elmerah rasped.

She heard the sound of water dribbling into a bucket, then a cool rag soaked her face, dabbing at congealed blood. Isara pulled the rag back through the bars, dunked it again, then continued her dabbing.

"The Dreilore will attack Faerune at first light," she explained. "Then we'll return to my brother in the Capital. I will appeal to him to spare you."

Elmerah swallowed, but it did nothing to soothe her burning throat. "You really are an idiot, aren't you? I will not be spared. I might not even live long enough to watch the elves be slaughtered, a small blessing, I suppose."

Isara reached something else through the bars. The spout of a waterskin touched Elmerah's lips.

She tilted her head to drink, but coughed and sputtered as soon as the water hit her dry throat. As soon as she could breathe, she tried again, drinking more slowly, though her body urged her to gulp the water down greedily.

"There's nothing to do about the elves."

Elmerah wanted to curse at her, but couldn't manage

enough fervor. "There's always something to be done. You are a coward."

Isara was quiet for a moment. "At least I'm not the one in a cage."

"Yet."

"You are right," she sighed. "But I cannot stand against him. I never could. Even if I wanted to, what could I possibly do to help?"

Elmerah thought of Celen, but quickly dismissed the idea. She couldn't risk Isara telling Egrin about the secret Arthali encampment. He'd destroy them all.

"Why did you do it?" Isara asked abruptly. "Why did you agree to help Saida and Alluin? The Arthali fell long ago, and no longer care for the affairs of this continent. What remains of your kin are in no real danger now."

"My mother was killed on the order of Soren Dinoba . . . who is actually Egrin, if I'm to believe your tale. Why wouldn't I want to depose him?"

"But you didn't know that at first. You didn't know it was Egrin who ordered the Shadowmarsh line destroyed."

"He did the same to Alluin's kin," she sighed. "I was fully prepared to sail away from the Capital forever, but Alluin found me. I helped him pile the corpses and burn them."

"That still doesn't answer my question," Isara pressed. "Alluin's kin were not your own. Why would you risk your life to help him?"

Elmerah almost smiled. "Because no one else would, you idiot."

Isara was quiet for several long moments, until finally she asked. "Do you think Egrin had my father killed? I was told it was the Dreilore, but we never found his body."

"Probably."

"Do you think Daemon let it happen?"

Elmerah stifled her irritation. At least Isara's inane questions were keeping her awake. "You tell me, he's *your* brother."

Isara was silent again.

"Did Daemon know about your father's theories?" Elmerah asked. "Did he know he thought Egrin a demon?"

"Yes."

So Daemon knew Egrin was something . . . evil, and stuck with him anyway, despite his sister and father running far away. "Well then I suppose you have your answer."

Isara stood.

Elmerah couldn't see her face clearly in the darkness, but imagined she was crying. A moment later, sniffling confirmed her suspicions.

Isara quietly left the tent, and Elmerah was left with nothing but her thoughts.

Tomorrow the Dreilore would march on Faerune. Saida's kin would be killed. Egrin would claim the magic of the moonstones, though for what evil purpose was anyone's guess. She would be powerless to stop him. She would watch the crystal walls fall. If Alluin and Saida had returned to Faerune, which she imagined they had, they would both die. And she wouldn't be far behind them.

She wasn't sure how long she'd been asleep when a soft rattling woke her. The tent's interior was still dark, so it had to be night. Her eyes cracked open, catching a dull flicker of light on Isara's round spectacles.

"I'm getting you out of here," she explained, her fingers working the lock. "I couldn't find a key, but this lock is not overly complex. I should be able to pick it."

Elmerah tried to sit up, but failed. "Not that I'm not grateful, but there's one problem."

Isara paused her movements to look down at her.

"I don't have the strength to stand, let alone run."

"Then I will carry you."

While the sentiment was nice, she doubted Isara could even carry a full sack of flour, let alone an Arthali witch. Though she wasn't about to stop her from trying. "I'll need you to remove my shackles first. Perhaps a measure of my magic has returned." She doubted it, but there was no way for her to tell until the shackles were off her.

The padlock holding the cage closed clicked open. The door moved with a deep groan.

She noticed the shadow looming up behind Isara

too late. Isara's breath whooshed from her mouth and she stumbled forward, landing atop Elmerah as she tried to struggle to her feet. The cage door slammed shut, and a female Dreilore latched the padlock back into place.

Elmerah rolled onto her shoulder and pushed Isara aside, only to watch as the Dreilore knelt and retrieved something from the ground.

She held up one of the small tools Isara had used on the lock. Her flickering orange eyes narrowed in distaste as Isara finally managed to stand. "Stupid girl. Dinoba told us to watch you."

Elmerah would have liked to stand too, but she couldn't find the strength. It was all she could do to brace her back against the bars. She'd have to settle for glaring up the length of the Dreilore's long legs. "Leave the girl alone. Not everyone thinks like a conniving eel in the reeds."

She couldn't quite tell in the darkness, but she thought she saw the Dreilore smirk. "Have fun sleeping in there together. We'll see if you still defend her in the morning."

Tears glittered on Isara's cheeks as the Dreilore let herself out of the tent, temporarily bathing them in a sliver of moonlight.

"I've failed you," she choked out.

Elmerah closed her eyes and leaned the back of her head against the bars. *You're definitely not the first*, she thought, but out loud she said, "Don't worry about it. I don't have the strength to run anyhow. At least now I know you're not *entirely* soft-bellied."

Isara removed her spectacles and wiped them on her dress.

"Though it might have been wiser to use your gifts to take down your cousin," Elmerah added. "You're likely the only person alive capable of sticking a dagger in his back."

Isara hung her head. "I could never do that."

"You'd be surprised what you can do when your life is at stake. You may soon have to test that theory."

Isara slid her back down the bars, sitting her rump next to Elmerah's in the small space. Their bent knees nearly touched. "He won't kill me. He doesn't waste useful things."

"And you're useful?" She regretted the words as soon as she said them. Isara seemed a sensitive sort.

"It's not only Egrin's magic I can nullify. I could do it to you, the Faerune priests and priestesses, anyone really."

"Can you do it to enchanted shackles?"

Isara turned to face her. Her slack jaw was faintly visible in the darkness. "I . . . I never really thought about it. Enchantments are powered by magically imbued metals, stones, or wood. In theory they should be the same . . . "

Elmerah shifted to put her back toward Isara, making the small space even more cramped. "Care to test the theory?"

"I can't remove them, how will we know if it works?"

"Just try. Even with the shackles on, if the enchantment is nullified, I should be able to call my magic."

Isara was quiet for a moment, then Elmerah felt the brush of her cold fingertips as she examined the shackles. A few more tense moments passed, then a trickle of magic bloomed within her core. It was weak, just the merest spark since Egrin had utterly drained her, but it was there.

Grinning, she shifted positions again, putting her back against the bars. "Get some rest," she told Isara. "I'll need as much sleep as possible if I'm to be of any use tomorrow."

"But shouldn't we escape now? I can nullify your shackles and you can use your magic on the padlock—"

"I'm too weak right now. We'd never make it past the Dreilore. For now we rest, and I'll have more strength come morning."

"What do you plan?" Isara gasped, lifting a hand to her mouth.

Elmerah's grin wilted as sleep reached out for her. She was getting better, *stronger*. The last few times she'd expended all of her magic energy she'd been unresponsive for hours afterward. She'd let herself grow weak in her peaceful little swamp, but she'd been flexing her muscles now more than ever before. With Isara's help to nullify the enchanted shackles, she just might have a bit of magic to use in the morning.

Her eyes fluttered closed. "Just be ready," she whispered. "I'll find a way to signal you when the moment comes."

She really had no idea what she planned, but she'd know it when the moment presented itself. All she needed was to catch Egrin off guard. If she could do that, she could save Faerune. She could save Saida, Alluin, and all the other elves.

She couldn't wait to see the look on Immril and Cornaith's faces when she did.

CHAPTER THIRTEEN

Saida

The sound of the ocean surf sent shivers of fear down Saida's spine like it never had before. She'd grown up by the sea. Its crystalline depths had always meant magic and mystery to her, along with delicious fish and oysters. Now it meant her doom. She knew if she boarded the Akkeri ship with Hotrath, she'd never escape him.

They'd walked the entirety of the night, and Hotrath kept a brisk pace ahead of them. She caught sight of the cresting waves in the dim light of predawn. Amidst them lurked a black ship, its mast and railings like jagged broken bones jutting up from the sea.

She dared not look back in search of Alluin or Malon. She wouldn't want them to take a glance from her as a signal to act. They were surrounded by Akkeri guards, as was she, their boots all slick from walking through the muck of the marshlands south of Faerune. She was unfamiliar with this territory, as the elves had no reason to venture south. Beyond the vast marshlands were the Southern Deserts, and Faerune horses were not suited for traveling across the arid expanses. They'd die of thirst long before they reached the Helshone, where larger cities provided refuge from the heat.

She shook her head as she walked. Her mind was addled and her feet were sore.

Hotrath glanced back in search of her. His milky white eyes found her quickly, not far behind him. "You, by my side. Do not make me kill your men."

Her shoulders hunched, she hurried toward him. She thought she could feel everyone's gazes on her, but she kept her eyes downcast. She had to think. There had to be something she could do to escape without getting Alluin and Malon killed.

A high-pitched whistle, like the mournful cry of a nightlark, sliced through the thin air of dawn. Hotrath marched toward Saida and grabbed her arm, pulling her toward him. She nearly gagged at the strong smell of fish. She finally dared to look for Malon and Alluin. She spotted them not far off, surrounded by Akkeri with their primitive weapons poised.

Another cry sounded. Malon seemed unsure of what it meant, but all the Akerri froze with apprehension.

Another cry echoed across the damp earth.

Hotrath shoved her away from him. "Get her to the ship!"

The nearest Akkeri wrapped thin arms corded with narrow muscles around her, then lifted her upward off her feet to secure her until two more Akkeri appeared, each snatching an arm. More closed in around her. She bent her knees and dropped her weight to thwart them, but it didn't stop her from being sometimes dragged and sometimes carried across the soggy ground toward the distant sound of the tide. More cries cut across the growing light as of the remaining Akkeri closed in around Hotrath. Her captors carried her over the hill until the others were out of sight.

On the descent toward the shore, one Akerri holding onto her shoved his bony shoulder into the Akerri next to him. That Akkeri stumbled, losing his grip on her arm. An Akkeri in front of the first turned with a hiss, but the first monster was already shoving his shoulder into the one across from him. All hands fell away from Saida. The air rushed from her lungs as she flailed, then landed hard on her rump. The Akkeri leapt upon the dissenter, flattening him to the ground. He was much smaller than the others and likely would not be long for this earth.

"Run Saida!" the small Akkeri cried.

A horrifying realization dawned on her as she rolled aside, narrowly missing a kick from an Akkeri boot. "Merwyn!" she shouted, staggering to her feet.

It couldn't be him, could it? Had he orchestrated this fortunate mishap? He'd disappeared again underneath a pile of fighting Akkeri. The rising sun blinded her as she looked toward where she'd left Hotrath, but the hill blocked her view. She knew the wise choice was to run, to save her own hide, but as people always seemed to be telling her, she wasn't terribly wise.

She knelt and picked up a roughly hammered fallen sword. The rust speckling the metal hilt bit into her palm as she lunged forward and shoved the blade into the back of an unsuspecting Akkeri. He rolled aside, taking the blade with him, revealing Merwyn underneath. Merwyn gasped for air, coughed up blood, then was immediately piled upon by the remaining Akkeri who didn't seem to care that one of their own had just been slain.

She heard shouting in the distance. Something was happening, but she could spare no time to figure out what. Finding no more fallen weapons within reach, she said a prayer to Arcale, then dove upon the pile of Akkeri who were attempting to beat the life out of Merwyn.

Alluin

M alon's shoulder bumped into Alluin's. "I sincerely hope these are friends of yours," he whispered.

Their Akkeri guards had their backs to them, eyes trained on the slowly approaching elves. Alluin couldn't help his grin. The call of the night lark was a well-known signal amongst Valeroot hunters. Those edging in were his kin, no doubt scouts sent to watch Faerune and the bordering towns. The Valeroot hunters were skilled trackers, and the Akerri were not difficult to track. They had probably picked up the trail where his party had been apprehended on the little used road near the temple.

Hotrath loomed over them. He said something in Akkeri, then Alluin was jerked backward by his collar through the mud. He scrambled to regain his footing as Hotrath grabbed Malon by his shirt and carried him in the direction Saida had been taken.

Alluin threw himself backward, surprising the two Akkeri manhandling him. One lost its grip on his right arm and he used the momentum to swing his fist around, punching his other captor in the jaw. He'd had no opportunity to communicate with Merwyn, but he'd spotted him amongst the Akkeri taking Saida to the ship. If Merwyn had actually managed to free Saida, then he had to buy them time to escape.

He could hear Malon struggling against Hotrath, though the High King would not be as easy to escape as his smaller counterparts. The Valeroot elves charged, a volley of arrows leading the way. A few Akkeri on the edge of the group went down screaming, but their screams were soon drowned out by the sharp clangs of steel on steel.

Seeming to forget him in their bloodlust, Alluin's

captors fell away, fearlessly meeting the Valeroot elves on the battlefield.

"Fools!" Hotrath roared.

Alluin turned in time to watch Hotrath throw Malon at him, but not in time to avoid the hurtling elf. Malon slammed into him, stealing his breath and knocking him into the mud. The blossoming sunlight danced over his eyes for a moment as he struggled to relearn how to breathe. Malon rolled off of him with a groan, then crouched at his side. Suddenly they were alone as the Akkeri all ran toward the battle, save their High King who'd retreated in Saida's direction.

Malon straightened and went after him, leaving Alluin lying in the mud.

Cursing the pomposity of Faerune, Alluin stood, then hesitated. In one direction his kin, possibly even Vail, fought the ruthless Akkeri. In the other, Hotrath might very well be dragging Saida toward his ship where more Akkeri waited to steal her away forever.

He clenched his fists and ran after Malon. He'd promised Saida's parents he'd keep her safe, and he had to have faith the Valeroot elves could defend themselves in battle. The sea came into view as he ran. Hotrath's broad back blocked any view of Saida, but she had to be in his arms considering he was marching toward a rowboat heading in to carry him to the larger ship. Malon was hot on his heels. There was another blue-sailed ship far in the distance, whether Akkeri or someone else, he could not tell.

Alluin might not have noticed the three Akkeri lying in the sand to his right, if one hadn't groaned in pain. He looked them over quickly, assessing the threat. One lay dead with a sword in his back, another unconscious or dead was sprawled beside him, and the third, badly beaten and bloody, was Merwyn. A few more Akkeri lay further down the beach.

"He took Saida!" Merwyn groaned. "Stop him!"

"I'll come back for you!" Alluin assured, then ran after Hotrath. He watched Malon intercept him near the tide, blocking the giant's path to his ship. Hotrath tossed Saida's limp body onto the sand, then held up a meaty hand toward the Akkeri in the rowboat. The Akkeri halted halfway into the water, then climbed back into their rocking boat.

Hotrath's head angled down toward Malon. "I will enjoy killing you with my bare hands, elf."

Alluin slowed his pace as he approached Hotrath's back. The High King had not yet noticed him. Malon caught Alluin's eye past Hotrath, and gave the barest of nods toward Saida.

Alluin nodded, then changed course toward Saida's unconscious form. He knelt beside her as Malon leapt into the air, aiming a well practiced kick toward Hotrath's jaw. Hotrath took the blow without flinching, grasping for Malon as he landed on his feet in the sand.

Alluin looked back down to Saida. Her face was purple with bruises, and her long blonde hair streaked with blood. Alluin lifted her carefully into his arms, fearing the worst. Before he could slip away with her, the Akkeri on the rowboat started shouting, gaining Hotrath's attention.

Hotrath took a fist to the gut from Malon without so much as a grunt. With a growl of rage he grabbed Malon's arm, using it to lift the elf over his head. He spun on Alluin and Saida, throwing Malon at them as if he weighed nothing. The three tumbled into the sand, pinning Alluin on the bottom. Malon was up quickly, but Alluin had to roll Saida gently aside before he could move.

Driven more by their instincts than the command of their High King, the four Akkeri dove off the rowboat into the water and splashed toward shore. Alluin rose shakily to his feet next to Malon, facing Hotrath, for what little good it would do. The High King seemed impervious to attack, and sounds of battle could still be heard in the distance. Were the Valeroot elves falling to the blind bloodlust of the Akkeri?

Arms splayed to catch the next attack, Hotrath approached. "You will die by my hands, elves. Not just you, but all of your kin. Once our curse is lifted, we will come for you. We will bathe in the blood of elves as we desecrate your temples, just as you desecrated ours. We will—"

A massive boom sounded toward the north, near Faerune. An explosion. The four Akkeri who had reached the shore froze, peering in the direction of the distant city. Shouts could be heard from the Akkeri ship, but

Alluin soon realized they weren't shouting about the explosion. The ship with blue sails was closing in. As it was absent an insignia, Alluin had no clue about its occupants, save one. There was a growing storm overhead. Dark clouds rolled in, thunder rumbling in their depths. Had Elmerah escaped Egrin? If she had, she would have returned to Faerune. It was a possibility. His heart filled with elation, far more so than he had expected.

Hotrath growled again, turning his sights away from the ship toward Saida where she lay forgotten in the sand. "You were lucky this time, elves." As he reached for Saida, lightning struck the shore, tossing him back. He landed with a heavy thud in the sand, but quickly got to his feet.

Alluin seized the opportunity to rush toward Saida. He lifted her into his arms with Malon at his back. Lightning rained down upon the shore, striking at the Akkeri from the rowboat before they could reach them. The lightning next turned toward the Akkeri ship, accompanied by harsh winds which caught the Akkeri sails, rocking the ship violently. The sharp twang of ballistas preceded a flaming volley of projectiles launched at the Akkeri ship.

The scene was so brilliant, Alluin nearly forgot Hotrath at his back. He whirled around, only to catch sight of Hotrath's broad back growing smaller in the distance, leaving his fellow Akkeri dead and injured on the beach. The assault of fire and lightning continued until the entire Akkeri ship was aflame despite the rain now pattering down across the sea. Flaming Akkeri screamed and leapt from the ship into the water.

Clutching Saida protectively in his arms, he turned toward Malon. "Care to rethink your opinion of the Arthali?"

Malon frowned. His right arm was limp at his side, and he leaned more heavily on his left leg, but he seemed otherwise uninjured. "I'll rethink it if we survive this oncoming encounter." He pointed toward the blue-sailed ship, and the large rowboat now headed toward shore.

He realized with great disappointment that it was not a Faerune ship with Elmerah on board, it was a ship entirely occupied by Arthali. Judging by the lightning, Rissine was the tall woman he could see standing at the bow of the rowboat.

"Alluin!" a familiar voice called.

Alluin turned, receiving yet another shock as he beheld his sister, Vessa. She was roughed up, her short hair, the same rich brown as his, dappled with Akkeri blood. She jogged toward him, a tight-lipped smile making her young features seem old and tired.

Reaching him, she glanced toward Malon, then out toward the Arthali ship, before returning her gaze to Alluin. "When we picked up that Akkeri trail I never thought I'd find you at the end of it."

"Are they all dead?"

She nodded. "Them, their nasty hounds, and many elves along with them," she bowed her head slightly before adding, "I'd love to hear your side of the tale, along with an explanation about the Arthali rowing toward us, but it will have to wait. I think Faerune is being attacked."

Her words were echoed by another explosion. He imagined the crystal walls toppling beneath the force of Dreilore fire and brimstone. "I believe Elmerah's sister is leading the Arthali," he explained. "Gather the remaining elves. We will reach Faerune faster by ship, I can only hope we are not too late."

"You will truly rush to Faerune's aid?" Malon balked.

Alluin glared at him. Even after all they'd been through, he still viewed the Valeroot elves as lesser. "The only way any of us will survive is to protect each other. I only hope that Faerune can muster the same honor as Valeroot when the time comes."

The Arthali boat reached the shore, carrying Rissine and three male Arthali. Alluin transferred Saida to Malon's arms, hoping she had nothing more serious than a concussion, then went to meet Rissine. He felt a little guilty making Vessa return to the field of their fallen kin, but he could not stand the thought of seeing them. Visions of the slain elves back in Galterra danced through his mind as he walked across the shore. Would the bloodshed never end?

Rissine eyed him with a smug smile as he approached, her boots and breeches wet from hopping out of the rowboat and helping her men drag it onto the sand. "I'm disappointed you let that giant Akkeri escape. I've never seen one so big."

He glanced in the direction Hotrath had fled, further south, away from Faerune. "Then you've never met their High King."

"Where's my sister?"

"I'll explain everything soon. Do you have more rowboats? We have more of my people heading toward shore, and we need to reach Faerune."

Rissine didn't move. The three male Arthali stood at her back, tattooed arms crossed. "Where. Is. My. Sister?"

They didn't have time for this. Faerune would still fall without aid from the Arthali. "She was taken by Egrin Dinoba. If I know anything about him, he will be there to watch Faerune fall."

Rage washed across Rissine's face. "Gather your elves quickly, we have no time to waste."

Elmerah

A warm wind sifted through Elmerah's hair, bringing with it the scent of smoke and ash from the explosions. To her right stood Egrin, and to her left Isara. Surrounding them were a bevy of Dreilore warriors, watching from a high hill as Faerune was assaulted by a mixture of magic and might. The magnificent crystal walls were chipped and cracked, but had not yet fallen, not that they needed to fall. The main assault had taken place at the gates, for all their might, they were weaker than their crystalline counterparts.

Elven archers rained arrows down upon the Dreilore warriors, and others dumped cauldrons of hot oil, but it would not be enough. Rows upon rows of Dreilore warriors marched onward. Elmerah wouldn't have guessed so many Dreilore existed in all of Salisfait, let alone hiding in the woods between Galterra and Faerune . . . yet, as many as there were, there would not be enough to easily overcome Faerune, a city nearly as large as the Capital. The Dreilore would be outnumbered by the elves twenty to one. They must have known something she didn't, because she did not for a moment believe they would attack unless they could win.

Egrin took a deep, satisfied breath, then slowly let it out. "You see, witch, this is what happens to those who stand against the might of the Empire."

Elmerah snorted, straining her hands against her shackles. "Don't you mean this is what happens to the Empire's allies? Faerune never stood against you. They supported the Empire since the Great War."

She sensed Dreilore warriors behind her, shifting at her words.

Egrin merely laughed. "They would never have willingly given up their moonstones. It's as good as standing against me. Just as you are doing by not divulging the secret to your magic."

"It's not my fault you're not smart enough to figure it out."

He casually backhanded her. Her body rocked back, but she managed to brace herself and not fall. Her cheek stung, and she tasted blood on the inside of her mouth. Egrin was thin and not overly muscled, but he'd hit her with the strength of a young troll.

The Dreilore down below hurried away from the iron gates, their alchemical explosives set at the base. Elmerah held her breath as the explosives erupted in a wave of blue and purple fire. The entire city of Faerune seem to shake, and the ground beneath her boots rumbled. A gust of wind cleared the smoke, revealing the ruined gates, no longer offering any protection to the elves within.

The Dreilore marched onward, over the corpses of their fallen kin.

Though they were surrounded by Dreilore guards, she could wait no longer. She subtly turned toward Isara and nodded.

She felt it as the enchantment on her shackles was restrained. She'd have to make this quick. She sucked in magic from the air around her, faster than was wise, so fast it made her dizzy.

Egrin turned toward her. She managed to gasp to Isara, "Keep going!" seconds before Egrin stole the air from her lungs. She called her lightning down, aiming it not toward Egrin, but the surrounding Dreilore. She felt the pulse of electricity at her back, heard the grunts of the stricken Dreilore, then her magic cut off. She gasped as air returned to her lungs, courtesy of Isara shifting her focus from the shackles to Egrin.

She took another deep breath as one of the Dreilore recovered and grabbed her shoulders from behind. She tossed her head back, breaking the Dreilore's nose. The Dreilore fell away, only to be replaced by another. She began to call out to Isara to nullify the shackles, when suddenly her magic returned. She spun toward the remaining Dreilore, summoning an erratic wave of flame ahead of her, then aimed a second burst at her shackles. The Dreilore fell back, rolling across the grass to put out the flames on their hair and clothing as the hot metal of her shackles scalded her wrists. The locks in the shackles broke under the heat and dropped to the ground. She tried to take another deep breath, but no air came in.

Isara tried to scurry toward her, but another Dreilore came up behind her and held a blade to her throat. "No more magic," he hissed in his thick Salisfait accent.

Isara nodded, her spectacles amplifying the terror in her eyes. Yet, Elmerah still had breath in her lungs, so she must not have obeyed.

"Clever witch," Egrin said as he stepped back between the two remaining guards. "Try that again I'll crush you so fully that your heart stops."

Ah, so Isara wasn't saving her, Egrin just wasn't attacking. She could attack now that her shackles were off, but that magic would do her little good now that Egrin was aware of it, and could deflect her attacks. She could attack the Dreilore holding Isara, but she'd risk harming Isara in the process.

She was fast running out of options, and Faerune was

falling behind her. She did the only thing she could think to do. She put her weight on her left leg then used the right to kick a rock near the toe of her boot. The rock sailed straight toward Egrin's face. In the split second it took him to reach out and catch it, she launched herself toward him, tackling him between the two Dreilore. The momentum was enough to send her and Egrin rolling down the grassy hill.

Egrin held on and they toppled over each other. She knew he could use his magic to halt their momentum, but he didn't. Was Isara helping her from up on the hill? She hoped so. The Dreilore yet with her wouldn't be able to tell unless Egrin informed them.

Egrin rolled over her, then she atop him. She thrust her elbow forward, slamming him in the jaw. He grabbed her hair at the back of her skull and yanked, wrenching her neck painfully as he toppled back on top. She cried out, but managed to take the opportunity to knee him in the groin.

With an *oof,* he lost his grip on her and went tumbling down the hill at a faster rate. She managed to right herself, digging her boot heels into the grass so she could slide the rest of the way down on her rump.

She didn't waste any time. The Dreilore would come running after them soon. She launched herself to her feet and landed a running kick to Egrin's jaw. He skidded across the grass at the bottom of the hill, blood flinging from his nose and mouth. She lined up for another kick. She knew Isara could be distracted from nullifying his magic at any moment, and she needed him dead or unconscious before that could happen.

Searing pain lanced through her left shoulder. She reached around and felt the hilt of a dagger sticking out of her back, piercing her dirty coat and the flesh underneath. The rest of the Dreilore, all but the one guarding Isara, reached the bottom of the hill and surrounded her.

"Don't kill her," Egrin groaned.

His words surprised her. She'd thought for sure she'd earned a death sentence from him by now.

The earth shook at her feet. At first she thought it was another Dreilore explosion, then a male voice yelled, "Down Ellie!" She dropped to the ground as a wave of arrows whooshed over her head. No, not arrows, she realized, but darts. Tiny darts, the type most commonly used in blow guns imported from the Helshone Desert, landed with light thunks into Dreilore flesh.

Her heart thundered in her ears as the Dreilore fell around her. The darts had to be tipped with a sleeping concoction, though she hoped it was something more toxic. She propped herself up on her elbows and nearly cried to see Celen running toward her. The protruding dagger made her shoulder feel icy and scalding hot at the same time.

Celen approached alone, but more Arthali stood near the tree line.

Though her adrenaline was waning, she forced herself to her feet, stealing a rapier from one of the downed Dreilore on her way up. Celen reached her as she reached Egrin. Egrin blinked up at her, his pale eyes vibrant against the blood coating his face.

With trembling hands she poised the rapier over his heart.

He smiled, revealing blood-coated teeth. "You'll come to me yet, witch."

She drove the rapier down to pierce his heart, driving its tip into the grass as Egrin seem to evaporate in a cloud of darkness. The darkness swirled for a moment, then was gone.

"Son of a Dreilore wench!" She snatched the rapier from the grass. "That bloody demonic bastard!"

Celen stared at her from across the space where Egrin had been. "So I guess he really is a demon?"

Elmerah wanted to cry, partially from frustration, but partially because she was so bloody glad to see Celen. She assured herself the tears had nothing to do with the dagger in her back. Reining in her emotions, she answered matter of factly, "Yes, we've established that." She looked up toward the hilltop as the Arthali approached from the tree line. Though her legs felt like thistle jelly, she started up the incline to find Isara. If Egrin had swooped in and taken Isara with him, she'd . . . well she didn't know what she'd do, but it would be rather unfortunate.

Celen followed her as she trudged up the hill. The sounds of battle raged on behind her, spurring her on. "Ellie! You know you have a dagger in your back? It seems a small blade, but still, we should probably get it out. You are losing blood."

She ignored him, though she felt lightheaded and on the verge of fainting. There was no time for delay. Swaying on her feet, she found Isara at the top of the hill, looking a bit dazed amongst the dead Dreilore, including the one who'd held her captive. The knife he'd held to Isara's throat now jutted out from his ribs. She had a key in her hands and was working at using it on her shackles.

Elmerah swayed on her feet again. "Well aren't you full of surprises?"

Celen moved past her to help Isara with her shackles.

Elmerah gestured toward her with the rapier still clutched in her hand. She'd nearly forgotten about it. "Celen, meet Isara Saredoth. We'll need to keep her alive if we still hope to carry out Alluin's plan, now let's go."

She turned without waiting for a reply, summoning every ounce of strength she possessed. Isara and Celen hurried after her as she tromped back down the hill. She didn't know what she could do for Faerune. Her sister had obviously failed to arrive, and she didn't know where Saida or Alluin were, but she couldn't just stand around and wait for the results.

Celen grabbed her good shoulder at the bottom of the hill where the other Arthali waited. "You cannot hope to take on so many Dreilore by yourself. The elves are as good as dead."

"We have to try."

He huffed. "Fine." Without warning, he gripped the

hilt of the dagger in her back and tugged it free. "Healer!" he called, motioning to the waiting Arthali.

She fell to her knees. That had *not* felt good. She hoped Celen had a proper healer, someone from the Greenfold Clan.

She had no idea what she would do once she could stand again, but she meant what she said. She had to try.

Alluin

Alluin braced his hands against the ship's railing as it swayed across the choppy waters. Vessa stood at his side, avoiding Rissine's glare. In all the chaos, he hadn't stopped to consider that Vessa had once worked for Rissine until he and Elmerah had messed things up for her. At least, that was probably how she viewed it. Personally, he still debated wringing his sister's neck for helping Rissine smuggle young women into slavery.

Of Vessa's scouting party, only eight of the original thirty still lived. They were outnumbered by the Arthali on the ship, but just barely. Malon was below deck with Saida and Merwyn, both too injured to stand.

Faerune was nothing but a cloud of smoke in the distance. He heard fighting, but it was already waning. They would be too late.

Rissine approached his side, opposite Vessa. "I fear there will not be much left of Faerune to save. Stupid elves should have let us in when we first arrived. Of course, if we hadn't been left out at anchor, we never would have seen you and you'd all be dead." Her dark eyes glinted with malice. "I'll need you alive if I'm to kill you for letting harm befall my sister."

Alluin didn't reply. They were too late, too late for everyone. He'd failed Saida just as he'd failed Elmerah. It seemed in the end the Arthali would be the only ones left standing, at least until the Empire hunted them all down.

Vessa clenched the railing in front of her hard enough to make the wood creak. "I told you uncle Ured's plan was folly. I told you from the start."

He still didn't reply. Maybe she was right. Maybe if he'd listened to her, Elmerah would be safe, Saida would be uninjured, and the Valeroot elves would still be living like rats trying to avoid Egrin Dinoba's boots.

Saida

Saida's eyes fluttered open to the creak of boots on floorboards. A lantern swayed gently from a hook on the ceiling. She was lying in a bed, though not a terribly comfortable one, and her head and body felt like she'd been hit by a horse. Her eyes slowly focused on someone walking toward her. She tensed, then relaxed when she realized it was only Malon.

He knelt beside her bed. He had one blackened eye,

and a bit of blood at his hairline, but he was still definitely in better shape than her. "I'm glad to see you're awake."

"Where am I?"

He smiled warmly. "You're on an Arthali ship. Probably not the best place to be, but better than an Akkeri one."

Her muddy thoughts slowly pieced together. "Rissine? Did she find us?"

He crossed his legs to sit on the floor beside her bed, eye level with her. "The she-beast, yes. She makes Elmerah look like a shining jewel."

Saida couldn't help her small smile. Rissine and Elmerah were both beautiful, but their manners left much to be desired, especially in the eyes of someone who had spent his entire life in Faerune. "What happened on the shore? Is Merwyn alright?"

"What's the last thing you remember?"

"Merwyn tried to help me escape. We fought the other Akkeri. I was hit on the head, but I vaguely remember Hotrath coming for me. Is Merwyn alright?"

He nodded, and she let out a sigh of relief. "He's on another bed right over there." He pointed across the dim cabin, though she could not see beyond the dome of lantern light.

She lifted a trembling hand to her forehead. Her skin ached, but was smooth and clean. Someone must have wiped away the blood. "What are we doing on this ship? Please tell me we're headed toward Faerune."

Malon pushed a lock of her dirty hair away from her face, surprising her with his touch. "Yes, I must inform you, the Dreilore assault has begun. We may not make it in time to be of much help. They are sure to act quickly."

Dizziness washed over her. Her mother, her father, they were being attacked and she should have been there to protect them. "How long? How long until we get there?"

"Soon," he soothed. "Does Hotrath have the circlet?"

His question gave her pause. Though the circlet was invaluable, why would he ask about it now? She almost reached for her belt pouch to see if it was still there, but hesitated. Hotrath had told her to hold onto it since she'd be wearing it at their marriage ceremony. Why would Malon, as a guardsman, not a priest, care about it?

"Hotrath took it," she lied. "Does he still live?"

"He escaped when Arthali attacked. I daresay he is the only Akkeri who survived this day, at least of his clan."

She shivered. She knew as long as Hotrath was alive he'd come for her, but that was a worry for another day. Her body felt so weak, so sore, she could barely move. She would be of no use once they arrived in Faerune.

She lifted a trembling hand and placed it upon Malon's shoulder. "Please, please promise me you will find my parents and protect them. I know it is not fair of me to ask, as your duty is to all of Faerune, but please, I cannot lose them."

He placed his hand over hers on his shoulder and gave it a gentle squeeze, once again surprising her. "Do you remember the time you became lost in the snow? You were but a girl, I'd guess around fourteen, maybe fifteen."

She furrowed her brow, then winced. "Yes I remember, I nearly died that day. I would have died if a guardsman hadn't found me—" She narrowed her gaze. "What of it?"

"I don't expect you to remember. I know all guardsmen are the same in the eyes of the priests and priestesses. But I was the one who saved you."

She gasped, then felt suddenly guilty. She remembered that day. She'd snuck outside the crystal walls after the first snow of winter. She'd wanted to sled down the large hill outside the city, but once she'd gotten out, everything have been so sparkly and dazzling she'd wanted to explore more. She's made it all the way to the edge of the forest, then went further in. She'd run from a wyrm. Then the snow came again, covering her tracks. She'd gotten lost.

She would have died, but a guardsman happened upon her. He'd made a fire to warm her before escorting her back to Faerune. She'd been very grateful, in fact she'd developed a small crush on him as he wasn't much older than her, but once she'd recovered she hadn't been able to find him again. She'd never even learned his name. And he was right, she'd soon forgotten about him, just another guardsman.

His brows lifted. "Starting to remember?"

"I can't believe I didn't realize it was you. That was

only what, five years ago? Less? I feel like such a fool, I apologize. I'd always wanted to thank you. But—" she hesitated, "why do you bring it up now?"

He gave her hand another squeeze, then allowed her to remove it. "Because now, priestess, I'm going to need you to trust me. I'm going to need you to trust that what I've done, I've done for the good of all elves. You may want to hate me, but things needed to change. The politics within Faerune are antiquated. Our class system is from another century. It has to change, and it will not be changed by allying with the Arthali."

The blood in her veins turned ice. "Malon, what have you done?"

He stroked her hair again, then pulled something out of his pocket, a small vial filled with red liquid. She recognized it as one of those her father had given her. Malon must have stolen it when they fled Isara's.

He flicked the stopper off the vial with his thumb, then brought it toward her face. "I'll see you again soon, priestess. I know your whole life you felt unimportant, not having your mother's magic, the magic of a Sun Priestess, but you are more valuable than you know, and not just to the Akkeri. I promise, this will become clear with time."

She lurched away, but there was only so far she could go. Her bed was against the wall, and Malon blocked the other side of it. He crawled onto her bed and placed a hand over her mouth before she could scream. She tried anyway, but knew with the sounds of the ship no one would hear her except maybe Merwyn, but he was obviously not conscious.

Malon pushed his weight against her, sealing her mouth closed and keeping her head still. She was too weak, and in too much pain to fight him. He held the vial under her nose, the smell was sharp and sweet. Before she knew it her eyes were closed, her thoughts were growing distant, and then Malon was gone.

She could hear everyone above deck, they must be getting ready to leave the ship. She had to warn them. She wasn't sure what Malon planned, but he'd said it would make her hate him. Her last thought as she drifted off was of that time in the snow. Of sitting across the fire from a handsome young guardsman. Of listening to his tale about how things would be different someday.

CHAPTER FOURTEEN

Elmerah

E lmerah scaled the rubble at the edge of the ruined gates, keeping a close watch for any who might still live. Bodies littered the once pristine street, both Dreilore and elves. The shining granite architecture she'd once found so awe-inspiring was speckled with blood and ash. Her shoulder ached, but Celen's healer had done a fine job mending it. With the healing herbs, a bit of magic, and fresh bandages, she'd at least been able to get moving again.

Celen was right behind her, along with Isara. The other Arthali were fanned out, some already within the city. With their small numbers, stealth was best, though Elmerah ached to lash out at something. She wasn't in top form unfortunately. Besides her wound, she hadn't fully recovered from Egrin's torture, and the scene on the hill had taken more of her strength than she cared to admit.

She crested the rubble, hurried down, then went behind the nearest building. She could hear more fighting further in, but so many were already dead. When immortal warriors were pitted against the prowess of elves, death happened quickly. Yet even with so many dead, there weren't enough bodies to account for all the Dreilore. There had to be many more within Faerune, even though the near silence made her doubt just how many she'd seen marching toward the gates.

Celen hovered over her shoulder as she leaned out and peered down the main street. His scarred face was set into grim lines. "Why would the Dreilore be willing to sacrifice so many? They might have overcome the elves, but just barely. Why would they risk coming so close to defeat?"

She shook her head. She didn't understand either. An alliance with the Empire was one thing, but to sacrifice so many Dreilore lives for the emperor's cause? The Dreilore had not survived so long by being selfless and loyal. "Egrin must have something they want bad enough to die for. Just as he did with the Akkeri. They were willing to die if it meant breaking the curse on their people."

"You believe the Dreilore are cursed?" Isara asked from behind Celen.

Elmerah had nearly forgotten her. She craned her neck, aiming her ear upward to better hear the distant fighting. "No, but it doesn't matter. It doesn't matter what they are willing to die for, it only matters that they are doing it. We need to see how many elves are still alive. Perhaps we can rally them to push out the remaining Dreilore."

"It still just doesn't make sense," Celen repeated. "Not just the Dreilore, but how quickly they overcame the city. Faerune has survived for a long time. Why were they so easily overcome?"

Elmerah leaned back into hiding, then turned and walked the other way, away from the main road. "There's only one way to find out. We need to get closer." She glanced back toward Celen. "Your people will remain hidden?"

Celen nodded as he fell into step beside her. "They will not act until I give them orders. If they come across any strays, they will quietly take them down with sleeping darts."

"Sleeping darts," Elmerah scoffed, "not exactly the Arthali style."

Celen shrugged. "Remaining hidden has been our priority these past years. Bows and darts work well to keep us protected."

Isara caught up to Elmerah's other side, lifting the skirt of her burgundy dress above her knees to step over rubble. "Aren't you two worried we'll run into Dreilore walking around like this?"

"No," they said in unison.

Elmerah heard a whisper from a nearby open window. Catching Celen's attention, she pointed.

He nodded, then took a side street toward the back of the small stone home. Elmerah stopped by the white-washed door. Though most of the stones were also white, this close she realized it was only paint. Granite was reserved for the wealthier homes and other buildings lining the main street.

She waited a moment to ensure Celen had time to reach the back of the house, then lifted her boot and kicked in the door. A yip sounded from inside, followed by frantic whispers. She hurried in, drawing her borrowed rapier, just as Celen came in through the back.

Three elves, a mother, father, and little girl, huddled in the kitchen. She felt a small pang in her heart. How many families like this one had already been slain?

"Please don't hurt us!" the mother gasped. "We have nothing."

Celen reached Elmerah's side as she explained, "We are not here to hurt you. Do you know what's happening further in the city?"

The father stood a little straighter and nodded. "I was near the High Temple when the Dreilore broke through the gates. The priests and priestesses locked themselves inside with our precious gems and irreplaceable artifacts. Many families fled to lock themselves up in the mines. I don't know if they made it. I had to come back for my family."

Elmerah nodded. These three were probably safer

than the ones in the mines, considering Egrin was after the moonstones. If there were magic artifacts in the High Temple, the Dreilore would be going there too.

Isara had finally entered the home, but hung back near the door. Elmerah turned toward Celen. "We'll head toward the High Temple. If anyone can rally the remaining elves, it's the priests and priestesses, but something else is going on here, more than what we realize. I can't really say what we'll find." She turned to leave.

"Wait," the father elf urged. "I heard something else as I was running back here. Some present at the gates claimed that over half the guardsmen didn't fight. They turned away from their duty, and let the Dreilore break through the gates. I don't know where these elves are now, but I wouldn't trust any guardsmen you come across."

Goosebumps erupted on Elmerah's arms. So that was it. The guardsmen had betrayed their city, and that was why the elves were overcome so quickly. She nodded her thanks, then turned back to Celen. "Let's go."

As they left the home she said a small prayer to Arcale for any other families like this one. They'd been betrayed by their own kin, and she knew exactly how that felt.

Alluin

Smoke plumes wafted up from Faerune, the scent mingling with the thick salt air. In a rowboat, Alluin stood next to Rissine, a borrowed bow in hand, and new knives at his belt. No one had had an extra sword to spare. Sitting behind them was Malon with another Arthali. Two others manned the oars. Following in their wake were more boats filled with Arthali and Valeroot elves.

He was glad Saida was staying aboard the ship. She hadn't even woken when he shook her. He wasn't sure what he'd say to her if she were looking at the scene ahead. There was still fighting, he could hear it over the slap of the tide, but it was the end of a lost battle. He almost hoped Elmerah was still with Egrin, because if she was within Faerune, she was probably dead.

He glanced at Rissine. Though she and Elmerah looked a lot alike—despite Rissine being a few years older with swirling tattoos up and down her arms—her presence was nothing like her younger sister's. Where Elmerah was like a passionate fire, her sister was like prickly ice. Both were dangerous and unpredictable, but at least the former was something you'd want to warm your hands beside.

"What?" Rissine snapped.

"Are you sure you can protect the boats if the Dreilore spot us? It seems risky rowing right for the docks."

Rissine turned her dark eyes toward Faerune. "We have several members of the Winter Isles clan amongst us. They can summon winds to deflect any arrows or incendiaries, and we have no time to spare. If Egrin has my sister, there's no saying how long she'll remain alive."

The choppy waves near the docks rocked the small boat enough that they had to crouch down. He looked back and saw the Arthali and Valeroot elves in the other boats doing the same. He continued scanning the boats until he spotted Vessa. Despite her tendency to make bad decisions, she'd come back to her people when they needed her the most. He wished he could have convinced her to stay on the boat with Saida, but she'd refused. Only Merwyn, a few injured elves, and three Arthali with little magic had remained behind.

With a few more thrusts of the oars, they reached the docks. As they moored the boats, Alluin waited with his ear raised upward, sure he'd hear the sounds of approaching Dreilore or elves any moment, but nothing came.

"Why is the city so quiet?" he muttered to himself. Most of the distant fighting had subsided. Faerune should not have fallen so easily.

"We'll soon find out," Rissine answered, though he hadn't been speaking to her. She was the first to climb atop the docks, the tiny trinkets draping her hips jingling with every step. She turned and looked back at him. "You'll come with me, elf. Each of your clan will be accompanied by one of mine, that way we'll have no surprises."

She might as well have said, *I don't trust you in the*

slightest, but he wasn't about to argue. If anyone would confront Egrin this day it would be Rissine, and he planned to be there when it happened. He climbed onto the docks, stretching his legs, which now felt wobbly from the short time at sea. He wasn't used to ships, not like the Arthali, who were born and bred on them.

He looked back to address the other elves and Arthali climbing atop the docks. "Most of you should head toward the mines. They're toward the southeastern end of the city."

Rissine curled her lip at him. "And where will you and I be going, oh great leader?"

He ignored her sarcasm. "We'll go to the High Temple. Any living priests and priestesses will be there. We need to find Saida's parents."

Malon reached his side. "I'll check the guard posts, without an Arthali escort, if you don't mind." He looked to Rissine. "I'll be able to address them better without them thinking I've turned traitor."

Rissine looked to Alluin, as if she might actually want to know his opinion.

He nodded. "Let him go. If there are any guardsmen left alive, we'll need their help, And he's the only one amongst us who really knows the city."

What followed from Rissine was a series of elaborate hand gestures like Alluin had never seen, but the other Arthali seemed to comprehend her meaning.

She turned and walked away without another word,

her boots echoing hollowly across the whitewashed docks.

Malon turned away too, without a reply, and Vessa was busy giving orders to the other Valeroot elves. Gritting his teeth, Alluin hurried after Rissine before he could lose sight of her. For all her confidence, she was making herself rather vulnerable to an arrow in the back, but perhaps she had skills he didn't know about. He wouldn't be surprised if she did.

Elmerah

E lmerah crouched behind a decorative partial wall between Isara and Celen. She'd been right in her assumption. The last of the Faerune guardsmen—at least those who'd chosen to fight—were being cut down on the steps to the High Temple. It was almost dizzying watching them fight. The elves were faster and more skilled than any human ever would be, but the Dreilore were even faster. Their icy white hair flicked and arced with their movements, standing in blurry contrast to their black leather armor. These were no mere foot soldiers, only the nobility and higher ranking officials amongst the Dreilore grew out their hair. Her confusion deepened. That the Dreilore were willing to risk their soldiers for whatever Egrin had offered them was one thing, but to risk their nobility?

She kept her eyes on the fighting, and on the blood running down the white steps. "Are you both ready?"

Celen grabbed her arm before she could stand. "Don't you see how their blades glow? They are enchanted. They might be able to nullify our magic before we can even get close. We shouldn't attack."

"Do you have a better idea?"

Isara cleared her throat. "I might be able to nullify the magic on their blades like I did with your shackles. You would be able to use your magic, but that will not make the Dreilore any less dangerous."

Celen squeezed her arm. "Are you willing to die for this, Ellie?"

It was a good question. She hadn't seen Alluin or Saida anywhere, but that did not mean they weren't within the temple. She could try to fight her way in, but doubted she could make it. Perhaps it would be noble to try, but she'd be doing no one any good—least of all herself—if she got cut down for no reason.

"You're right. Rushing in is stupid, but if Isara can nullify their enchantments, we can attack from a distance. It will undoubtedly catch them off guard and give the elves a fighting chance. We can't just hide here and do nothing."

They both nodded their agreement.

Celen backed away from the decorative wall, then cursed. "Well I honestly couldn't be more surprised if I saw a walking whipfish."

Elmerah tilted her head up to view what Celen

seemed to see. Rissine strode down the street bisecting the main thoroughfare, making no effort to hide. She marched right toward the Dreilore, and there was someone behind her. Elmerah's heart leapt into her throat. *Alluin*.

"Um," Celen began, "they are about to get themselves killed."

Elmerah stood up straight, her feet stanced for action. "Isara, block the Dreilore's enchantments. Remain in hiding and do not reveal yourself no matter what happens. Keeping their enchantments suppressed is our only hope."

The Dreilore continued their slow advance up the steps, leaving elven corpses at their feet. She wasn't sure if Rissine couldn't have come at a better time, or a worse time, but all they had was right now. She called out to her magic, hoping in her weakened state it would be enough.

Celen's voice seemed distant, though he was standing right beside her. "I guess we're doing this then."

She felt him calling his magic. It wasn't as strong as hers, and almost nothing compared to Rissine's, but it was a different type of magic, which sometimes could count for more.

Rissine stopped walking just outside the Dreilore's field of vision. Her eyes went wide. She pointed in Elmerah's direction, and Alluin's eyes landed on her. The look on his face as he realized she was still alive was not what she'd expected. He blinked at her for a minute, then grinned.

She gave him a quick wink, then focused on her magic. She felt suddenly invigorated, and more hopeful that they would succeed. Thunder seemed to shake the very foundation of Faerune. She felt her sister's magic melding with hers, while Celen's earth magic was just a distant throb behind her. This was the true reason the Shadowmarsh clan had been so dangerous. Alone, each witch was a force to be reckoned with. But together? Enough Shadowmarsh witches could destroy an entire city in minutes. They could sink an entire fleet of ships. Maybe they could even kill a single demonic emperor.

The Dreilore on the steps regrouped, their orange, burning eyes searching the surrounding streets for the source of the building magic. As one, they seemed to realize that their swords were no longer glowing. Every elf around them lay dead at their feet. Three Dreilore ran for the unguarded doors.

The pressure built until Elmerah felt like she couldn't breathe. With a resounding *clap*, her magic fully melded with her sister's. The steps beneath the Dreilore shook with Celen's earth magic, then brilliant lightning rained down. A sudden downpour of moisture followed, drenching the entire city. More lightning crackled as the smoke disappeared in the rain. Four Dreilore were down and unmoving. Elmerah could hardly believe her eyes as the remaining three evaporated into clouds of darkness. The two that had raced toward the top of the stairs had gone inside.

"What in Ilthune's name was that!" Celen called over the sound of the rain.

Isara stood, removing spectacles made worthless by the downpour. "That was demonic magic!"

Elmerah didn't need the explanation, and Celen shouldn't have either. They both had witnessed Egrin disappear right before she could drive her stolen rapier through his heart.

Alluin and Rissine jogged over to them. Her sister looked at Celen like she had spotted a particularly disgusting bug.

Celen stared back at her defiantly, even though Rissine could potentially crush him like that aforementioned bug.

Elmerah noted the scuffs and bruises on Alluin's face. "We need to follow those who went inside, but be wary. They may have a bit of Egrin's power to them."

Alluin nodded, then followed her as she hopped over the low wall, leading the way to the High Temple. There were so many things she wanted to ask him, namely *where was Saida,* but there was no time.

She ignored the bodies, both elven and Dreilore, as they hurried across the street and up the High Temple stairs. Their boots splashed in quickly forming puddles of water, washing away the blood. Isara, Rissine, and Celen followed.

Reaching the top of the stairs, Elmerah looked to Alluin, who nodded. Together they each manned one of the heavy double doors, throwing them open. The silence inside was deafening in contrast to the heavy rain. They stepped inside.

Elmerah turned around to address the others. Her eyes landed on her sister. "I'll go with Alluin and Isara toward the left wing, you and Celen take the right."

"Why do I have to take *him*?" Rissine whined.

"Because he can protect himself, and I don't trust either of you to protect anyone else."

Footsteps thundered up the stairs outside, echoing the patter of rain. Everyone instinctively faced the threat with weapons drawn.

Malon ran inside, his wet boots skidding on the white tiles. He lifted his hands in front of him at their raised weapons. "It's only me. There were no guardsmen in any of the outposts. Everyone must be deeper in the city, or holed up in the mines. That is where those unable to fight are instructed to go in case of attack."

Elmerah wanted to ask questions now more than ever, like where in Ilthune's name was Saida? But expediency in locating the Dreilore remained vital.

"There are Dreilore in the building," she explained to Malon. "You go with Rissine and Celen." She turned away and strode down the long hall of the left wing, confident Isara and Alluin would follow.

As the others took off toward the right wing, she heard Celen introducing himself to Malon.

She turned her attention forward, scanning the hall. There was no blood decorating the pristine white interior. A good sign.

Alluin reached her side, his bow held casually, though she knew he could nock an arrow in seconds. "You're as good as sacrificing Malon sending him with those two."

"I'm guessing by your demeanor, Saida is all right?"

"She's on Rissine's ship, injured but alive. We had a run-in with the Akkeri."

"You'll have to tell me about that later." She stopped outside the first door and placed her ear against it. After a moment she pulled away. "Isara, listen at the doors. The priests and priestesses have to be somewhere in here, perhaps locked in a vault somewhere, hiding while their people are murdered in the streets."

Isara nodded a little too quickly, then hurried to the next door on the other side of the hall.

Alluin jogged toward the end of the hall, then pushed his ear up against the nearest door.

Elmerah moved toward the next door closest to her. She hoped there were only the two Dreilore somewhere in the building. She didn't relish the thought of an ambush, especially now that she'd used up most of her magic outside.

She was just about to lean against the next door when she heard a familiar voice, muffled as if several rooms away. "You shall not have it!"

"Solana no!" another familiar voice called.

Alluin was already at her side as she kicked down the door in front of her. She scanned the rows of books within, then broke into a run with Alluin and Isara trailing her. She came to another door just as a pain-filled scream sounded on the other side.

She kicked the door open, then drew her rapier. "Be ready!" she called back, hoping Isara realized her words were meant for her, but all she found was another room filled with books.

"There." Alluin pointed.

A bookshelf at the end of the room cut diagonally across the floor, clearly out of place against the other neat rows. She ran toward it, discovering a secret doorway.

She charged inside, barely managing to light her rapier. Solana Fenmyar lay in a pool of her own blood. The crimson puddle rapidly expanded across the white granite tiles.

Ivran backed into a corner, clutching a velvet box the size of a large book to his chest. Tears glimmered behind his round spectacles.

The male Dreilore in front of him aimed a glowing sword toward his heart. "I will have the box, elf. You may live or die, it is all the same to me."

Ivran's entire body trembled. "You killed her! You murdered her like her life meant nothing!" Spittle flew from his mouth. "Her life meant everything!"

"Hey Dreilore!" Elmerah called. "Let us see how you fare against an armed opponent you little gnat."

The Dreilore turned. His eyes seem to burn brighter than any she'd ever seen. His blade lowered from Ivran's heart as his body angled her way. "You dare address the High Lord of the Dreilore in such a manner?"

Elmerah stepped forward, hoping to edge closer to Ivran, or to at least draw the Dreilore away from him. "I don't care if you're Arcale himself, no one attacks my friends and lives to tell the tale."

The Dreilore launched himself toward her without hesitation. An arrow twanged from Alluin's bow, but sailed right through a cloud of darkness where the Dreilore should have been.

"Soft-bellied muckdweller," Elmerah cursed.

The Dreilore appeared again, right next to Ivran.

"I'll get him," Isara's whispered behind her.

Alluin aimed another arrow, but the Dreilore snapped his arm outward, placing the tip of his blade at Ivran's throat. "You seem to care for this one. Will you allow your bravado to cost him his life?"

Alluin's bow did not lower, nor did he release his arrow. The Dreilore were even faster than elves. Could he slit Ivran's throat before an arrow could pierce his heart?

The Dreilore's blade did not waver. "I will have that box now." He extended his free arm toward Ivran.

Ivran shook his head, his gaze dutifully avoiding his wife's body on the floor.

Elmerah let the flame on her blade go out before the magic sapped all her strength. "There are four of us. There is no way you will escape here with that box alive, even with your borrowed demonic powers. So, it is you who must make a choice. Leave now, and keep your life, or kill Ivran for the box, and die in the process. We can stop you from avoiding the next arrow."

The Dreilore laughed. The sound of it slithered down her skin. "I have more than borrowed powers, Arthali bitch. Dinoba has made me truly immortal. Fetching his jewels is the price we pay, but for this one thing, I am willing to play lapdog."

Elmerah's palm began to sweat around the hilt of her rapier. He couldn't truly be immortal, could he? Her eyes narrowed slightly, realizing if he were, he would have already slit Ivran's throat for the box. His hesitance pointed to his fear that an Arthali witch might be able to defeat him.

She took a step closer. All she had to do was lure him away from Ivran. "I killed many of your lords and ladies outside. They didn't seem terribly immortal to me. Now will you face me, or are you a coward?"

The Dreilore growled, then launched toward her, almost too fast for her to follow. Alluin loosed another arrow. It struck the Dreilore in the shoulder and he fell mid-leap, surprise painted all over his grayish face.

He staggered to his feet and tore the arrow free from his shoulder. "How!"

Another arrow cut across the room toward him, but instead of disappearing in his demonic cloud, he rolled across the bloody tiles.

Elmerah darted between him and Ivran, then held her rapier at the ready.

The Dreilore went for Alluin instead. Alluin dove aside, narrowly missing the tip of the Dreilore's blade. The magical blade cut into the stone wall with a flurry of sparks.

The Dreilore recovered quickly and slashed at Alluin, forcing him into the corner across the room from where Ivran stood.

Elmerah raced across the room, desperate to save Alluin. He was a skilled fighter, but this Dreilore was faster than any she had ever seen.

Isara, far closer to Alluin, cried out as the Dreilore's blade narrowly missed Alluin's throat. She ran toward the Dreilore's back, though she had no weapon to bear.

Elmerah reached the corner at the same time. The Dreilore swung his elbow back. Elmerah managed to duck, Isara did not. His elbow connected loudly with her jaw.

Isara fell back, landing hard on the tiles.

The Dreilore turned partially toward Elmerah, lifting his free hand and clenching it into a fist. Alluin gasped, then clutched at his throat. Slowly, he crumpled to his knees behind the Dreilore, but the Dreilore's eyes were all for Elmerah.

"Demons are beings of air and darkness. You cannot hope to stand against them. Now I will have that box."

She didn't dare take her eyes off the Dreilore, but she could see out of the corner of her eye that Isara wasn't moving. She'd be no help in suppressing his magic now, nor the enchantment on his blade.

She did the only thing she could do with Alluin slowly suffocating. She slashed her rapier toward the Dreilore. He countered it easily with his sword.

Growing desperate, she slashed again. "Let him go! If you kill him I will hunt you to the ends of this earth. Every day you have left will be spent looking over your shoulder for me, because I will have your head!"

She slashed furiously, though every attack was easily parried by the smug Dreilore. She summoned a burst of flame into her rapier, knowing it was the last of her magic, and probably the last thing she'd ever do.

Her blade connected hard enough that her rapier flew from her hand, but the Dreilore lost his grip on his sword too. The Dreilore reared away from her, then a bolt of lightning struck him in the back. His body went skidding past her across the tiles, propelled along by Solana's blood.

"Elmerah move!" Rissine charged into the room, leading with her cutlass sparking with electricity.

Blood-smeared and with static in his hair, the Dreilore climbed to his feet, let out a frustrated growl, then disappeared in a cloud of black.

Elmerah raced back across the room, then knelt beside Alluin. His shoulders shook with a rasping breath.

Tension eased out of her body. She put her hand on his shoulder as he panted. Finally, he looked up at her, then past her toward the rest of the room.

Isara still lay splayed across the floor near Solana.

Ivran knelt beside her, clasping the velvet box, his head bowed. His shoulders shook with tears.

Celen and Malon followed Rissine into the room.

Celen glanced at Ivran, then approached Elmerah and Alluin. "We would have come sooner, but we found the other Dreilore."

"Dead?" she asked, her throat feeling oddly tight.

He nodded. Beyond him she could see Malon gently taking the velvet box from Ivran. As soon as his hands were free, he gathered his dead wife into his arms and slowly rocked her back-and-forth. To him, at that moment, no one else existed.

Rissine sucked her teeth. "Well this was an utter disaster, though I don't see any other bodies around here, so the priests and priestesses must still be hiding somewhere. We should head toward the mines."

Elmerah nodded. She wanted more than anything to escape Ivran's gentle sobs. Saida was going to be crushed. She would never forgive herself for not being there—for leaving Faerune.

Celen clasped her shoulder. "You did all that you could."

"Yes—" Alluin began to agree, but cut himself off. He glanced around the room. "Where is Malon?"

Elmerah whipped around. Ivran was still on the floor, rocking his wife, but Malon was gone . . . and so was the velvet box Solana had been willing to die for.

She ran toward the door and careened outside, finding only rows and rows of undisturbed books. She raced through the rows to the next room, then went down the hall and out to the steps, but Malon was gone.

Alluin reached her shoulder, gently panting. All of the pieces fell into place in her mind as she stared out at the slowly clearing rain.

She shook her head, feeling like a fool. "It all makes sense. All of it. Over half the guards left their posts and did not defend the city against the Dreilore. Malon arrived at the Akkeri Temple just after the witch hunters. Inside, he knew all about the Ayperos. He knew all about *demons,* and I saw in his eyes how much he wanted that circlet. I thought he just wanted to be the one to return it to Faerune, but I was wrong. He was the traitor. He was the reason the guardsman did not defend their own city. He was the reason the Dreilore knew just where to go. And *he* was the one who hired the witch hunters to take me. Who knows what he would have done with me had they succeeded."

Alluin's breath fogged the cool damp air beside her. She could hear the others approaching at their backs.

"But why?" Alluin breathed.

"Because who would want to be a lowly guardsman kissing the feet of high priests when he had it in his power to change *everything*?"

She was shocked to feel a hot tear rolling down her cheek, but felt too numb to swat it away.

She turned at the sound of sniffling. Ivran had joined them in the Great Hall. His eyes were red rimmed, his spectacles missing. "They took them all, all of our powerful artifacts. There may be some unrefined moonstones left in the mines, but it's not enough. The magic of Faerune has been stolen from us."

He didn't need to say anything else for Elmerah to understand. Not only had Faerune's magic been stolen, but it had been given to the demon who would destroy them all.

She rubbed her throbbing brow. "What was in that box, Ivran? What was Solana willing to die for?"

Ivran stared outside with hollow eyes as the sunlight slowly returned, chasing away the last of the rain. "It was the Crown of Arcale. The most powerful artifact that has ever existed, guarded by Faerune elves since before Faerune even existed."

She looked to Alluin again, who nodded. They had been dealt a near-fatal blow, but at least they were alive. And as long as she was alive, she would find Malon. She would find him and reclaim the crown from his cold dead hands.

Elmerah

Smoke from the funeral pyres blotted out the evening sun. Elmerah stood next to Saida, who stood next to her father, saying their final goodbyes to mother and wife. Saida had awakened on the ship to

Elmerah standing over her, the only one brave enough to explain what had happened.

Elmerah had assumed that someday she and Saida would find something in common. It was unfortunate that that thing was dead mothers, brutally slain.

The remaining members of the High Council and their families had been hiding deep within an underground vault beneath the High Temple. Solana and Ivran should have been there too, but they'd gone after the crown, hidden in a separate vault. Sadly, the crown might not have been found had they remained in safety, but Solana felt they could not risk it. It had cost her her life.

Though the casualties were heavy, many had escaped to the safety of the mines. The Valeroot elves and Arthali had arrived before the Dreilore could break through, but Nokken in disguise, allowed through by the traitorous guardsman, had cleared out many of the moonstones before the battle began. Other survivors had emerged from hiding places throughout the city once it was clear the battle was over. The survivors now moved the littered bodies outside what remained of the crystalline walls where they could be burned.

Elmerah spotted Rissine carrying a body toward the pyres with the help of a male Arthali. She didn't know the Arthali man's name, nor did she desire to. While they needed the Arthali's help, any of them could have been involved in her mother's death. She could never fully trust them.

She squeezed Saida's shoulder, then walked around

the gathered elves toward Rissine as she and her cohort tossed the body into the fire.

Spotting her, Rissine nodded to the other Arthali, who walked past without sparing Elmerah a second glance.

Rissine wiped her hands on her breeches, then wrapped her arms around herself, sealing her fur-lined coat close to her body, as she stood shoulder to shoulder with her sister. "So many would not have died if they'd let us into the city when we arrived."

Elmerah's eyes slid her way. "Watch your tongue." Her brow furrowed, she shifted her stare to the nearest fire. Her own coat had a hole where her back had caught the dagger, and the garment was torn and tattered besides, letting plenty of cold evening air through to chill her bones. "They have been punished for refusing you tenfold. They do not need to hear any more of it."

Rissine looked side to side, then turned to her with a raised brow. "Am I to understand you've developed affection for these elves? More than just for your handsome Valeroot companion?"

Her shoulders stiffened. "No one deserves to die like this."

Rissine laughed softly. "No, I suppose they don't, but this bloodshed will not end until Egrin is slain."

She spotted Isara with a group of elves gathered in front of another pyre. The stench of burnt flesh growing thick, but it was customary to wait while the bodies burned to see their souls off to Arcale. "With

Isara's help, I think it's possible. She can suppress his magic."

"So I've heard." Rissine turned toward her. "Oh don't look so affronted. I'm not spying on your conversations with your elves. Celen told me."

Elmerah's shoulders relaxed. "She doesn't want to kill her brother, but he'll need to die too if we're to make her empress."

Rissine huffed. "We'll decide who should be empress when the time comes."

"No one on this continent will accept *you* as ruler."

Rissine's laugh drew glares from the nearest elves.

Elmerah elbowed her in the arm. "You definitely won't be empress if the elves kill you here and now."

Rissine laughed again, more quietly this time. "Do not fret, dear sister. I have no intention of becoming empress. I only meant that Isara seems a bit . . . fluff-headed to rule over the Ulrian Empire."

Elmerah shrugged. "She's smarter than she seems, very smart in fact, and she has a good heart. She tried to save me when we were trapped in the Dreilore camp. She could have taken Egrin's protection, but chose to save me instead."

Rissine watched Isara, who didn't seem to notice the staring. "I suppose that does have to count for something. She's better than an elf, at least."

Celen approached, bringing their conversation to an end. He'd found a fur-lined coat somewhere, much warmer than Elmerah's dirty and torn black coat. She'd need to find a replacement soon enough, as well as another weapon. The loss of her jeweled cutlass, stolen from a pirate captain, still stung. The Dreilore rapier was still at her belt, but she wasn't accustomed to rapiers only sharpened at the tip. She liked her blades sharp all the way down.

Celen leaned his elbow on top of Elmerah's shoulder. He was one of the few people around who could make her feel small. "You'll need to get that wound in your back properly tended, Ellie."

Rissine snorted at the affection between the two, then walked away toward a small gathering of Arthali.

Celen watched her go. "I see your sister is still just as prickly as ever."

"That she is." His weight was beginning to feel heavy on her shoulder, but she had to admit, it was nice to have him around. "Most would say the same about me," she added.

"Oh not at all. I'd say you are far less prickly these days."

She sneered.

"Especially toward Valeroot elves," he added. "Or at least, toward *one* Valeroot elf."

She side-stepped out from under his elbow. "Don't you start too."

He let his arm fall with a laugh. He looked past a few elves to where Saida and Ivran stood, now joined by Alluin. "I suppose they're all nice enough. It might have taken them awhile, but they've welcomed us into the city while they rebuild. Together, we will all be stronger."

She nodded. "We'll need that strength. Egrin may back off for now, but the Akkeri still want Saida. I don't think we missed our only opportunity to meet their High King."

He turned back to her. "Don't worry, Ellie. Our blades will not discriminate between Dreilore flesh and Akkeri." He extended his arm, this time wrapping it around her shoulders. "Now let's find you a healer. They are set up with the injured, including your Akkeri *friend,* at the main inn."

She smiled softly. She'd been mostly indifferent to Merwyn, but he very well may have been the sole reason Saida wasn't taken aboard the High King's ship. While he'd not fully recovered from the Dreilore poison, and likely never would, she was glad he was still alive.

"Just a while longer," she said, her gaze back on Saida and Ivran. They both silently wept, overcome by their grief. She knew exactly how they felt.

Celen gave her uninjured shoulder a squeeze. "Take as long as you need."

She watched Saida for a few moments more, then looked up through the smoke toward the high hill where she'd stood with Egrin. As the last rays of sunlight disappeared, she made a solemn vow. She would make Egrin pay, and she wouldn't be doing it for herself, or for the Arthali, or even for the Valeroot elves. She would do it for Ivran and Solana, and for their daughter, who had unexpectedly become one of her dearest friends. Because vengeance for any other reason would be a hollow victory, while vengeance for those dear lives lost meant . . . she grasped for the proper word, then found it deep in her heart. *Everything*. It would mean everything.

CHAPTER FIFTEEN

Elmerah

Later that evening, Elmerah, Alluin, Saida, Ivran, and even Merwyn sat near a fire in the living room of Ivran's home. They drank burrberry brandy and told stories of Solana's life. Well, Saida and Ivran told stories, often interrupted by tears, while Alluin and Elmerah listened quietly side by side. Elmerah was pretty sure Merwyn had fallen asleep in his chair, the one nearest the fire.

Eventually the stories faded into silence, until Saida raised her gaze to Elmerah.

She'd been about to refill her cup, but remained seated, watching Saida instead.

Saida looked down into her cup, then back up, this time encompassing Alluin in her gaze. "I should have realized what Malon was planning. He saved me once when I was younger. He spoke about one day no longer being a lowly guardsman, but I didn't remember. I didn't realize it was him. I should have known." She hung her head.

Ivran rose from his seat and walked toward Saida, then placed his hand on her shoulder. "It was not your fault, none of this was, so do not blame yourself. Everything that happened here today was the fault of one man alone. Egrin Dinoba."

Saida wiped the tears from her eyes with her free hand, then nodded. "I have something to show you, father. Perhaps it will be of some value now that all of our other artifacts have been stolen."

Her father had to help her to stand. She was still injured from her run in with the Akkeri, and bone-tired besides. She really should have been in bed. Elmerah was glad they'd all be staying in Ivran's home, where she could protect Saida.

Saida hobbled toward her small pile of belongings brought in from Rissine's ship, just a large belt pouch, more of a satchel, really, and her torn shirt which had been replaced by one of the Arthali's while she was on the ship. She knelt, then reached into the pouch and withdrew the circlet they'd found in the Akkeri Temple.

Elmerah looked to Alluin. They'd both assumed it had been taken by Hotrath, and hadn't had the heart to ask Saida about it.

She handed it up to her father.

He took it in hand and examined it closely, then gasped. "My girl, where on earth did you find this?"

She stood, then hobbled back to her seat. "We found it in the Akkeri Temple. The High King of the Akkeri had it hidden there, guarded by Ayperos."

Ivran walked back toward the fire, then examined the circlet. The moonstones glinted in the warm yellow light.

"Do you recognize it?" Elmerah asked, unable to contain herself.

Ivran nodded, his gaze on the circlet. "If I'm not mistaken, this is the Crown of Cindra. It is meant to be paired with the stolen Crown of Arcale. This is extremely old, and extremely powerful." He blinked back tears. "If only Solana could have seen it."

Elmerah looked to Alluin, knowing his thoughts would mirror hers. The circlet would be something Egrin would want above almost anything else. She had no doubt the primary item he'd been after was the Crown of Arcale, a task he'd entrusted to none other than the High Lord of the Dreilore.

Yes, he'd want this circlet badly, but she'd be cursed, drawn and quartered before she'd ever let him have it.

Saida

S aida woke panting and drenched in sweat. She sat up in her bed, blinking as her eyes adjusted to the darkness. Her dream still clung to her skin like oil, a pleasant memory turned dark. She touched her hot cheeks, expecting them to be cold from the freshly fallen snow in her dreams. She'd dreamed of that night, where she'd first met Malon, but she'd never learned his name. He'd seemed so kind. He'd protected her and kept her warm.

He'd saved her life.

She tossed her blankets aside and padded barefoot toward her window. Smoke still hung in the air from the funeral pyres. Her heart ached for her lost mother. If only she'd remembered Malon sooner. If only she'd remembered his words that night, and had noticed the bitterness beneath them. Maybe she could have stopped him before he'd turned half the guard against the city. Maybe her mother would still be alive.

She leaned her hands heavily against the windowsill. Why her? Why had Malon deemed her important? Why had he asked her not to hate him? There was no way she could not hate him now.

She clenched the edge of the windowsill until her fingers ached. She supposed she would find out eventually. He hadn't kept her alive without reason. He'd said she was important.

She'd wanted her whole life to be important. She'd need to learn to be more careful what she wished for.

EPILOGUE

Elmerah sat at the edge of a balcony jutting out
from the High Temple, her legs hanging through
the railings to kick back and forth in the cool morning
air. The breeze was scented heavily with the first blossoms of spring, blossoms normally helped along by elven
magic. It was odd, that spring would still come after all
the darkness of the previous weeks. The seasons didn't
care about demons though. Nor did the trees, nor the sea
waiting to carry her sister away in search of more
Arthali, leaving most of those she'd gathered behind.

In the streets below, the elves were rebuilding the
city, not just Faerune elves, but Valeroot as well, and a
solitary Akkeri, who ignored the glares he received.
More Valeroot elves arrived every day, sought out by
Alluin and Vessa's scouts. She'd spotted Vail among the
most recent arrivals. The healer from the Valeroot settlement hadn't bothered to greet her, though she knew she

saw her. Not that Elmerah had particularly wanted to speak with her either.

The door behind her, heavily adorned with blue and yellow stained-glass, opened. Alluin walked outside and seated himself beside her, draping his legs through the railings. The bruises on his face had begun to heal, and he looked more rested and less thin than when they'd first been reunited. The deep green silk shirt and deeper green linen breeches, so deep a green they were almost black, suited him, though more rustic Valeroot garb suited him better.

She observed him for a moment longer, then looked outward. "So, would you ever have expected in beginning your grand scheme that you'd be facing demons?"

Alluin leaned forward. "No, but it doesn't really change things, we still have to kill Egrin."

Elmerah gripped the railings above her legs and stretched her back, grazing the ends of her loose black hair across the granite tiles. She sat back upright and took a deep breath of the flower scented air. "Any idea how we're going to do that?"

He laughed again. "I was hoping you knew. You know him better than any of us now, except maybe Isara."

She watched those below them. "I never truly thought it could work, but here they all are: the Woodfolk, the Moonfolk, and Arthali all in one place."

She spotted Celen walking below, carrying a sack of grain like it weighed nothing. He looked up at her and gave her a militia salute. She smiled. Now where on earth had he learned that? She stiffened as she realized Alluin was watching her, then glared.

"What?" she snapped.

He smiled and shook his head.

"*What?*" she asked again, giving his shoulder a shove.

He playfully shoved her back. "Must you ruin every decent moment?"

She snorted. "You ruined my decent moment the second you walked your pointy ears out here."

"I owed you a ruined moment. I owe you a million ruined moments for sacrificing yourself to Egrin like that."

Elmerah opened her mouth, hoping another scathing remark would pour out, but nothing came. "Am I to believe you were worried about me?"

He shrugged, not looking at her. "Just a bit."

She watched him, waiting for him to reveal that he was only joking. When he did not reply, she turned her gaze back out to those working below. "I might have been ever so slightly worried about you," she admitted. "With only two Faerune elves to watch your back you were as good as dead. I'm shocked you survived."

His shoulders slumped. "Yes, especially considering one of them was a traitor. Out of all the people who could've betrayed us, including each other, he was one of the last I would have expected. He seemed to care so much about Faerune. I can't believe he would betray them all."

"I don't find it hard to believe. How would you feel,

watching the priests and priestesses up here in their high Temple?"

He shrugged. "I can't say, Valeroot has no such hierarchy. We assume the roles to which we are best suited, while the eldest make the final decisions for their clans."

"Well regardless, we'll kill Malon too. What's one more name on the list?"

"Nothing to an Arthali witch."

She grinned. "You're incorrigible."

They sat like that for a long while in companionable silence. Perhaps they should have helped the workers below, but Elmerah felt entitled to rest while she could. She was the one who had to figure out how to kill a demon, after all, with help only from the elf at her side, a naïve priestess, and a fluff-headed scholar with demon blood running through her veins.

Really, it was more help than she'd ever had in anything else, so she supposed it wasn't too much for her to take on. If anyone was going to get to tell the tale of how they killed a demon, it was going to be her.

To be continued...

WARD OF WINTER

A MOONSTONE CHRONICLES SHORT STORY

Saida tossed and turned in her sleep. In her mind, she hurried out into the freshly fallen snow away from the crystalline walls. She glanced back over her shoulder as she ran, dragging her wooden sled behind her. Her mother had strictly forbade her from going out that day. It was the Lunar Festival, a sacred rite to Cindra as she was welcomed for the darker months. Saida was one of two Moon Priestesses—someone born to a Sun Priestess, but without actual magic—currently alive in Faerune. The other priestess, Nilasanndre, was over two-hundred years old. It was the responsibility of Moon Priestesses to blow out the final candles at the Lunar Festival, for they represented the darkness, whereas the Sun Priestesses stood for the light. The ritual was boring, and embarrass-ing, and she hated it. To a fourteen year old girl, the snow held mystery and adventure. She would not miss it.

Saida slipped further into the dream. Her boots

crunched as she ran across the freshly fallen snow toward the tall hill overlooking Faerune. When she'd woken that morning to snowflakes, she knew she simply must conquer it, though her mother expected her to be preparing for the festival all day. Her fur-lined white coat kept out most of the cold, reinforced at her wrists by woolen gloves, and at her throat by a bundled up lilac shawl, pilfered from her mother.

She glanced over her shoulder again as the crystalline walls grew smaller in the distance. The guards hadn't questioned her when she exited the gates. Her father was at the coast that day, searching for rare specimens that only came out after the first snow of winter. She'd told the guards she was only bringing him a message from her mother, though no such message actually existed.

She looked up at the hill as it loomed over her. It would be difficult to climb in the snow, reaching nearly the top of her boots, but it would be worth it.

She started up, laboring to drag her sled behind her. Her breath fogged the air in front of her face, and her lungs stung with every inhale. Her cheeks began to burn with every labored breath, but she kept going.

Her legs began to go numb about halfway up, but she'd come this far, there was no going back now. She would not endure her mother's scolding with nothing to show for it. By the time she reached the top, her legs felt like jelly. She fell to her knees in the snow, then dragged her sled close, but couldn't quite bring herself to climb atop it.

Just a few moments of rest, she told herself, then she'd slide down the hill and return to Faerune. She might even make it back before her mother realized she was gone.

While she waited to regain her strength, her eyes danced over her glittering surroundings. It was breathtaking. The snow reminded her of the magic she'd never have. The Sun Priests and Priestesses could make the flowers grow, they could make rivers run more fierce, irrigating the crops of the surrounding villages. They could also form beautiful moonstone artifacts, which would then amplify the creator's magic in turn.

She sighed. Her mother was always telling her she was still important, despite her lack of gifts, but her words fell on deaf ears. Saida knew she'd never be as important as her mother—a Sun Priestess *and* one of the six ruling members of the High Council—and it weighed on her every day. Eventually she would have to take on the duties of the High Council herself, with none of the power to show for it.

Her gaze reached the distant forest, the treetops glittering in the murky sunlight. She could see snowflakes still lightly falling in that direction. She closed her eyes, imagining how dazzling it would be to stand amongst the trees while it snowed, their boughs glittering all around her.

She opened her eyes and looked down at her sled. She felt rested enough now to climb atop it, but would it really be so bad to go see the trees first? She'd already climbed the hill, she was more than a quarter of the way there.

A twinge of guilt plucked her stomach as she glanced back at the crystalline walls. She could be gone a little while longer. The festival wasn't until dark. She'd make it back with ample time.

She stood and started walking, leaving her sled behind. She'd return to it soon, and slide down the hill on her way back. Though the snow up here was deeper, the journey was easier without an incline. She picked up her pace, jogging is much as the deep snow would allow. The trees grew nearer and nearer.

Eventually her lungs began to scream at her and she slowed her pace, but she continued going. She was getting close to those dazzling trees. The forest could be dangerous, but she'd make sure to stay on the edge. Nothing would happen to her while the crystalline walls were still in sight, she was sure of it.

She let out a heavy sigh as she reached the trees. Snowflakes fluttered around her face. She stepped into the edge of the forest and looked up. Her spirits wilted slightly. It wasn't quite as dazzling as she'd imagined . . . but it was still beautiful. She felt far away from the responsibilities which constantly weighed her down.

She decided to walk just a little bit further. She'd come all the way out here after all, she might as well make the best of it.

Her boots crunched across the snow, fresh enough that there were no other prints. It made her feel safe. The monsters of the forest would not venture this close to the border.

Eventually the woods began to grow dark and dense, and she realized she'd better turn around. She spun around, then staggered, blinking at her surroundings. All she could see were snowy trees and the thickening storm clouds overhead. She'd lost sight of the crystalline walls. Panic lanced through her.

She started walking back toward the city, following her own tracks, then stopped abruptly at a low *hiss*. Her heart thundered in her throat as she searched for the source of the noise, then she saw it. A long, cylindrical body wove its way through the trees, not twenty paces ahead of her. She could not see its head, nor the end of its tail, though she did see the front set of legs as they passed. It was a snow wyrm, she could tell by its pure white scales nearly blending in with its surroundings. They only came out in the winter, and hibernated during the warmer months. They were blind, but had excellent hearing and sense of smell. As it continued on, she began to relax. It had already crossed her tracks and hadn't followed them. If she waited for it to pass, she should be safe, but . . .

The wyrm stopped moving forward. Saida held her breath as it stood eerily still for several long moments. With a sudden flurry of snow, it started backing across its own tracks.

No, no, no, she thought. This was bad. She backed

away slowly. The wyrm blocked her path toward Faerune, and she didn't dare run past it.

She turned and fled in the other direction, running deeper into the woods. Maybe if she ran east for a while, then turned south, she could circumvent the wyrm, along with the high hill, and come out of the forest closer to Faerune.

The deep snow tugged at her boots and the flakes grew larger overhead, blurring her vision, but she hardly noticed, so intent was she on listening for sounds of the wyrm's pursuit. The wind howled almost deafeningly, pushing her faster. Her breath steamed the air in hot clouds as she staggered. Soon every step forward felt as if it took all of her strength, but she somehow managed another step after that, then another step after that. The snow grew deeper as she walked. She was beginning to realize the great peril she'd placed herself in. Wyrms were dangerous, she was right to flee, but now she might have made her situation even worse. If she became lost in the woods, she could easily freeze to death once night fell.

She wrapped her arms around herself, pressing her white coat closer to her body, and walked onward, veering south. At least, she hoped it was south. The snowy trees around her had begun to all look the same, and her tracks were beginning to fill in behind her. Now, even if she chose to go back toward the high hill to see if the wyrm had passed, she was not sure she could find her way.

The heat she'd built up under her coat while she ran started to evaporate into the icy air. The slower she walked, the more her warmth left her, but she also couldn't make herself go any faster.

She blinked back tears. All she wanted now was to be wrapped up in her mother's warm embrace, when only that morning she wanted nothing more than to get away from her.

Saida sat in the snow, her back leaned against a tree. She didn't remember sitting down, but here she was, and she was unable to get up. The snow had stopped falling, but she was still freezing, and utterly lost. She would have cried if she had any more tears left to shed, but her mouth was utterly parched. She knew she could melt some snow in her mouth for moisture, but would that be the final thing to push her over the edge into hypothermia? She looked around at the snow that she thought so pretty just that morning. Now it seemed harsh, not soft, and bleak, not enchanting. The elves back home would all be getting ready for the festival. Would anyone even realize she was missing before it was too late?

Her eyes caught movement in the distant trees. Something tall and dark, not the snow wyrm. Distantly she felt panicked, but knew her heart rate was slower than it should have been given her fear. She wanted to get up and hide. *Get up, just get up*, she thought, but her body didn't move.

The shape neared, and slowly came into focus. She breathed a weak sigh of relief. The elf, clearly a guardsman judging by his charcoal gray shirt and breeches partially covered by a heavy gray winter cloak, spotted her and hurried over.

He knelt in front of her. "Priestess Saida, what are you doing so deep in the woods?"

His silver eyes made her think of a gentle river glittering in the sun, complemented by the long, silvery-blond hair pulled away from his face. She'd guess he was only a few years older than her, maybe eighteen, so he was likely new to guard service.

She opened her mouth to speak, but only a painful croak came out.

His eyes filled with worry. "We need to get you warm, *now*."

He tugged the satchel slung over his shoulder around to the front of his body, then dug through it, coming up with a fire-striker. He stood and glanced around at the trees. "We'll have a hard time finding any dry wood, but we'll have to make do."

He kicked away the snow in front of her, rounding out the indentation until dark soil was revealed below, then he walked away.

She wanted to call out to him not to leave her, but her body didn't move. She just stayed seated in the snow.

It felt like hours until he returned, twigs and branches

piled up in his arms, but realistically she knew it had probably only been minutes.

He knelt back in front of her, dropping the branches into the snow, then pulled around his satchel again. He dug out a wad of fresh white bandages.

Her eyes widened slightly. Was she injured?

Instead of searching her for wounds, he dropped the wad of bandages into the open pit in the snow he cleared, then delicately stacked the twigs and a few branches atop it. "The bandages should burn well, hopefully long enough to dry the twigs and light them." He looked up at her with his silver eyes. "You'll be alright, Priestess Saida, I promise."

She managed a slight nod.

He turned his attention to lighting the bandages with sparks from his fire-striker. The first hints of smoke had her hopeful, and the first little burst of flame was the most beautiful thing she'd ever seen, far more beautiful than the snow could ever be.

Soon she sat near a roaring fire. The guardsman stood on the other side.

He looked down at her. "Do you mind if I move you? It will be easier for you to get warm if you sit atop my cloak and not in the snow."

She nodded.

He removed his cloak, then spread it across the snow before walking around the fire. He lifted her, cradling her like a child, then pivoted and placed her upon the cloak. The warmth of the fire seeped into her, bringing her back to life.

When she finally felt she could speak, she looked up at the guardsman. "You should sit on the cloak too," she chattered. "It won't do either of us any good if you catch hypothermia instead. I fear I don't know my way back out of the woods, and I'm not sure I could carry you."

He spread out the edge of the cloak, then sat beside her. "You would try to carry me?" he asked, clearly amused.

She inhaled sharply. Was he mocking her? "Of course. I wouldn't just leave you out here to die."

"Why not? It's not like you know me."

She leaned forward, warming her numb cheeks and nose. "Well you don't know me either, yet you're still here taking care of me."

He lifted his hands toward the fire. "Yes, but you are a priestess, and I but a lowly guardsman. I'm sworn to protect you, but you owe me nothing in return." His words—no longer holding amusement—were tinged with bitterness.

She furrowed her brow and turned away from him. "I don't care what I owe you, I wouldn't leave you out here to die, and you know nothing of my life, so perhaps you should not be so quick to judge me."

He laughed, startling her. "I was not judging you, simply making an observation. You owe me nothing. Are you warming up?"

She glanced at him. He seemed young to be so bitter,

but she supposed she could not presume to know anything about his life either, just as he knew nothing about hers. "Yes, I'm beginning to feel my face again, thank you. *And*," she added before he could speak, "don't tell me I don't owe you my thanks."

He laughed. "You're not like any Sun Priestess I've ever met."

"That's because I'm not a Sun Priestess, I'm a Moon Priestess. Surely you know this?"

He blinked at her. "My apologies, this is my first year in the service. So you'll be performing the rite to Cindra this evening? This is the first year I'll actually be close enough to see it."

She looked upward, searching for the sun as it began its slow descent. "Yes, along with Nilasanndre. That is, if we make it out of these woods alive."

"We'll make it, priestess. I just want to make sure you get warm enough before we leave the fire."

As her body warmed and her thoughts began to clear, she had a sudden realization. "How did you find me out here? The snow should've covered up my tracks."

"I saw you leave the gates before my shift began. Your father returned after the guards switched shifts, but you did not. I became worried and walked to the high hill where I found your sled piled up with snow. Since I could see you nowhere from the hill, I assumed you must be in the woods. After that, it was sheer luck that I found you."

She watched the light of the flames flickering on his

pale skin and hair as dusk closed in around them. "I suppose I'm very lucky then, but if you were so worried, why did you come alone?"

He smiled mischievously. "I suspected you might be out here without your parents' permission. I did not want to get you in trouble if you were simply walking in the woods." He looked up past the snowy tree boughs toward the sky. "Speaking of walking, do you think you're warm enough to go? We'll want to get back before full dark when the Fossegrim and snow wyrms come out."

She nodded as sudden fear snaked through her stomach. "The Fossegrim only dwell deep in the Illuvian forests, but I did see a snow wyrm earlier. That's how I got lost, it blocked my path out of the forest."

"Ah, it's all beginning to make sense now." He stood and offered her a hand.

Once she was up, he lifted the cloak, flicked off the snow, then wrapped it around her shoulders.

She greedily pulled it close around her neck, then hesitated. "But won't you get cold?"

"I'll be fine. Now Faerune is roughly that way." He pointed. "I'll go out and fetch your sled tomorrow. We'll need to head right back if you're to make it in time for the ritual."

She nodded and started walking. "You're very kind."

"You should not say that, priestess. You hardly know me. I could be a wolf in disguise."

She thought it an odd thing to say, but decided he

must be joking, considering he'd come all this way to save her.

The warmth Saida had gathered from the fire soon left her. It didn't take long for her to lose the feeling in her toes, then her feet, then all the way up her ankles. The guardsman didn't seem bothered to be walking without his cloak, so she kept it tightly gathered around her.

Suddenly, he stopped walking and extended his arm, holding her back. "I hear running water beneath the surface. We must be approaching the stream bed, watch your step."

She looked around. Her boots were wet enough already, she *really* didn't want to step in any water. "How could you hear it over the sound of our footfalls?"

The guardsman shrugged. "Spend enough time in the woods, and you learn to listen for such things. It wouldn't have been an issue had you come out a day later. I'm sure it will freeze overnight."

She followed him as he picked his way through the snow, trusting he'd know where to step better than she. "You've spent a lot of time in the woods?"

"I grew up in a small village, not within the crystal walls."

She watched his broad shoulders as he walked ahead of her. Usually elves became guardsmen because their fathers were guardsmen. "How did you come to live in the city?"

"My parents were killed, and I was left with nothing. Enlisting with the guard was my only hope of survival."

She was sorry she'd asked. His words held no emotion, but given his age it couldn't have been *that* long ago that his parents died. It had to still sting. She couldn't imagine losing her parents.

The thought made her suddenly homesick. She didn't know why she was always trying to get away. Her mother might have been a little overbearing, but she still loved her. She'd lived a comfortable life compared to what this guardsman had experienced.

She knew she had already overstepped, but couldn't help herself from prying. "What would you have done if things were different—" she hesitated, "if you hadn't become a guardsman, I mean."

He was quiet for a moment. Their boots crunching in the snow seemed suddenly loud.

"I'd probably be a farmer," he answered finally, "or a drunk. My mother's sister was an exile. While my family could technically enter Faerune . . . " he trailed off, then shook his head, keeping his eyes on their path, "you know how it is," he finished. "Just because you can enter a place, does not mean you are welcome."

She felt suddenly guilty. It took a great crime to warrant the exile of a Faerune elf. An exile's family was usually guilty by association. This man had likely been a child when his aunt committed her crime. He might not have even been born at the time, but the taint of an exile followed his parents, and by extension, him.

"Will you be running the other way now?"

She startled at his words. "No!" she blurted. She stopped walking and turned toward him. "That's not what I was thinking. I was only thinking how hard your life must have been. I cannot even imagine how that might feel."

He shrugged. "It's better now. With my parents' deaths, my connection to an exile faded. I was allowed to enlist. Some day I may even become a Guard Captain."

She knew she should start walking again, but, "You didn't mind swearing an oath to a city that treated you and your family so poorly?" She bit her tongue. She was such a brazen idiot. If her mother had been around to hear her words, she would have washed her mouth out with soap.

The guardsman had a strange look in his eye. "You know, no one has ever asked me that."

"I shouldn't have—"

He held up his hand. "No, it's alright. A part of me will always resent how I was treated." He looked down at his feet and gently shook his head. "But if I would have stayed in Fallshire, if I would have become a lowly farmer or a drunk . . . " He looked up. "Then they would have won, now wouldn't they?"

She blinked at him. "You did it to prove Faerune wrong?"

He shrugged. "Perhaps. Or perhaps I just did it

because I don't like living in squalor." He gestured for her to keep walking.

She did, though her mind was a violent blizzard of thoughts. She hadn't experienced much of life outside Faerune, but she was beginning to think she wouldn't like it. She suddenly felt like an ungrateful idiot.

The guardsman abruptly stopped walking ahead of her, then put his hand on the sword at his belt.

She glanced around them, but could not see far in the growing darkness. "What's wrong?"

"Shh."

She wasn't used to being shushed, but sealed her mouth closed. He gripped the pommel of his sword and silently unsheathed it.

"Hissssss!" It was like the sound of an arrow being loosed. It was their only warning before the slithering white shape crashed through the snow.

The guardsman threw himself between her and the snow wyrm, slashing at it with his sword.

The snow wyrm reared back, lifting its thin front legs into the air. The midsection of its body curled and writhed, keeping its serpentine head balanced. Though she knew the creature was blind, the tiny pockmarks serving as eyes seemed to land on her.

The guardsman slashed at it again. "It must have tracked you!"

Saida remained frozen in place, unsure of what to do. The wyrm seemed sentient enough to know the guardsman's blade would do it harm. It bobbed and weaved, trying to get around him to Saida.

The guardsman lunged, opening up a crimson gash across the wyrm's belly.

"Hisssss!" It writhed more erratically. It swung its head, knocking the guardsman in the shoulder. His sword flew from his grip and landed in the snow. He staggered back into the wyrm's path. It struck at him with a sharp-toothed maw dripping venom.

Saida finally motivated her body to move. She dropped the guardsman's cloak and dove for the discarded sword, but it was buried in the deep snow. She flung her gloves aside, then scrambled on hands and knees, searching for the sword while the guardsman narrowly avoided the wyrm's attacks.

Cool metal bit into her hand, slicing open her palm. She withdrew her hand, then used the other to more gently search for the hilt. Sword in hand, she stood, clenching her injured fist against her chest.

The smell of fresh blood seem to drive the wyrm wild. It knocked the guardsman aside and dove for Saida.

She forced her injured hand around the hilt, holding the blade two-handed in front of her. It was almost too heavy for her to wield.

"Saida no!" the guardsmen shouted. He produced a rock from the hidden stream bed and threw it at the wyrm, hitting it in its back near its head.

The wyrm whipped around, striking at him. Saida said a silent prayer to Arcale and lifted the sword over her head. She leapt forward, landed, and used the momentum of her leap to propel the sword into the wyrm. The sharp blade sunk through the wyrm's scales, making a deep gash in its back.

The creature screamed an unearthly scream, knocked Saida aside with its tail, and fled, leaving a trail of bright crimson against the white snow. She scurried back to her feet, sword held at the ready, but they were now alone. As quickly as it had arrived, the wyrm was gone.

The guardsman staggered toward her. "Are you injured?"

Her hands began to tremble so badly that she dropped the sword into the snow.

"Your hand!" the guardsman took her sliced hand and balled it into a fist. "Hold it over your head."

She obeyed while he retrieved his cloak, then used his belt knife to cut a thick strip from the hem. He reached out for her hand. "It's not ideal, but seeing as we burned all of my bandages, it will have to do for now. A healer can properly attend it once we return to the city."

She lowered her fist and extended it toward him.

He peeled back her fingers, then winced at the sight of the deep cut.

Saida winced too, feeling a bit queasy.

Quickly schooling his expression to a reassuring smile, the guardsman gently bandaged her wound with the damp strip of cloak. "You know, if not for you I'd be dead right now."

His words were so ridiculous to her she had to laugh.

"If it weren't for me, you wouldn't have been out here in the first place."

He smiled. "Perhaps." He tied of the makeshift bandage around her hand. "There, that should do for now." Their eyes met.

She wasn't sure why, but she felt her cheeks burning with a blush.

The guardsman quickly averted his gaze. "Faerune should not be far off, and I don't want to wait around for that wyrm to return. Let's hurry."

She shivered at the thought. "Yes, let's."

She waited while he cleaned his sword and resheathed it, then they started off again. Though she was shaken and injured, she was beginning to feel equally thrilled with the idea of being on this small adventure with a handsome guardsman.

The sky was pitch black by the time they reached Faerune. Saida glanced at the guardsman as they trudged through the snow, catching a glimpse of his reflective eyes. The festival always occurred on the first new moon of winter, so the torches at the gates seemed almost blinding against the dark sky.

The first of the guards spotted them, then started shouting.

She looked to her friend. "You won't be in trouble, will you?"

He shrugged. "Not unless you tell them that I didn't find you by happenstance."

She smiled. "I won't tell. I swear it."

An older guard whose name she did not recall was the first to reach them. "Priestess Saida, we've been searching everywhere for you. You must prepare for the festival."

She held her roughly bandaged hand behind her back, then turned back to the guardsman who'd rescued her. "I fear I must hurry or my mother will have my head. Will I see you at the festival?"

He smiled. "I would not miss it."

She bit her lip and looked at the older guard, wishing he hadn't reached them so quickly. More were rushing toward them.

She removed the too big cloak, and handed it to her new friend. "I just realized, I never learned your name. I'll need to know it to find you again and properly say my thanks."

Her new friend shook his head as more guards approached. "My name is not important, and I told you, you owe me nothing. Now you must hurry, priestess. I'll be there to watch you perform the ritual, I promise."

"But—"

"Saida Fenmyar!" Her mother's voice cut across the dark, crisp snow. She marched out of the gates and toward Saida, her white-blonde hair cascading freely past her pointed ears. She was already dressed in the customary white gown priestesses wore for the Lunar

Rite. "Where in the name of Arcale and Cindra have you been? You need to get dressed, *now*."

Her mother grabbed her arm, then dragged her through the snow back toward the gates, leaving the guards behind without any acknowledgment.

Saida looked back toward them longingly, knowing better than to disobey her mother now.

Her new friend watched her go with his cloak in hand. Or perhaps he wasn't really her friend, since he'd refused to give her his name, and since he had reason for bitterness toward Faerune. She made a silent vow to herself to seek him out. Somehow, as the daughter of a High Priestess, she could make amends for the wrongs he'd suffered. She knew he worked his shifts at the gate, he shouldn't be too hard to find.

She hurried up so her mother wouldn't keep dragging her. She hadn't even noticed her daughter's injured hand.

Saida gritted her jaw. While her adventure had been somewhat terrifying, and she was currently frozen to the bone, she couldn't help but wish she were still out in the snowy woods, sitting by a fire with a handsome young guardsman.

Saida stood at the head of the procession, next to Nilasanndre, who dwarfed her with her height. She hoped she still had a few more years to grow, as she was short for an elf. Her flowing white festival garb had needed to be hemmed so it wouldn't drag through the dirt. Her mother had eventually noticed her injured hand and had ordered it freshly bandaged, but didn't ask what had happened. There was no time. Saida was sure she'd get the lecture of a lifetime later.

Three elves strummed lutes behind her, and the fourth attendant handed her and Nilasanndre each an ornate glass lantern, flames already burning brightly within. The flames symbolized Arcale's light, ready to be swallowed up by Cindra's darkness for the winter.

She started walking down the steps of the High Temple. She could hear the crowd murmuring in the expanse of the eastern gardens where the rite would take place. Her injured hand ached where she gripped the heavy lantern, but she held it high, refusing to give her mother anything else to lecture her about.

As she and Nilasanndre reached the crowd, followed by the musicians and two rows of priests and priestesses, she searched the excited waiting faces for her guards-man. She scanned the excited pudgy cheeks of children, and the less excited, but still happy faces of older elves. She noted many guardsmen amongst the crowd, but not her new friend.

She continued to look for him as she approached a dais glowing with lit candles. She turned her back to the candles as the priests and priestesses formed a circle around her and Nilasanndre. She looked over their heads while the eldest member of the High Council, Cornaith, recited the sacred rites that were said every year.

It seemed to take forever, but for all the time it took, she never managed to find her guardsman. When Cornaith finally stopped speaking, she turned and started blowing out her half of the candles, while Nilasanndre took the other half. The ritual was meant for more than two priestesses, but few Moon Priestesses had been born over the past century, and no others since Saida.

Once the candles were out, her duty was finished. More music played, and the crowd began chattering. Food and drinks were dispersed through the crowd, carried by white liveried servants.

She walked toward the edge of the gathering, giving up on finding her guardsman. He wasn't there. He'd broken his promise.

Eventually her father found her with her head slumped, a glass of burrberry juice in her hand.

Her father adjusted his spectacles, then clapped her on the shoulder. "You did a fine job, my girl, but I hear you ventured into the woods today?"

Her head hung lower. "I only wanted to see the snow. I had every intention of returning well before the festival started, but then a snow wyrm crossed my path. I fled and became lost."

Her father's eyes lit up. "A snow wyrm? How marvelous. You don't happen to have an estimate of its length, do you? I've been tracking migration patterns of the wyrms for years."

Finally, she smiled. Her father always had that effect

on her. "My apologies, father. I was too busy fighting for my life."

"It attacked you?" he gasped.

"Yes, but a young guardsman saved me. I suppose I saved him too in the end. You wouldn't happen to know of someone enlisted recently from one of the nearby villages? He said his parents were killed."

Her father stroked his chin. "I can't say that I make a habit of learning the history of all of our guardsmen. Perhaps you can find him tomorrow, that is, if your mother doesn't lock you in your room."

She laughed. "Nothing some knotted silks tossed out the window can't solve."

"Ah, so that's how you got out."

She enjoyed the rest of the festival with her father, and eventually gave up looking for the guardsman. Though she tried to find him over the next few days, and occasionally whenever the mood struck her in the following weeks, eventually she forgot about him. He became just another nameless face, and she convinced herself that he'd only been doing his duty to Faerune, and had never really been her friend at all.

Saida awoke with a gasp and sat up in her bed. Her dream still clung to her skin like oil, a pleasant memory turned dark.

She tossed her blankets aside and padded barefoot

toward her window. Smoke still hung in the air from the funeral pyres. Her heart ached for her lost mother. If only she'd remembered Malon sooner. If only she'd remembered his words that night, and had fully comprehended the bitterness beneath them. Maybe she could have stopped him before he'd turned half of the guard against the city. Maybe her mother would still be alive.

She leaned heavily against her windowsill. *Why her?* Why had Malon deemed her important? Why had he asked her not to hate him? There was no way she could not hate him now.

She clenched the edge of the windowsill until her fingers ached. She supposed she would find out eventually. He hadn't kept her alive for no reason. He'd said she was important.

She'd wanted her whole life to have adventures and be important. She'd need to learn to be more careful what she wished for.

Fallen
Fury
Forged
Found

The Thief's Apprentice Series
Clockwork Alchemist
Clocks and Daggers
Under Clock and Key

The Xoe Meyers Series
Xoe
Accidental Ashes
Broken Beasts
Demon Down
Forgotten Fires
Gone Ghost
Minor Magic
Minor Magics: The Demon Code

Printed in Great Britain
by Amazon